Fragile Angel

Stefaunia Dhillon

Dedicated to

My lovely daughters Jennifer and Angie, my dear friends in England James and Christine Mason, Viv Green and Georgie, as well as Jennifer Ball, Jo Graham, Sharlene Hansen and Jamillah. Thanks to all my amazing co-workers, who supported me and encouraged me along this amazing journey and Melody Chase for the amazing formatting of this novel. Also, thank you to Jim Bezoski for sticking with me through the long-haul and never losing faith that this would not be accomplished.

Foreward

This story is true. It's *my* story. Names have been changed to protect the innocent, but it remains my story nonetheless. There's a purpose for everything and there's no such thing as coincidence. What we think becomes our reality. My story depicts both an exciting and confusing time for me, when my heart—no, my very soul!--was shaken to its core. Challenged and made to question my true purpose, instead of focusing on the external world I was asked to dive deep within--which is where I'd hidden my gifts and talents and allowed others to take away my power.

My lack of confidence and low self-esteem left me wide open and vulnerable. Others manipulated and controlled me sometimes in very subtle ways that I mistook for love.

Only by falling in love with myself was I able to take back my power and my space, and grab hold of the reins of my own life. Living in England proved a cure for my soul, as it was where I was forced to dump old beliefs and the kind of mindset that could have kept me in the dark forever.

This book is testimony to the fact that now I honor my true nature and what I really came here to do. A story of my past life and the spirits who revealed themselves to me, *Fragile Angel* was written about my many experiences while living in a 13th Century gothic church in the English countryside, where accelerated healing of my karmic contract and ancestral past occurred.

Forever grateful this service was provided to me, I did not realize its full blessing until I returned home and began to recount the story in its entirety. I have laid it out here for all of posterity to honor Catherine, David, and Aggie, and all the souls who aided me on my journey, both now and in centuries past. They are elated that *Fragile Angel* is available now for all to read, and that my story—*their* stories—may live on in the hearts and minds of readers for many years to come...

Fragile Angel

Prelude

Distant thunder clapped as jagged streaks of lightning shredded the evening sky, giving me the first glimpse of my new home; an ancient Gothic church, abandoned and forgotten until the day of my arrival. Weathered gargoyles, sentinels of a distant past perched eerily atop its gabled bell tower, cast dark foreboding shadows across the crumbling exterior. Mesmerized as I was by these guardians of the church, it was their inhuman faces that sent the first pang of fear rushing through me. Faded grave stones, markers of the dearly departed, jutted up through patches of thick lush fern and ivy, which seemed to have a stranglehold on both the living and dead. I'd always felt comfort and peace when visiting a cemetery, but here, in this place, something hostile stirred beneath the surface.

As I walked along the narrow gravel drive toward the entrance, I thought I heard laughter drifting down from the guardians perched on the tower. Were they mocking me? Or was it some kind of warning? I quickly pushed the thought to the back of my mind, yet the soft whispering continued and swirled around the bell tower, subtle as the wind. Just my imagination, I'd stick to that for now. I'd mixed feelings about living in a foreign country, after leaving so much I loved behind. My husband Michael stood beside me, yet his presence didn't help to lighten the heavy burden I carried inside.

Chapter 1

"Ladies and gentlemen, this is your captain speaking," boomed the pilot's voice. "Welcome aboard Delta Flight five-zero-seven, nonstop to London. Please secure all luggage in the overhead compartment or underneath your seat as we prepare for takeoff."

This was it. No turning back now, I thought, as I fastened my seatbelt and watched in quiet fascination the flight attendants spring to action, point to exits here, oxygen masks there, and--God forbid should we need them--floatation devices to use if some mishap took place as we journeyed the five thousand miles across the Atlantic Ocean. Powerful engines roared to life, sending a rumbling, vibrating pulse through the cabin. I gripped the arm of my window seat tight as a rush of anxiety coursed through me. I tried to shake it off as nothing more than excitement and perhaps exhaustion.

Newly married for a grand total of forty-eight hours, give or take, to husband number three! *Hopefully the third time's the charm,* I mused. I'd spent most of my life screwing things up, not intentionally of course, as much of it had been out of my control. I managed to exorcise the demons from my past, lay them to rest, and now was embarking on a new chapter and adventure in my life.

"Evie! Evie!" Michael's soft British voice whispered sotto voce, breaking my reverie.

"Hmm--what?"

"My arm, darling, do you think you might release the

1

talon's grip?" he chuckled. My nails had pinched tightly into Michael's forearm.

"Sorry," I mouthed, drawing close to give him a quick kiss.

"Pre-flight jitters?" he asked, casually stroking my breast with his fingers and giving my nipple a firm twist.

God, what this man did to me, I thought, my nipple now hard and standing at attention. Seriously, Evie, have you no shame?

"Michael!" I gasped, as I scanned the cabin quickly for prying eyes, raised eyebrows, or inquisitive stares. Not to worry, all eyes faced forward. Everyone seemed deep in thought, as some chatted quietly while others adjusted seats and plumped pillows, readying themselves for takeoff.

One last glance out the small oval window as I whispered my heartfelt goodbye to Salt Lake, the city I'd known for most my adult life. Our wedding ceremony was perfect and beautifully executed, but bittersweet. Family, friends, and co-workers all gathered for one last toast, one last goodbye. Michael was such a sweetheart and wonderful host, giving me space to mingle with well-wishers and say my last farewells. Everyone pointed out to me how my life was like a fairytale--the romance, marriage and, soon, life in a completely new place.

But fear comes in many forms, many guises...I felt the first shudder of it when I said "I do," but couldn't explain why. I rationalized part of it as leaving behind my two daughters, but they were grown women now and completely independent and happy in their own lives. Change is a constant and things can't always remain the same. I'd grown into a self-assured and strong woman, to which I can only credit the hardships and experiences of a tainted past. Today was not the day to dwell on darkness, or depressing thoughts that held absolutely no power over me anymore.

I brushed aside all thoughts of negativity and darkness as the plane bolted forward and glided down the runway. I closed my eyes, held my breath, and allowed the rush of the rapid ascent to sweep me away with its sheer intensity. I remember being told once it's not the take off you need to fear but the landing. I wasn't afraid of either, I loved the adrenaline rush; it made me feel alive.

I'd barely caught my breath and unbuckled my seatbelt when once again I was hit with a wave of anxiety, accompanied by a familiar voice from the past—one I thought had been laid to rest. *Deep breaths, Evie, it's over, he can't harm you from the grave!* Flashbacks rolled over me with extreme force. *Are you kidding me?* I thought. *Not here, not now! Leave me alone! Go away!* I screamed inside my head. I'd worked hard to clear myself of the memories and damage caused by the emotional abuse and scars he'd inflicted on my heart.

"Champagne?" asked Michael, leaning close.

God yes! I thought.

"Are you sure you're okay?" he asked, as we clinked glasses thirty-five thousand feet in the air.

"Absolutely," I replied, knowing full well it was an outright lie. But I was damned if I'd allow my father's power and control to reach out and destroy me from the grave. I found it strange that Michael never asked me about my past. He didn't want to know, said it wasn't important. He fell in love with the woman I was now. Had he done me a disservice by not allowing me to share my past? He knew nothing about my father or mother, nothing about my losses. This worked both ways--had he known of my past would I now be his wife? The past is what carved out and molded me into the woman sitting before him today.

I glanced over at Michael, now fast asleep beside me,

thank God, through air turbulence and all. How did he do it? He was always so calm, self-assured, and confident. Nothing seemed to ruffle his feathers. This was a rare quality I completely admired about him. I managed to work myself up into a nervous ball of energy. I signaled the flight attendant for more champagne. I would silence the voice. He would not control my life anymore! He wasn't in charge, damn him! I wasn't the helpless small child from the past. He did not have that power, nor would I give him the power to control and dominate me any longer! I felt the warm touch of my Michael's hand as he squeezed mine. It was as if somehow he'd read my mind, and this small gesture of affection brushed away the darkness, at least for now.

Chapter 2

Gray overcast sky and a light misty rain greeted us as we exited Heathrow Airport, Terminal One. I'd been fighting a nagging headache and a bout of anxiety when I de-boarded the plane. The fresh air temporarily kept the jackhammer pounding in my head at a tolerable level. I reached inside my bag for an umbrella but quickly decided against it. The rain felt cleansing and I allowed it to wash away the last remnants of dark memories. I think I could have stood for hours this way.

"Welcome to England!" Michael shouted above the deafening roar of jumbo jets flying overhead as he grabbed my outstretched hand and maneuvered me through the crowd of weary travelers anxious to get home. I eased into his black Mercedes and wished the drumming in my head would go away. Michael pulled from the curb quickly and, once engaged on the open highway, kicked into high gear sending the little car speeding down the wet pavement. I watched as lush rolling hills, dense forests, and thatched roof cottages whizzed by until everything became a blur.

I lay against the headrest, closed my eyes, and tried to fight off the ping pong match being played inside my head. A loud clap of thunder jolted me upright and I watched in fascination as Michael veered off the main road. A few twists, turns and sharp curves later he pulled the car into a narrow graveled drive. The next flash of lightening illuminated the

13th Century Gothic church that was to become my new home.

As we emerged from the car, I pushed a few stray locks

of blonde hair from my rain-streaked face and walked along the narrow gravel drive that led to the entrance of this place. Was this really happening or had I just stepped onto the pages of a Gothic novel? I never imagined anything quite like this! The church was breathtaking in an unsettling kind of way. A slight chill embraced my slender shoulders, but passed as quickly as it had come, sending a nervous shudder through my entire body.

The wind whipped through the branches of a lone pine spurring restless birds into flight. Pelting rain smacked my cheeks and blended with the tears sliding down my face. The soft crunch of gravel beneath my feet, and the last hollow rumble of thunder released me from wishing back the past. I stood facing an old oak door and brass knocker. An electric current shot through me the instant my hand grasped its cool, smooth surface, and I jumped away quickly, but not before I could stop my scream. I felt foolish once it escaped, though rubbing my hands together didn't release the intense tingling that still ran through my fingertips. The atmosphere was powerfully charged and the smell of ozone hung heavy in the damp air.

"Did you say something?" shouted Michael above the roar of the storm.

I shook my head and wiped away the rain. He reached out toward me and placed a large heavy skeleton key into the palm of my quivering hand, which still throbbed from whatever possessed the brass knocker. A light mist swirled through the graveyard, bringing with it an overwhelming sense of sadness, causing my heart to flip-flop with intense anxiety. Suddenly, I didn't want to be here. Every cell, every beat of my heart, every breath screamed at me, "*get out!*" Michael must have sensed it and slowly wrapped his warm hand around mine. I was thankful he couldn't read my mind.

Along with the worried glance he shot at me, I sensed the dead beginning to awaken. And what the hell was up with that knocker? Had that been a warning? I placed the key inside the rusty chamber and wondered if somehow I'd regret it. *Deep breaths,* I thought, and pushed the thick oak door open wide. An overwhelming smell of rot and decay assaulted my nostrils and sent me bolting back outside into the pouring rain. The fresh air did little to wipe away the oppressive odor. I took in deep breaths and tried to hold it together. I knew this place had been abandoned for years, but I wasn't expecting this! It smelled like something had crawled inside the church and died. I wasn't sure I could go back in.

Michael said nothing, just gave me a quick wink, squeezed my hand, and ducked into the eerie darkness. I truly envied his casual calm, as I struggled with a deep urgency to flee. I gathered up my courage, stepped back inside, and was immediately devoured in darkness. Just my luck, no power! I felt my way slowly through the pitch black foyer, as cold, moist air swirled around my ankles. *Please, please, please, let me meet nothing that goes bump in the night,* I thought, as I continued to feel my way through dark empty space. Suddenly I sensed I wasn't alone in the foyer; in fact whatever was in here with me was approaching fast. I stood still as a statue and hoped it would pass.

"Say hello to your new home," it whispered, as it pulled me close and tucked its chin into the nape of my neck.

"Jesus, Michael!" I screamed. "You almost gave me a heart attack!" I squirmed to push myself out of his tight embrace. I managed a quick hard slap to his shoulder.

"Relax," he laughed, releasing his hold. "There's nothing here but you and me, Evie."

I stood frozen in the dark foyer for what seemed like hours while Michael explored the rest of the church. I felt foolish just standing there and I'm sure Michael thought I was overreacting, but I couldn't shake the uneasy feeling that things were about to go seriously wrong.

Chapter 3

The church was completely vacant, with the exception of Michael's four poster wrought iron bed that I could see--as he began to place candles strategically throughout the living space-- he'd situated in the far southeast corner of the loft. Golden blue flames sparked to life, sending slender bursts of grey smoke spiraling toward the high beamed ceiling and, with the light, the tension and uneasiness I felt when I first crossed the threshold began to melt away.

Then I noticed the old smelly green velvet chair, the kind with clawed feet, emerging from the shadows as candle light filled more and more of the space inside the church. *Seriously,* I thought with raised eyebrows and a smirk, as I smacked layers of dirt from its surface.

"We're getting rid of this!" I remarked as I plopped down onto the threadbare chair.

"What, you don't like its charm?" laughed Michael. "I think the previous owner left it. Some artist from Greece," he added, as he eased down beside me.

"I suppose he's the one that left the artwork too?" I asked, pointing to the lovely scripts and scrolls painted across the ancient stone walls.

"Hmmm," he mused, as he nuzzled up close and buried his chin next to mine.

When Michael purchased the church prior to our wedding without consulting me I was hurt, but didn't show it. He'd stumbled across it while surfing the net and was immediately smitten with its unique charm. He acted on impulse--his words-- and called it our "heaven on earth." I had hoped we'd choose something together that we could both enjoy, but when he told me about it, I didn't want to rain on his parade.

Not a big fan even before we arrived, I glanced around at the surroundings now, and it was more than clear we didn't share the same vision. Already this cold empty shell felt more like a "hell on earth..."

"Michael, why'd you buy this place without me?" I asked. "I don't mean to sound ungrateful--I just wished you would have waited."

"Why are you bringing this up now?" he asked nuzzling in a bit closer. "It was a great find, so I bought it. That's what I do. No big deal. My friends love it, why can't you?" he asked.

Friends? "What friends, exactly?" I asked.

"It doesn't matter now," he replied, as he stepped up from the chair and began to pace the loft. He turned his back on me, refusing to make eye contact. "Just leave it alone," he whispered.

"What *friends?*" I repeated.

"Clare," he replied. "She absolutely fell in love with it. I brought her here, we had a picnic—nothing fancy, just some Cristal and brie--and checked the place out. It was a great day."

"Clare--you're ex-girlfriend Clare?" I asked, incredulous. I pushed myself up from the chair. "What the fuck, Michael?" I screamed. "Jesus Christ, how could you? Are you telling me you needed to get the seal of approval from *her?*"

"We weren't married yet, Evie!" he yelled back. "I wasn't bound to you yet!"

I couldn't believe what I just heard, his words ripped through my heart like a knife.

"Did you sleep with her?" I continued in my rage.

"I told you, she's just a friend! I don't want to discuss it anymore! I'm not your ex-husbands-- don't put me in their category!" Michael knew about my ex-husbands and their betrayal--or my mistakes or imperfections, and he didn't want me to compare him with them. "It's all about trust, Evie!"

His intense brown eyes stared at me as he ran his fingers nervously through his thick brown hair, which I learned later was a sign he did not want to talk. I needed some air. I needed to distance myself from him and this conversation. I stomped outside, slamming the old oak door behind me.

Clare, really? I fumed. She was an artist, painted mostly nudes. Hey, I'm not a prude, whatever floats your boat. Michael had talked about her a lot prior to our wedding. He said she was just a friend. I'd picked up more than that, but dismissed it quickly. I didn't want to come off as the jealous controlling type.

It set my blood to boil that he'd had the nerve to share this place with Clare! Did he bring anyone else here as well? Damn him! To me, this was a betrayal. He'd blemished our relationship with someone who should have remained in the past. They picnicked in the surrounding graveyard, nothing fancy, just Cristal champagne and brie! *And was she also on the menu?* I thought angrily as I paced the gravel drive and tried to regain my composure. *Damn you, damn you, damn you!* And why the hell hadn't he come outside after me? Although the rain had stopped, it was now freezing out here! In my fit of rage I hadn't thought to grab a jacket.

I should have confronted him the night of our wedding, but I believed in him. I didn't want to rock the boat. His cousin, Rachel, who attended our wedding, spilled the beans. She asked me if I'd met Clare, which of course I hadn't.

11

"Fair warning," she confided. "She's a man eater, so beware."

What the hell did she mean by that? I looked at her directly. "Why are you telling me this?"

I wasn't going to let her get away without explaining. For all I knew she was just trying to stir the pot. Maybe she thrived on drama and gossip. She hadn't struck me as that kind of person. I liked her, but I loved Michael more.

"Because you're different," she answered. "I know Michael loves you Evie, and we were all very pleased when he shared the news about your marriage. But I was also quite surprised," she said as she placed her arm gently around my shoulder.

I didn't like where this conversation was going.

"Michael sees what he wants and takes it," Rachel continued. "He's used to getting his own way. Don't let him walk all over you or take advantage. He has women 'friends' all over the world. To tell you the truth, I never thought he'd get remarried."

I couldn't believe what I was hearing! I'd just said, "I do!" Had she considered that maybe Michael was tired of that kind of life? That he'd sown his wild oats and was ready for a real commitment? My mind raced a hundred miles an hour as I soaked in this revelation. He charmed the pants off of me. Wined and dined me, opened my eyes to an entirely different world than the one to which I'd been accustomed. I'd felt special, desirable, and--most important—loved! I wasn't going to let this woman burst my bubble.

"That was the past," I responded impatiently. "I can't accept that he's like that now."

"They were lovers at one time," Rachel continued, undaunted. "She wanted him to let her use the church--your new home--as her art studio."

"I don't believe that!" I cried. "No way! Michael wouldn't do that! This conversation is over!"

But the seed of doubt had been planted, and I knew that dwelling on it would only cause it to fester. I wasn't about to let that happen. I trusted Michael completely. He would never hurt me that way! Difficult as it was, I pushed what she shared with me to the farthest corner of my mind and made the decision that--until Michael proved otherwise—he had my complete devotion and trust.

And now here I was standing outside the church, beyond pissed--but mainly at myself. How in the hell had I not seen this? Was I that naïve? I admit that often I trusted too easily and without question, which sometimes left me vulnerable and wide open to deception. I seemed to repeatedly make the mistake of thinking that everyone else was like me. My heart's like an open book and, even though people used that fact to their advantage in the past, I still tried to see the good in everyone.

Now my head pounded as Rachel's words resounded through my mind. *What if the roles had been reversed?* I wondered. Would *he* have remained calm? Ex-lovers and husbands were not on the menu, I'd completely given my heart to him. The thought of sharing his heart with anyone else never entered my mind! Was I supposed to just laugh this off, dismiss it as if it was nothing, just as he said? After all, he picked *me*. He married *me*. Perhaps I was blowing things out of proportion, but this little disclosure of his shot like an arrow straight to my heart, from which suddenly issued memories of my father's transgressions.

God, I could barely hold back the bile as I thought back to the time he cheated on my mother: The day I arrived home from school to find her barely breathing, empty pill bottles scattered about her bedroom floor. I was eight and it seemed—

sensitive or not—I was destined to soak in every ounce of my mother's pain. Thus the seeds of distrust for my father were planted, while simultaneously the fear of losing my mother sank deeply into my psyche.

The last thing I wanted was to go back inside, but as much as I desired to avoid the inevitable, it was freaking cold, so I walked reluctantly back in. Michael sat in the smelly green chair in the loft reading a book. *Not smart,* I thought. Relaxed and calm as he slowly turned the page, he glanced up only when I planted myself in front of him and took away the book.

"You know, Michael, when you purchased the church I was hurt, but I didn't want you to think I was ungrateful. Was this place really going to be for Clare?" I waited and watched as he shifted uneasily in the chair.

"Darling, please let's not fight." He looked up at me earnestly as he began to pull me down close to him in the chair. Emotionally exhausted, I allowed it. Then, as if nothing had transpired between us, he lifted me up and escorted me to our four poster bed.

Whoa, I thought, *if you think we're going to have makeup sex, you're sadly mistaken!* Suddenly I realized I was beyond spent. There was no power. We had no heat. The church felt like the bloody Arctic. I could actually see my breath as it circled around in the chilly air. I shed my clothes, as exhaustion and frustration wrestled for my attention, and dropped onto the welcoming folds of the satin sheets. I lay silent as Michael discarded his clothes and climbed in naked beside me. As pissed as I was at his little confession and all the negative memories it brought to the surface, I spooned in close against his chest...I couldn't let this get between us. We vowed never to go to bed angry. Our bedroom would remain untainted with the day's events. If Clare was truly just a friend —he assured me previously that the romantic part of their relationship had been severed—then I needed to swallow my stubborn pride, set aside my fears from my painful past, and allow us to move forward.

I turned toward him and brushed my breasts up against his bare chest. He pulled me quickly on top of his very hard erection. The lovemaking was slow and sweet. *Now it's my turn to christen this God awful place,* I thought, as I shivered with an intense unexpected release. I lay in his arms, watching as he slowly drifted off. Soft moonlight filtered down through the skylight above the bed, casting a pale lemon glow throughout the loft. The patter of soft rain on the slate roof and the whispery hoot of a night owl nesting in a nearby pine softly lulled me to sleep.

Chapter 4

Michael was showered, shaved, ready for work, and staring down at me with a sullen smirk.

"What time is it?" I mumbled, as I lay sprawled naked across the satin sheets, rubbing the dregs of sleep from my eyes.

"Early," he replied. "I gotta run--I'll check in on you later, sometime mid-afternoon!"

"You're leaving me here by myself?" I know he planned on returning to work today, but hadn't actually considered he'd leave me here alone!

"Don't be silly, you'll be fine."

No way! the voice in my head shouted. *Take me to work with you! Drop me off at the nearest pub so I can drink myself into utter oblivion--at least then if I see any ghosts I'll know they're only drunken hallucinations!*

Michael obviously had no idea how vulnerable I felt, knowing I'd be left alone in this disturbing place as--with a quick kiss to my cheek--he bounded out the door. I watched from the window as his black Mercedes backed from the drive and disappeared from view. Suddenly, I missed my daughters and my friends. It had been easy to give up my house, job, and material things, but giving up the warm hugs, smiles, and closeness of family was much harder than I thought it would be. I realized now I was homesick, and felt lost and out of touch with my emotions.

Still overwhelmed with the move from America--the

16

only things I had from home were stuffed into two suitcases full of clothes and as many memories as were allowed on the plane, and now my heart began to ache. I was supposed to be happy; instead I felt anxiety and dread. I had journeyed into the unknown and my comfort zone was five thousand miles away across the Atlantic Ocean.

I didn't want to fail with Michael. Unlike any man I'd ever known, he was a God send when he entered my world. For the first time in my life, someone wanted to take care of me and spoil me and make me feel like a queen. I was grateful when Michael said he did not care to know about my past. I loved his take charge personality and the fact that he was a lot of bling and loved to show others his acquisitions, and yet at the same time was so humble. Only now was I beginning to suspect that maybe I didn't understand him emotionally as well as I thought I did; that he was a dichotomy--more surface, and yet not. I really loved him, though, why else would I have given up everything to move to England with him? But my entire world had flipped topsy-turvey--a complete 180 degrees upside down--while Michael's lifestyle remained much the same. His daughters, friends, and career were here, and the fact that our home wasn't refurbished yet didn't seem to faze him.

My thoughts returned to our new home. Now isolated and alone without a television--Michael didn't believe in them, hadn't owned one in years—and unable to figure out his complicated stereo system, I vowed to keep myself busy in order to make time pass more quickly. Once up and dressed I made use of this quiet time as I began to clear away dirt and debris from inside the church. The beautiful intricacy of hundreds of spiders' webs clearly illustrated that these creatures claimed this place as their home, and that they would not be evicted easily.

After a few exhausting hours, I gave up fighting the spiders' attempts at world domination. It was clear I needed a change of scenery, so I slipped on my favorite leather boots, grabbed a fleece jacket, and stepped outside. Fresh air slapped me hard in the face, and it felt damn good. The graveyard, covered in a carpet of snowdrops--small delicate white flowers that sprang up in thick patches everywhere—looked like it lay under a blanket of freshly fallen snow. Disturbingly thick ivy had grown and wrapped its vines around the tall pines like suffocating lethal weapons. I'd felt like that minutes earlier inside the church.

I needed distance, and found myself retreating to the quiet sanctuary of the nearby woods. This place fired up my imagination. It begged to be explored! The lush rolling green hills, dotted with plump woolly sheep grazing along the English countryside, enticed the old soul in me to explore the secrets hidden there. The smell of lush conifers and pine mingled with damp soil and fern proved a heady and intoxicating combination. I felt solace in the enchanted medieval forest surrounding the church and out of range of the energies that dwelled in my new home.

As a child I would lose myself for hours in the thick woods that surrounded our home in Virginia. I had this uncanny--my sister Nickie called it "freaky"--ability to connect with nature. Said it wasn't normal for someone to spend all their time roaming the woods. Dolls and tea parties were not my thing. She was the proper lady—me, I was the tomboy always inventing a new form of thrill that usually ended in disaster!

Thank God our mom was a nurse and always prepared for the bloody knee or nose. Worst case scenario was the time I cut my thumb on a barbed wire fence. I remember it dangling from my hand on a thin loose thread of bloody skin. My sister passed out--she couldn't handle blood and gore. I, on the other hand, shared the story with my classmates for weeks. I managed to outgrow my tomboy days and to mature into a delicate young woman, but my passion for, and fascination with, exploring nature remained intact.

As luck would have it, I noticed dark grey clouds circling above me and threatening rain, so I reluctantly made my way back home before the heavens spilled open. As the church came into view, I stopped dead in my tracks as I realized the truth: I'd been introduced to this church and its unusual residents' at least six months before I actually left America! That was when ghostly specters began to visit me in my dreams. At first, I blew it off as pre-marriage jitters--until these hauntingly surreal dreams became more realistic and increasingly disturbing. I asked Michael to research this church for me--much of what I got centered on the bell tower and crypt of a young woman named Catherine. Her energy reached out to me from five thousand miles away.

As a young child, I used to think that something was terribly wrong with me. I learned early on that I was different, but because I felt too intimidated to open up, I did not share my experiences with anyone. When stressed or anxious--especially when self-doubt and feelings of worthlessness set in--I'd awaken unexpectedly in the middle of the night and see my bedroom infused with a soft soothing light and beings of light, people not of the living, standing next to my bed. There was no fear; I sensed they were there to protect and guide me to a higher purpose.

I had this thing for stuffed animals--my favorite was a pajama cat with emerald green eyes. I displayed them along the headboard of my bed. I remember the time I forgot something in my room and, as I walked in to retrieve it, I witnessed the most bizarre event: My pajama cat levitated from the headboard and landed on my bed; the rest of the stuffed animals followed and were thrown across the bed by some unknown force!

How was this even possible? I remember thinking. I stood there, amazed at first, until the adrenaline kicked in and I was out of there and down the spiral staircase in a flash. I refused to go back into my room until my sister arrived home from school. After that, there was something about that stuffed pajama cat that spooked the hell out of me. Eventually, I had to throw it away.

I did not know at the time anything about the "gifts" belonging to a psychic medium, so I kept a lot of my experiences to myself. It didn't help that my father always told me I was overly sensitive and that I'd be a failure, that no matter what I did it was never good enough--so when I discovered I had psychic sensitivities, I found it hard to believe because I trusted that my father's words must be true.

I managed to make it to the entrance of the church as the first drops fell from the darkening sky. I glanced up at the smiling, disquieting faces of the gargoyles as they peered down at me, their clawed feet clinging to the tower, and an involuntary quiver rushed down my spine, as if someone had just stepped across my grave. I quickly shrugged it off. *It's broad daylight for hell's sake, get a grip!* I admonished myself.

Now, as I stood at the threshold of this church, the instant I stepped inside I felt the unearthly welcome of the residents' cold embrace, and immediately remembered my dreams of the recent past. Each night became a continuation of the night before, and always someone who called herself Catherine tried to make contact--she would not go away!

The dreams all started out the same: I found myself standing in front of a rusty black wrought iron gate, two flowering plum trees--their branches weighed down by delicate pink flowers in full bloom--positioned opposite one another. Before me was a narrow gravel drive surrounded by an old cemetery. The gate opened of its own volition, inviting me through, and closed quietly behind me after my entrance. I walked slowly down the long drive, soaking in the peaceful solitude of this place, not a cloud in the sky. Warm sunshine filtered down upon me and enticed me further down the drive. Quickly, I realized I wasn't the only one there. A young woman, back towards me, head bowed, stood in front of an old, crumbling crypt.

I didn't want to disturb her, and yet some invisible force propelled me towards her. As I drew closer I heard soft whimpering, but I could not see this woman's face. I reached out—a gesture meant to find out if she was okay and if there was anything I could do to help her--and suddenly the atmosphere within the cemetery shifted, and a cold wind began to stir. The sky blackened with clouds that blocked out the sun. The young woman turned toward me slowly and, though it took a moment to register, I realized I was not looking at a stranger--I was looking at my own face, as if a mirror image of myself reflected back at me! The woman pointed slowly toward the crypt. I saw a name, barely readable, etched across the surface.

Complete darkness surrounded the two of us; it came swiftly with the wind. "Catherine," she whispered softly, "Catherine..." Then she was gone, swept up in the darkness. I ran toward the gate and saw that the plum trees had shed their delicate flowers, which-- shriveled and brown—were now being carried by the wind. The trees stood barren and black, branches broken, brushing up against the rusty gate. I woke always in a sweat, my heart throbbing wildly, head pounding; the clock on my nightstand always registering the same time:

five minutes past three a.m.

A dream is only a dream when it fades away quickly. But this dream haunted me throughout the day. Visions would appear to me—preceded almost always by a headache which grew into the intensity of a jackhammer, and what I referred to as a ping pong match in my head—during my waking hours, often as I lay on my couch. At first, I thought I had brought these dreams and visions upon myself--caused such unbelievable emotions to awaken--because I was caught up in a romance with Michael that seemed too good to be true. They did nothing for my beauty sleep; however, love is blind, and at the time I refused to acknowledge my intuition and heed the warning signs.

Whether communicating with the dead is my curse or my blessing, there was no doubt this place amplified my sensitivity. Upon entering the church again, I swear I heard them whisper "welcome home, Evie, welcome home..."The chill of their soft voices unnerved me, as an entirely different world began to present itself. It was as if a tear opened in the fabric of time, unleashing a menagerie of spirits, both dark and light. Suddenly I realized I could no longer dismiss my previous experiences as just a series of dreams, and knew with certainty they'd been visions of things to come once I crossed the Atlantic.

I had no sooner grasped the latch and entered the foyer when an uneasy feeling rushed over me, and I heard a low monotone hum that stopped me dead in my tracks. *What the hell?* I rounded the corner into the great room, just as a sudden swift darkness descended from high in the rafters. An army of black winged creatures swarmed directly down at me, taking me completely by surprise.

I screamed, and as I raised my hands to protect my face, saw my cell phone on the table nearby. I grabbed it and bailed to the safety of Catherine's tomb outside, where I plopped down to catch my breath before making the call to Michael--otherwise I knew I'd sound like a raving banshee when he answered. Suddenly, I was startled yet again when a swarm of blackness exited the church, and I ducked behind the tomb, wishing them away.

Convinced this was an orchestrated attack, I realized in a flash there was a disturbing presence that remained isolated on the third floor of the bell tower. Yet its energy disrupted and confused the others who I sensed dwelled here with me. I began to fear this place would either destroy me or forever change me. However, I resolved I was going to stay. I didn't believe in coincidence. I'd been brought here by extremely powerful forces that reached out now and begged me to stay.

I felt I wasn't alone in the fight; there was another presence here with me. *Catherine is that you?* I gazed about the graveyard, searching for a hint of her silhouette, anything that would prove she was here. Nothing, dead silence, that's when I made the call.

When Michael picked up, all I could manage was a forced whisper: *"P-l-e-a-s-e* come home..."

Chapter 5

Michael summarily dismissed the otherworldly by reminding me we'd turned on the heat to rid the place of damp and mold, and that the warmth must have caused thousands of blowflies' larvae to hatch. The church had become a mini incubator for the little beasts, nothing more. He could rationalize it all he wanted; I wasn't spending another night in this wicked place!

We spent the night at The Blue Heron on the Lake, a charming, quaint, out of the way inn surrounded by a pristine lake, nesting herons, and white swans. It was mid-week, the place was fairly deserted, and I welcomed it with open arms. Michael went all out. We dined outside on the deck. Our table faced the lake and I watched, mesmerized, as graceful swans sailed by. They glided to the edge as I tossed small bits of French bread, which they gobbled down with delight.

"What is it with you and nature?" Michael teased, inching a little closer as we sipped a delicate rose wine. "You're like Snow White," he smiled. "Salute" he said as, reaching across the table, he grasped my hand and rubbed his thumb across my wedding ring. "I'm sorry," he whispered, looking at me with somber brown eyes.

You should be, I thought, *for leaving me all alone in that God-forsaken, spirit-ridden church all day!* Easy, Evie, rein in that temper! Instead of speaking my mind I replied "it's okay, Michael," in a somewhat convincing tone. "Maybe once I've settled in things will calm down." *Yeah, sure...*"I could use another glass of wine, though," I smiled, and slid my crystal goblet towards him. He winked and immediately poured another glass for me.

I sipped the deliciously fragrant wine and watched as the last rays of sunshine dipped behind the horizon. Dusk had descended, and the lake was still. Michael escorted me to our chambers where he surprised me by drawing a hot bath. I soaked in the deep French tub until the water grew cold. Michael walked in as I stepped from the tub, and drew me near. Naked and quite wet, I allowed it. After drying me completely from head to toe, he carried me to the warmth of the bed and tucked me in. Once he bathed, he joined me. I slept like a baby without fear of dark dreams or things going bump in the night. It wasn't until we headed for home that the uneasy feelings began to creep back in and I noticed I was developing a slight headache.

Michael had hired a man to spray the place while we were away. He warned us we might return to two or three inches of dead flies. If only he knew that was the least of my problems! It took us several hours to vacuum up their little carcasses. I watched in relief as Michael emptied them into the bin. Unfortunately, unlike the flies, the spiders were still alive and kicking. They'd busied themselves constructing newly formed webs high in the rafters and shadowy corners of the church.

We settled back in to life at the church, and the next few weeks proved uneventful. I knew that if Michael had his way this place would remain an empty shell, since he had absolutely no sense of urgency about making this place into a home. So far, I hated the church. Left alone here ten hours a day while Michael escaped to work--no TV or other form of entertainment--I felt so alone. No furniture, no kitchen, stove, fridge...he didn't understand I wanted to feel secure in this place, I needed my own things! Everything belonged to him--his books, his stuff. He hadn't given up friends, family, or country, yet in the past six months I'd given up a job of eighteen years, sold my car, my home, and all the belongings I'd collected for more than forty-five years, remarried, and moved to a foreign country! I was in unknown scary territory and I felt lost...

However, I intended to keep my sanity intact! In order to escape boredom and the loneliness I felt when Michael was away at work for so many hours a day, I contacted local builders to meet with me to discuss the remodeling of our home. I hoped they'd be open to committing to such an unusual project, as I refused to live under these conditions any longer! I assumed that Michael finally realized how important having a real home was to me, since he did not protest. Still, I wondered if we'd ever achieve transforming this place into one that was all warm and cozy.

Shortly after, I managed to gain the trust of the local Council and Church Wardens, both of whom had to be onboard before we could make any progress toward renovating the church. All plans had to be approved by the church and city council before we could begin. Strict guidelines had to be met and specific rules followed, since the church was a landmark. We had to promise to respect the church as an historical landmark, and that we'd adhere to all of their guidelines. We were informed that we could not construct new walls and create separate rooms; we had to have an open floor plan. And, since we knew the surrounding cemetery was still a working one, there was no need to remind us of the importance of respecting the dead.

I continued to make use of my time fighting the never-ending battle of the arachnids as they persistently spun their webs over and over again despite my efforts to clear them out once and for all. I still missed my family and friends, but realized I'd been resisting everything from the time I set foot into Heathrow airport. I decided I would try to make the best of my new home, new life, and new country.

Michael hired three architects he'd met while visiting a good friend in Bulgaria. Skeptical at first, I was wary of the fact that they were all women. Unpleasant, not-so-distant memories of his need to have ex-girlfriends over before I'd arrived surfaced. Now he wanted women to design the place-- *God, Michael, what is it with you and the need to be constantly surrounded by feminine energy?* I marveled. The urge to confront him rushed once again to the surface, though I paused long enough to consider my confusion: Was I confronting Michael, or my father? *Easy, Evie!* Past fears that still hadn't healed, nothing more. I managed to submerge my fear from whence it came--at least for the moment. These women came highly recommended and were well known in London, I should at least give them a chance...

I sat next to Catherine's tomb and watched in fascination as three women exited from a black van. The eldest glided past me and flashed a toothless smile. *Okay,* I thought, *no competition here!* The others approached. Hmmm, they were quite lovely--sisters perhaps? They smiled and sashayed past. When Michael approached, the quiet solitude of the graveyard was suddenly pierced by their shrill giggles. I had to admit he was a good-looking specimen. *But really, girls, aren't you going a little over the top?* I don't usually judge others, but their dark gypsy-like appearance was a bit unnerving, not to mention the fact that they flirted openly with my husband. *Hands off, girls!* I thought, though I pretended not to notice.

When they reached the entrance to the church, all hell broke loose. I couldn't understand what they were saying— apparently, they were speaking in their native tongue. By her actions, I sensed the toothless one did not want to go inside. She crossed herself repeatedly, while the others mumbled something about the evil eye. It took a lot of convincing on Michael's behalf to get them inside. Of course, I'm sure the sisters would have followed him to hell itself had he asked!

Immediately, they set to work designing a spiral staircase and oval balcony which led to our bedroom in the loft. It faced a huge twenty-five foot rectangular window that once housed beautiful stained glass panes, long since removed and now on display in a museum in Winchester. Simple glass pane replacements still captivated, especially in the morning when golden rays of sunshine filtered through, making it a more than suitable replacement.

Over the course of a few weeks I managed to set aside my fears and found the eldest sister begin to warm up to me. A very strange and beguiling woman, she reminded me of an old gypsy fortune teller. She kept her thick dark hair wrapped tightly in a red silk scarf, and large gold earrings dangled from her tiny ears. Upon completion of the plans, she presented me with a gift.

"Take zis," she insisted, as she flashed her toothless smile and pressed into my hand a small circular medallion that hung from an intricate silver cord. "You vil need it," she whispered in her soft, barely audible English. The look in her deep-set brown eyes disturbed me. Was this her way of telling me she felt the presence? She said nothing more, just withdrew her liver-spotted hand from mine and, smiling sweetly, walked away to join the rest of her motley crew. I found out later from a dear Bulgarian friend of ours that she had given me a charm to protect me and my home from the "evil eye." Immediately I dug it out of the kitchen cupboard and hung it on the inside of the old oak door...

Chapter 6

One night, eager to get some fresh air--Michael settled comfortably in the loft working on some papers--I decided to take a walk. Streaked with golden amber highlights, the sky reflected the fading globe of the sun as it disappeared beyond the horizon. I noticed the cemetery was unusually quiet. Previously I'd seen small rabbits and red deer grazing in the field, but tonight the thick mist weaved its wispy tendrils around my bare ankles. I'd forgotten to grab my wrap before coming out, and when I reached to grasp the door handle to go back inside and get it, I found myself standing in the empty field behind the church!

How the hell did I get here? I marveled. I'd had no warning whatsoever! No usual jackhammer signaled an impending vision, no ping pong match played in my head. *Had I drank too much champagne and this was my imagination running away with me?* Thick grass pushed up tightly against my legs, and a bone-chilling dampness sent nervous anxiety coursing throughout my body. Invisible fingers seemed to push me further into the field and bring me stumbling to the edge of the thick, black woods.

The sick feeling in the pit of my stomach alerted me to that fact that I was being watched. I thought I glimpsed a hint of something just up ahead, but the mist and dense darkness had a way of playing tricks on the eyes. For all I knew this was just a wild illusion or nightmare into which I'd dreamed my way! *I'll probably wake up and be standing by the old oak door,* I mused. The unsettling crack of a tree branch and the sound of heavy breathing a few feet away confirmed that I was not alone. This illusion, nightmare—whatever I wanted to call it--was *real!*

The mist parted, and I could make out the barest details of a slender silhouette. It appeared to be a young woman standing several feet away. Her long golden hair cascaded down past her shoulders; she was barefoot and dressed in a thin white gown. There was the slightest hint of lavender and sage in the air that mingled with the damp mossy ground and rich, wet earth. It was her eyes that were most captivating, their deep rich emerald pools drew me in. Paralyzed and unable to speak, I hadn't expected to witness a full body apparition! Yet here she was, almost waif-like, and regarding me with such an intense demeanor.

The chill of the mist became almost unbearable as it surrounded the two of us in its otherworldly embrace. She motioned me to follow, but my hesitation and disbelief about what I was seeing must have scared her away. It was as if she was there but moments later dissolved into the swirling mist.

The contact with this ethereal woman stirred a memory buried deep within me. *Was this Catherine?* I wondered. I thought I recognized her from my dreams, but there was something else about her that struck a chord deep inside my soul. What happened next was most difficult to fathom. I reached out into the darkness in hopes she'd return and that's when I realized I was no longer in the woods--I lay now in our four poster bed in the loft, the dark stillness of the church all around. The hint of lavender lingering in the air, I heard the soft familiar sound of Michael snoring-- paralyzed, I couldn't move or make a peep. Then I realized I was screaming but no sound was coming out!

"What's happening?"I squeaked. It felt as though I was

wrapped in a straight jacket and held down by powerful, invisible hands; a deep bone-crushing weight pressed down hard on my chest. This *thing,* whatever the hell it was, was smothering me!

"Get off me!" I croaked as, disoriented and blindsided, I tried to fight off my unseen attacker. My screams wouldn't come, my breathing was shallow and constricted, and fighting seemed only to make things worse. The darkness was all around and the smell of decay assaulted my nostrils. I went limp as a rag doll, trying to bring my breathing under control. As quickly as this thing had come, it was gone. I lay in the darkness, waiting for my muscles to respond. After several minutes I was able to move once more. I rolled over slowly and saw Michael fast asleep, snoring. How could that be? Had this all been nothing more than a nightmare? I'd heard of night terrors and the extreme fear and paralysis people experienced —is this what happened to me? It seemed so real...

I stepped quietly from the bed, careful not to awaken Michael. The pale lemon glow of a full moon filtered through the skylight above the bed, lighting my way as I slowly descended the spiral staircase. The rest of the church was silent. I made my way to the kitchen and stopped short of switching on the light when a chill so devastatingly cold nearly knocked me off my feet.

It's not over, I thought. My blood curdling scream "GET OUT!" was so loud, Michael nearly broke his neck racing down the staircase to see what in God's name was happening.

"Over there!" I cried, pointing toward the dark foyer.

Michael wiped the sleep from his eyes, and switched on the lights. Nothing; the only sound was that of my heavy breathing.

My mind raced a hundred miles an hour. *This can't be happening! This isn't real!*

"I don't understand what just happened!" I cried. "There was something down here with me--it was cold and smelled terrible--as if something dead passed through! It followed me from the woods," I mumbled.

"What are you talking about?" Michael stepped toward me but the look in his eyes made me back away.

"I know what you're thinking," I whispered. "I'm *not* crazy!"

"Sweetheart, come here--I don't think you're crazy, I think you had a bad dream." He wrapped his arm around my bare shoulders and guided me back upstairs to the warmth of our bed, tucked the down comforter around us both, and pulled me close.

"Earlier, while you were busy reading, something drew me out into the woods." I shivered as I related my experience. *Please don't think I'm crazy!* Now, more than ever, I needed him to believe me, no matter how bizarre and absurd my story sounded.

"It was only a nightmare," Michael responded. "You've been having a lot of those lately." He looked down at me worriedly as he crawled across me to his side of the bed.

"No!" I protested. "It was real! Something wanted me out there in the woods! I remember going out just after finishing the dishes--*something* led me out to the woods!"

"No," Michael said, almost sternly. "After you finished the dishes I watched you go upstairs. I expected you to come back down but you never did, so I figured you were tired and fell asleep. When I came up to join you, you were snoring softly and I snuggled in next to you."

"No," I insisted yet again, "that's *not* what happened! That *couldn't* have been what happened--it seemed so real!"

"Darling, it's been a major adjustment to a new home and country--not to mention that I realize now I should have had more work done here before we arrived." He took my chin in his hand and tilted my face up until my eyes met his. "It's completely understandable, with all of these changes, that you've just spread yourself too thin." He looked at me intently with his deep brown eyes and smiled. "Once we get the house in order things will settle down, I promise...now close those pretty green eyes and get some sleep."

I snuggled up close to him. He felt safe and warm. "You're probably right," I responded wearily, as he wrapped his arms around me. I had learned from my past to keep my paranormal experiences to myself; that those who never experienced such happenings had a hard time relating. In fact, they often shut me down before I had an opportunity to share. And then it was my father all over again, telling me there was something wrong with me, that I'd never amount to anything if I continued to speak about such nonsense. It was as if a metal door within his mind slammed shut, and bolted and sealed itself from any exposure connected with the invisible world. Having seen these otherworldly specters from an early age, this rejection of my reality only made me doubt myself even more, and I realized how strange I must appear to others and to Michael right now. But it hurt that he didn't believe me, and I thought *oh no, Michael, not you too...*

"You'll see," he continued. "Things will look better in the morning. And what you've told me simply isn't possible," he added, almost as an afterthought. "It was definitely a nightmare, nothing more."

I closed my eyes tightly and tried to forget about the night's events, and a few minutes later Michael's soft snoring began to ease me back to sleep. As I began to drift away from consciousness, I could swear I felt something cold and wet brush up against my cheek, and a soft, barely audible voice whisper "good to have you back," just as I fell into a deep sleep.

Chapter 7

I awoke the next morning to the familiar sound of Michael's whistling as he busied himself in our still rudimentary version of a kitchen. The deep, rich aroma of fresh brewed Italian coffee drifted up to the loft, nudging me from my sleep. Michael and I loved our Italian coffee, and when I insisted we at least be able to make that fresh in our own home, he did not argue. The rest of our breakfast he'd picked up from a local diner, and I had to admit it smelled damn good as well.

All was quiet in the loft—normal even. I almost had myself convinced that what happened last night was only a terrible nightmare. After all, night terrors were not uncommon--thousands of individuals experienced them throughout history—and I shouldn't be too quick to rule that out. My rational mind was all for that theory, although my heart and intuition emphatically screamed *"no way!"*

Whatever had happened, it was over now, thank God. Michael said things would look better in the morning, and I guess he was right. However, as I pulled the sheets away and climbed out of bed, I noticed small patches of dried dirt scattered everywhere. Perhaps I'd ventured out without Michael's noticing? He was so involved in his reading, perhaps I'd passed him undetected? I wasn't in the habit of sleep walking--at least that I was aware—so I most definitely I ruled that out. As relieved as I was to discover the soiled sheets, panic gripped my heart just the same. Something inexplicable had happened last night, and one way or another I'd get to the bottom of it!

I stripped the bed and tossed the soiled sheets into the laundry basket, made the bed quickly, and joined Michael downstairs for breakfast. I didn't mention anything more about last night's events to Michael, nor did I bring up the soiled sheets. I decided from then on to keep my otherworldly experiences to myself, especially since I felt our marriage already on shaky ground once he'd shared his little story about Clare. He'd tried to set things straight since then, and was being far more supportive in his actions, so I pushed the incident to the back of my mind and vowed to move forward and make this our home.

We ate in silence, both savoring the English breakfast which consisted of eggs over easy, pork sausage, toast with marmalade, pork and beans, and our Italian coffee, of course. I reminded myself that the remodeling of our home was about to commence--Michael and I had finally felt comfortable enough to choose a contractor, an electrician, and a plumber to handle the job of renovating the church. I knew only an extraordinary crew could take on this place, and they were scheduled to arrive today! I grinned like a Cheshire cat as I envisioned the church about to get a drastic face lift!

Michael drank the last drop of coffee, kissed me on the cheek, and headed off to work. I walked outside to watch him back his car from the graveled drive, and as soon as he disappeared from sight I felt an overwhelming sense of despair and sickness wash over me. The urge to throw up all the breakfast I'd just devoured was overpowering. I managed to hold everything in but, gazing around, noticed the morning mist swirling around my ankles. Something didn't feel right; I felt a malevolent presence bearing down on me. The smell of decay was thick in the air. This was the same depressing heaviness I'd felt the night before.

The loud cackling of the disgruntled rooks rescued me from further psychic attack. I sat on Catherine's crypt and tried to figure out my next move. I scanned the cemetery for intruders; there was absolutely nothing to fear.The sentinels eyed me from their perch on the tower.

"You don't scare me anymore," I whispered, as I continued to survey my surroundings. I stopped when I detected slight movement on an ancient headstone a few feet away and, though at first I doubted my peripheral vision, I saw an object take flight and glide gently past.

"Holy crap!" I ducked instinctively and covered my head, then laughed when I realized it was only an owl. What the heck was he doing out during the day? Owls were omens of the underworld and magic--perhaps he was a harbinger of things to come? Or was I letting this place get to me? I thought back to when I was a small child. Why was my psychic sensitivity coming back now after such a long time?

What the...? My thoughts were interrupted suddenly by the soft whimpering noise that seemed to come from the tower. What was this, another trick of my imagination? I hadn't the courage to investigate that part of the church yet-- every time I walked past it an intense wave of nausea swept over me. It seemed much of the activity in the church centered itself up there. I heard strange noises coming from the tower late at night, when complete silence enveloped the church. Michael assured me it was nothing more than birds nesting in the eves or--worst case scenario--rats. He promised to have someone take a look.

I was really letting this place get to me! It seemed to be tugging at the threads of my sanity! It was as though I was living two realities--one married and starting a new life with my charming new mate, and another that reeled me back in time. What part of the puzzle did I play here in a country so far away from home? Who was this young woman I saw barefoot in the mist at the edge of the woods last night? And, most disturbing of all, who or what was this evil presence that seemed bound and determined to send me away--or perhaps push me to the very edge of my sanity?

A light drizzle of rain began to fall. I didn't want to go back inside, but I didn't relish the thought of sitting out in the rain. Cold air rushed past as I entered the foyer and a silky thread from a spider's web brushed against my face. A low mournful sound echoed throughout the church, its origin the bell tower. I refused to let this scare me and walked into the warmth and safety of my kitchen. The slightest hint of a headache niggled inside my head and a bout of vertigo swept quickly over me. The walls within my kitchen began to close in around me. I felt as though I'd left my body and was seeing through the eyes of another. I knew I was standing there but everything seemed so blurry and far away.

As I fought to focus my eyes, suddenly before me materialized a colorful market place! Amazed to hear the sound of dogs barking in the distance, the smell of chimney smoke and urine assaulted my senses. The call of venders hocking their wares rang through narrow alleyways.

"Fresh baked bread, warm and sweet!" they cried. The intoxicating smell of freshly baked bread made my mind swirl. I watched as a horse and his rider trotted along the cobbled streets. How was this possible? I could see everyone, but they could not see me! Was I caught up in a time long ago? Everything transpired in slow motion, as if time itself stood still.

This isn't happening! I thought. My head began to pound, and the walls of my kitchen began to spin out of control and close in on me ever so slowly. "What's happening?" I screamed, as I felt the familiar caress of blackness surround me and I slipped slowly away.

Chapter 8

The builders found me lying on the cold marble kitchen floor. I began to regain consciousness when I heard them come through the door. Apparently, I left it wide open and when no one answered their call, they ventured inside to find me lying here.

As I regained my senses and began to see straight, I found myself looking up at three men whose concerned faces stared down at me. Still lightheaded, I blinked and tried to make sense of everything that had taken place while a damn jackhammer did a number in my head.

"Pardon me, miss'us," said one, "but are you all right? May I help you up?" He stared down at me with kind twinkling grey eyes. I smiled weakly, embarrassed now, and allowed him to help me to my feet. I patted myself down, still a little disoriented, but discovered no bumps or bruises, thank God, and I realized this was John, the head builder Michael and I had hired to carry out our remodeling.

"Thank you," I said, grateful for his assistance. "I guess I've been so exhausted from settling in here and fighting these damn spiders—I-I'm sure that's why I fainted," I said with a reassuring smile. That ought to satisfy them for a while, I thought as I grabbed a cold wash cloth and placed it on my head.

"I wouldn't be caught dead living in a place like this," mumbled one of the builders softly underneath his breath.

"That's enough of that," barked John, as if to say, don't

scare the young lady any more than she probably is already.

"Well, it's true sir, it gives me the willies," the young man replied.

I remembered now how much I liked John when we'd first met him. His tall, lanky body appeared almost comical-- his feet and hands seemed too large for the rest of his slender body, and he looked like a giant, albeit hunched over a bit now with age.

"Alright, show's over!" John informed his crew, which consisted of two younger men who'd come through the door with him. "I don't pay you boys to sit on your arses, so let's get started!"

His gruff voice was comforting as he turned to me and said "let me make you a cup of tea, miss'us, that will make you feel better, I'm sure."

"No, no, not at all," I protested. "It's I who will make tea for us all!" At this point I noticed all eyes were still on me. "Really guys, thank you, but I'm fine." Then I smiled and threatened to fire them all if they breathed a word of this to Michael. "I've been working a little harder than usual--that's the only reason I fainted. Capisci?"

"Understood mum," replied John, patting my hand. He turned to his crew and barked "alright let's get to work now-- and not a peep to anyone about the happenings here today! Do I make myself clear? Rob, let's get the tools out of the truck and show the rest of the crew where to start, like we discussed on the way over."

He turned to me once more and, scratching a day or so worth of gray stubble on his narrow chin, added, "I've lived in several countries during my seventy years, and it was hard for me too, miss'us." Then, without missing a beat, he turned back to bark more orders at his crew.

I spent the next few hours dusting as John's crew of

builders began to pound, hammer, and drill their way toward the church's renovation. I began to feel better as I turned my attention to the spiders and my mission of sweeping away their newly spun webs. We were going to have to come to some kind of understanding once and for all! I threatened to Hoover them away if they didn't respect my boundaries. This was so comical it made me smile; here I was in a strange country, with no friends or family, battling things out with hairy little eight-legged creatures in a haunted church.

The more I thought about this, the more I didn't think anyone back home would believe me without experiencing this for themselves. My friends would dismiss it as over imagination and exhaustion. They already thought I was living the good life and felt I was acting ungrateful. "Give it time, enjoy the adventure," their words echoed through my mind, "things will begin to settle down in time."

I decided the only way to clear my mind was to take a walk. I loved the woods and hoped I'd feel refreshed and ready to face the church when I got back. I slipped on my walking boots and a jacket and told John I'd be gone for a while.

"You're goin' by yourself miss'us?" I thought I detected a flicker of worry in his eyes.

"Yes, why?" I replied.

It was as if he'd spoken out loud unintentionally and just now realized that I'd heard him.

"I'll be fine," I assured him and, before he could even answer, added "I love the woods and the fresh air and a walk will do me good."

I noticed again the flicker of concern in his deep set grey eyes. This set me on edge a bit but I wasn't about to show it. "Have it your way," he said, and with a wave of his large hand disappeared back inside the church.

As I began to walk I pondered my experience back in

the church kitchen. I knew I'd been transported to another time and place, one that existed centuries ago, and that, in fact, something strange and very profound had taken place! No matter how I tried, I could not explain this away. I needed to find out what triggered this vision, and how it was possible I could be swept away to another time and place! The entire experience blew my mind, and yet I'd felt no fear. One thing was certain--I sure as hell was not going to confide what had happened to Michael!

To get to the woods I had to make my way through the large field behind the church which meant dodging stinging nettle--its bite is sharp and leaves nasty welts on the skin for days. Then I remembered Trevor, the very cranky and formidable sheep farmer (a.k.a. pheasant wrangler!) I'd run into while exploring the woods one day. It seemed he was worried I might steal his pheasants. He made it very clear this was his livelihood and he didn't need any strange American woman snooping around!

His thatched roof cottage was the only other building within miles of the church. I decided not to let him bother me —I was convinced his bark was worse than his bite--but whenever I heard him puttering around on his four wheeler I'd duck behind the nearest tree to escape the scolding I knew he'd cherish giving me. It was quite entertaining to watch him scour the woods in search of trespassers, his round squat body jiggling each time he hit a bump or dodged the rabbit burrows scattered throughout the fields!

The only other way to get to the woods was along the narrow road that--even though we lived out in the country-- always appeared to be busy. A very popular road where kids raced their bullet bikes, it nevertheless seemed not to lack its fair share of fatalities. Already, I'd found a dead deer, fox, rabbit, and the occasional badger who'd met their demise along this road, their lifeless bodies curled up along the edge of the pavement. This always broke my heart, so today I found myself sneaking across the empty field, my fingers crossed I wouldn't meet with "Trevor the Terrible," my nickname for him.

I'd walked before to Ellisfield, a small village about two hours away. There was a great pub there called the Fox and Hound that served the best fish and chips I ever tasted, along with an icy cold pear cider that really hit the spot. I was tempted to go there, but my feet turned in the opposite direction.

"Okay, this way it is," I said, laughing and shaking my head.

Things began to seem almost normal again in my world now as I walked along the dusty road that sliced into the rolling green countryside. The smell of rape seed fields and fresh newly cut hay drifted through the air. I felt safe and once again at peace as I eased into my walk.

After walking for more than an hour, I stumbled upon an old abandoned stable. Its crumbling stone walls and caved-in roof had provided a grand opportunity for the rats and winding ivy to take up residence. It seemed the perfect spot for a rest before turning back and heading home.

I sat down on what appeared to be a once proud and magnificent tree that had fallen and now lay naked, stripped of its leaves, its burial ground a thick patch of delicate ferns that carpeted the forest floor. The woods were thick here and only patches of sunshine managed to push their way through the dense foliage.

Who owns this place? I wondered. For a brief moment an image of the stables filled with the bustling of stable boys and magnificent, spirited horses snorting impatiently after a long ride in the woods appeared before me. The horses stomped their hooves nervously on the cobblestone floor as they anticipated oats and fresh cut hay. The air was filled with the smell of fresh sweat and leather. Polished saddles and bridles hung next to each of the stalls, ready for their next ride through the woods. Off in the corner a very plump orange tabby--the stable's mascot--groomed its whiskers of recently consumed freshly churned cream, no doubt his daily reward for keeping the population of pesky mice and rats down. The vision slowly faded away.

I walked through what once must have been the wide stable doors onto a level that, had the roof not caved in, might have been the loft. Above the threshold a date was inscribed in flint stone: 1695. Beneath the date it looked like someone's name had been etched. I could barely make out the first letter "H" as I dusted off the stone. The rest was worn away from centuries of harsh weather and age.

Just past the stables was a narrow path leading to an open meadow covered in thousands of tiny bluebells, and in the distance beyond that loomed the most magnificent mansion I'd ever seen. Surrounded in a grove of tall pines and birch, no one would've noticed it unless they'd stumbled across it like I had. I stood there for several minutes drinking in its beauty.

As I did so, the sun dipped behind a billowy cloud sending the slightest hint of anxiety surging through me. As the familiar feelings of déjà vu swept over me, I recognized having been here before! *Impossible!* I thought, yet the strength and force of my recognition came in waves. I felt the slightest bit of a headache coming on, and closed my eyes to wish it away. The pain released its vice-like grip and I continued on my way.

I drew closer--the sad faces of the gargoyles perched lazily atop the balustrades of the home were not unwelcoming, but gave me goose bumps just the same. Purple lace wisteria clung to the faded gray bricks and the inviting smell of lilacs and lavender filled the air. No longer hesitant, I was anxious and excited to explore. There were no cars in the graveled drive. I hoped the owner wouldn't mind my trespassing.

The grounds were huge with expansive plush green lawns and manicured gardens. Roses of every variety and color graced the property. Hidden among tall cattails and ferns was a small pond brimming with lily pads, moss, and tiny gold fish that occasionally leapt to the surface, snatching up a clueless fly. Beyond the pond, nestled in a grove of silver aspen and pine, was a tiny church. This, of course, intrigued me since I was living in one now.

Damn! The slightest bit of nausea washed over me. *Not now!* I thought. Candle light and incense greeted me as I pushed open the heavy oak door and was enveloped instantly in a wave of peace and warmth. Drawn to the center of the room, I stood where rays of sunshine streamed in from the four small windows and illuminated the pew with golden light. No shadow people here! No dark energy threatened to evict me from this enchanting place!

I hadn't felt this peaceful or calm since I moved to England. For the first time since then I allowed myself to really feel my emotions. Before I knew it, the floodgates opened, and I found myself sobbing in shaky waves of emotional release. *Wow, where did this come from?* I wondered.

I knelt to feel the smooth cold surface of the stone and, as I did so, caught the slightest movement of a shadow. Perhaps it was the flickering candles playing tricks on my eyes? I was about to dismiss it as my imagination when from out of the corner of the small chapel a form appeared. Suddenly I panicked, thinking *my God! The owner of the place has been here all along! I'm trespassing!* How would I explain this?

"Catherine?" The deep baritone timbre was hypnotic. It seemed to come from nowhere, yet it was everywhere, as if the chapel breathed the name. I crouched, frozen to the spot. Who the hell was in here with me? Heavy footsteps clicked against the stone floor and the outline of a tall figure glided toward me. The dim candlelight made its face appear distorted and grotesque. This thing, whatever it was, was almost on me! I wasn't sure if I should run, or stand my ground and plead my case. A number of scenarios raced rapidly through my mind.

Then my brain screamed, *move your ass, Evelyn!* Just as I was about to make my get away, I found myself caught in its embrace.

"Catherine," it whispered, its soft breath tickling my ear. The warmth of his touch sent waves of recognition racing through my body. *"No! No! No!"* screamed my brain, *"I don't know you!"* Incredibly strong, he pulled me close, crushing my body against his.

"I'm *not* Catherine," I winced as I pushed myself away, breaking the trance. I turned and ran from the chapel, this stranger not far behind. I made it as far as the tiny pond then stopped in my tracks. Clearly he'd mistaken me for someone else--I was the intruder! Oh God, time to face the music. Had he been in the chapel the entire time? I must have looked like a complete fool blubbering away there! Perhaps he'd hidden in the shadows not wanting to scare or embarrass me. Either way, geez, I felt like such a fool...

He stopped a few feet behind me, giving me the opportunity to collect what was left of my dignity, and to get a good look at him. He stood well over six feet tall with a slender muscular frame. His deep set amber eyes stared right through me. His angular unshaven face and deep olive skin hinted toward Italian, or perhaps French, ancestry. I found his dress unusual, old fashioned, and outdated. His dark wavy hair just barely skimmed his shoulders. What I found most shocking was that he was completely covered from head to toe--none of his skin was exposed! The left side of his face bore a deep jagged scar. This did not detract from his handsomeness, however; rather it enhanced it and added a kind of vulnerability. I'm not sure how long we stood there staring at each other, but when I finally found my voice it was barely a whisper.

"I'm sorry," I said casting my eyes toward his beautiful face. "I'm trespassing?" I waited for his reply. Our eyes still locked, I grew nervous. *Come on, come on, be the gentleman, say something...*I started to pace, my eyes still locked with his. I felt like a trapped animal with nowhere to run.

He continued to stare with a puzzled, almost amused, look on his face. *Right,* I thought, *keep staring at the crazy American woman!* A hint of anger began to rise to the surface. He'd caught me sobbing my eyes out in what I'm sure was his chapel. I could only imagine what was going through his mind. Obviously I was not leading with my best foot forward here ...

"Say something!" I pleaded. "Anything..."

In response, he burst into laughter.

"I'm sorry, this is funny? I asked, distraught. "You find this amusing?"

"Forgive me," he replied. "When I saw you in the chapel, you reminded me of someone I knew a very long time ago. The similarity is amazing! Your face and eyes brought back memories. Even your temper matches hers. All such fine qualities in a woman!" he laughed.

"Please allow me to introduce myself," he continued. "I'm David Hawksworth, and yes-- in answer to your question--you are trespassing but I think I can be persuaded to forgive you if you agree to a guided tour of my estate." I felt the embarrassment and anger drain slowly from my body.

"I don't get many visitors nowadays," he added. "What do you say?" I nodded my head and agreed to his kind offer. He reached out his gloved hand and grasped mine gently in his. I pulled away, but as I did he held my hand tighter.

"Madame," he said, pulling me close, his deep intense amber eyes inches away from mine. "I refuse to take you any further until you tell me your name."

"My name is Evie," I stammered, and gently removed his gloved hand from mine.

"Short for Evelyn," he mused. "Hmm, I believe Evie suits you just fine! Come, my lady," he said, as he made what I thought was a slightly comical bow. "I inherited the Manor after my parents died unexpectedly in a stable fire," he explained.

"I'm so sorry--that explains the condition of the stables," I replied. "I kept horses back in the States at one time but our stables were not half as lovely as yours must have been." I found it odd that he lived here alone, but it wasn't my business to pry. After all, we'd just met.

For the first time in a long time I felt relaxed, and began to enjoy myself with this complete stranger. No intimidation or pressure to be anyone but me, and it felt good! I enjoyed listening to him as he shared the history of his home. We walked side by side along the green expanse of his land as I admired his estate.

There was something unsettling about him that I couldn't put my finger on. I felt perfectly safe--that wasn't the issue. Rather, I was drawn to him and felt guilty. I liked the feel of my hand in his. I was married, I loved my husband, and yet this man seemingly stirred memories and emotions deep inside of me I didn't know I had.

So engrossed was I, that I completely lost track of time.

I'm not sure how long we'd been talking, but the sun had already begun to set beyond the horizon. Its temporary replacement, the familiar deep liquid purple and gold, would soon paint the sky, and I knew I needed to get back. Twilight—the in-between time of not yet dark but no longer light--when those who slept during the day crept out of their burrows to play amongst the shadows of the approaching night—would soon be in full swing.

I didn't want to leave this man or this place--there was so much more I wanted to see! I enjoyed the company--I felt as though I'd met him somewhere else a long time ago.

"I've got to go, David," I said, and thanked him for his hospitality.

"Must you?" he replied. I nodded.

"Well, it would be my pleasure to escort you home--the woods are not safe at night," he warned. "Even the most courageous can lose their way. It wouldn't be any trouble for me to see you home safely."

"No, thank you, I'll be fine."I turned my gaze to the approaching evening sky and, as I glanced back to wave goodbye, he was gone! *How odd,* I thought. *I guess he had enough of this American woman for one day...*

Strange that he warned me about the woods. My mind's eye flashed on that flicker of concern I'd seen in John the builder's eyes earlier today. It wasn't the first time I walked through them alone at night. Michael traveled quite a bit for business since our arrival in England, and whenever he was away I found myself out walking. I didn't always know what drew me there, or even how I got there sometimes. I just knew I'd be alright. I found comfort and solace in the woods and with the creatures that lived there.

The darkness in England was different than back in the States. The stars, a shining backdrop in the evening sky, led me home. I had the walking paths memorized by now, anyway, and the familiar outline of aged trees that appeared like skeletons stretching out their branches pointed the way. Off in the distance the hooting of owls echoed through the woods and an occasional bat brushed past my head as he hunted with reckless abandonment for unsuspecting insects.

Chapter 9

I knew I was getting close to home when I smelled the smoke from the pot belly stove, and saw the yellowish light shimmering dimly from the windows of the church. I picked up my pace when I reached Trevor's field. I did not fear his wrath; rather an overwhelming uneasiness and dread overcame me as I felt caught out in the mist alone. There was a dark place in the field I wanted to avoid at all costs. I noticed that the sheep and rabbits avoided it as well. The only things that grew there were the miserable stinging nettle and occasional clump of thistle. Everything else on that small patch of land appeared barren and dead.

I began to climb over the barbed wire fence that separated the woods from the field when I heard galloping hoofs approaching. Who was out riding this late at night? My legs froze and for a moment I was unable to continue. I straddled the fence, temporarily paralyzed. As the wind brushed lightly against my cheek I swear I heard it whisper faintly *"beware!"*

Within seconds two men arrived on horseback, their horses snorting and stomping wildly as they sent dust and rocks scattering through the air. They stopped just short of a twisted old oak then disappeared from sight. *Where'd they go?* I wondered. Still frozen to the spot, I tried willing my legs to move, but nothing happened. *Is this real?* I panicked. *Perhaps I should have heeded David's warning!*

In the distance more hoof beats pounded on the forest

floor, and several more riders appeared on the scene. They hopped from their horses and disappeared into the woods. Finally able to move, I walked hesitantly toward the old oak careful not to spook the horses. I listened for any sounds that might lead me to where the others had so mysteriously disappeared. It seemed almost too quiet, as if the woods and all its creatures held their breath in anticipation of what was to come. My head pounded and the slightest wave of nausea washed over me. The eerie quiet was deafening.

It didn't help that there was no moonlight, and the few stars that graced the night sky had taken refuge behind thick clouds. I struggled to make my way through the thick foliage, dense thickets, and biting nettles. Finally I came to a clearing.

In a matte r of moments I was to witness a most bizarre event...as I peered ahead I saw five women and four men take shape as they danced around a circle of fire and chanted softly in an unfamiliar language. I pressed the palm of my hand to my head--the jackhammer had returned and thumped wildly through my skull, distorting my vision as everything swam before me in a filmy haze. *I must be going out of my mind!*

One of the men, very tall, staggered and swayed and shouted out words in this strange language that the others then repeated. It sounded like some kind of evil prayer, if there could even be such a thing! The fire's flames flickered and cast long distorted shadows, making him and the others appear as grotesque giants against the backdrop of the woods. I could barely see his face, though I thought I noticed a long scar that ran from his check to his jaw, and a small golden cross that dangled carelessly around his neck. His prancing and shouting became wilder and more erratic when suddenly he drew a small silver dagger from beneath his cloak. Pointing it upward in the direction of the four corners of the earth--north, south, east and west—he sliced invisible symbols in the evening air.

A slender young woman entered the circle slowly, as if in some kind of trance. She looked frightened, but seemed unable to shake herself loose from the grip of invisible forces that pushed her further into the circle. I hadn't noticed her before--where had she come from and why was she here? Suddenly and without warning, the disfigured giant leapt toward her and slashed the small dagger across her throat, sending blood spraying everywhere! The others rushed toward her and immediately began to lap up the blood from her severed neck. Like a pack of wolves, they took down their prey. I stood there stunned--I'd never seen such hunger and cruelty! My stomach churned, threatening to heave.

Oh God, not now! Please get me out of here! Get me out of this nightmare!

"Come this way," a woman's voice whispered close to my ear.

I turned to look quickly, but no one was there. *Was I hearing things?* Perhaps the rustling of leaves tickled by the wind as it brushed through the aged oaks? But no, there it was again, the soft whisper of a woman, entreating me "come, follow me..."

I looked again, and there she stood. Cloaked in the darkness and the rising mist, just barely visible, was Catherine. I was certain this was the same woman I'd seen several nights ago out in the woods. Barefoot and skimpily dressed, her emerald green eyes beckoned me toward her.

She turned and ran into the mist. I couldn't move, couldn't breathe. My chest felt heavy and constricted, my body paralyzed. Suddenly I became aware of the murderous group as they crept toward me. *"Oh my God!* I realized their dark soulless eyes stared past me into the dark night. Frozen in fear to the spot as they approached ever closer, I watched in amazement as, one by one, they walked right through me and their specters evaporated into the thick swirling mist!

I don't know how I made it back to the church, but I did. My hands shook so badly I could barely open the heavy oak door. I hesitated at first to walk through the dark foyer, but I managed it and placed my boots firmly on the stone floor as I closed the door quietly behind me and walked into the warmth of my inviting kitchen.

Michael sat on the sofa reading one of his favorite books and sipping a glass of red wine. The pot belly stove was lit and the warmth of its fire immediately began to melt away the chill of my experience.

"You're out late," he smiled up at me, then immediately returned his attention to his book.

"I was out walking," I mumbled, my voice still shaky from my bizarre encounter. "I guess I lost track of time."

Without looking at me, he patted the sofa with the palm of his hand--his way of asking me to join him. How was it that he couldn't see or feel the fear that still rippled through my body? How could he be so disconnected from what was taking place around me?

"You're cold," he said, and offered me a sip of his ruby red wine. He kissed me softly on the lips and turned back to his reading once again. I curled up next to him, thankful for the warmth of his body, but I knew better than to share what had just happened. Besides, how would I even approach the subject? *Oh darling, I think something keeps transporting me to a different time and place?* Or, *sweetheart, I think a ghost named Catherine is stalking me and showing me horrible visions from her life!* I heard how crazy it sounded in my head, never mind spoken aloud! I knew he'd never understand...

I wondered now why Michael seemed so distant and aloof when I desired his comfort, support, and advice most. I began to realize he almost never questioned my whereabouts.

In fact, he never seemed worried when I came home late, never asked where I'd been. Frustrated, I felt invisible, lonely, and confused.

Why had he married me? At times he seemed more like a stranger then a lover or a husband. I knew him to be intelligent and charismatic--someone who often needed to be in the limelight and at the center of attention, but his need to explore new places and acquire new things was foreign to me, and frankly, pretty exhausting. I had to admit ours had been a whirlwind romance—he swept me off my feet. Perhaps I'd gone in with blinders on, when I should have tested the waters a bit more.

We met on the internet, of all things. Friends talked me into online dating, even though I thought only desperate people turned to that. I wasn't looking for a relationship. My job was terrific, I made excellent money with great benefits and had just purchased my first home. I was so proud--I wondered in the back of my mind if my father would be proud of me too, though I doubted it as to him I was always worthless...

Content with my life, I excelled at what I did, even received awards from my company, but something was missing. I'd been single for ten years at that point, and I wanted to be in love again. Hesitant and out of my comfort zone, I placed my picture and bio online anyway, and every now and then I'd venture into this unknown world of cyber dating.

Online one evening I received interest from Michael. He posted his picture and said he really liked mine. We began to chat over a period of several months. Never in a million years did I believe anything would come of it. He lived thousands of miles away. Very intelligent, Michael was born in India and moved to London at five years old when his parents immigrated to England. He attended the finest schools there and obtained a degree from Oxford University, including a master's degree in banking and finance, the field in which he now worked.

We communicated via email and chatted online for more than eight months before I felt comfortable enough to speak to him on the phone. Looking back, I think I gave him my heart the first time he called--he sounded so gentle and sincere, in addition to being so kind and intelligent! I loved his accent, and we talked for hours sometimes. Eventually, he called at least three times a week to chat for a few minutes and touch base.

He knew, of course, where I worked, and every Friday began to send me one dozen long stemmed roses, lilies, and sunflowers--my favorites. The wooing began quite earnestly. My friends were blown away by his persistence. He knew I loved to read, and he picked out books he thought I would like and sent them to me. He sent me music and pictures of himself and his family, too. He'd call me at work before I started my day so we could chat. Yet always in the back of my mind there was this tiny, stupid voice telling me this was too good to be true. I dismissed it, though--it sounded a lot like my father's voice saying I did not deserve true happiness.

It wasn't long before he insisted we meet. I refused, I knew that he and I came from two different worlds and that it would be foolish for me to get involved with someone who lived so far away. I told him we could be friends--long distance. Unfortunately, that did not go over well with him. I did not talk to him after that, as I saw no point in going down a road that would probably go nowhere in the end, and I really didn't need another broken heart.

So when my daughter invited me to lunch one day, it seemed unusual—normally I was the one to ask her--but I thought what the heck? I loved that she wanted to spend time with me. We sat at the table in a cozy restaurant in town and I faced the archway where guests entered. I happened to look up as I was about to take the first bite of my meal, and there beneath the archway I saw this beautiful, dark, mysterious, bearded man smiling at me.

Michael had flown all the way from England to meet me! He made his way over to our table, thanked my daughter, bent down and kissed her on the cheek, and sent her on her way. Turns out he'd arranged a week off with my boss--all without my ever knowing! During that whole week he romanced and bedazzled me—bought me the best wine and champagne, my favorite flowers—literally swept me off my feet!

What a magical time that was for me--I'd never been treated as though I meant something so special; told I was beautiful and that I shined! He won my heart when, on the final night of his stay, he carried me over my threshold and said someday he'd marry me.

Even still, he had to return to England, and many of my friends said he probably had women all over the world with which he did this kind of thing. I knew I needed to get my feet back on the ground and chalked this experience up to a whirlwind romance that would never amount to anything.

Months went by, and when Michael told me he was moving from England to California on a contracting job, he asked if I'd join him after he settled in. I refused his offer, worried that his stay would be short-lived. It turned out I was right.

Eventually, he called me from California to inform me he was moving back to England; his contract had not been renewed. He wanted me to join him for his last week there-- said if we were ever going to have a relationship, it was now or never. I threw caution to the wind, flew down there, and once again he swept me off my feet. Every morning we'd walk by the ocean and watch the sunrise, sit on the beach and watch the seals play, hunt for seashells along the shoreline. After breakfast at a small café along the pier, we'd go to the farmer's market, drink fine wine, sip Irish coffee, and always he'd tell me I was his beautiful Italian American angel.

On our last evening together I knew I had fallen deeply in love with this beautiful man. He treated me like an angel, was so gentle and kind—but now he was going away, leaving to return to England! He said we'd keep in touch, and for a time we did, but eventually he told me I needed to forget about him, he had his life in England, I had mine in America, and it would never work. It broke my heart, but I tried to accept the fact that he'd come into my life to share a short romance--at the end of the day, bittersweet but memorable...very memorable.

He contacted me several times over the course of the next few months, just to tell me what he was up to and ask how I was doing. I did not respond--I needed to protect my heart.

When New Year's Eve arrived, I found a huge vase of four dozen long stemmed white roses waiting for me! Delivered to my neighbor's house, she brought them to me when she saw me pull into my driveway. I could barely lift them, they were so heavy! He called that night to ask if I'd received them. I thanked him, and told him I was overwhelmed. He said he'd been thinking of me, he was calling me from a friend's home in Austria, and wished me a wonderful new year.

Many months later I received an email that blew me away. He told me he was in love with me—said he hadn't been able to get me off his mind—and that he couldn't find a woman who kissed the way I did! He wanted to know if I was involved with anyone, had I found and fallen in love with Mr. Right?

I told him I was happy but did not want to see him. I knew my heart could not take that kind of risk again. He called and emailed on a regular basis trying to convince me to change my mind. Finally, as the end of that year rolled around, he asked if I'd consider spending the upcoming New Year's Eve with him. He told me he had a surprise for me and needed to see me. After much coaxing, I told him we could meet, and after work on Dec 31 I met him at the hotel in town where he'd arranged to stay. He had champagne chilling when I arrived, presented me with my favorite perfume and, again, long stemmed white roses.

At midnight that evening after we returned to the hotel, he got down on one knee and asked me to marry him. I broke down and cried. I couldn't believe he wanted me to be his wife! Of course, I said yes. The next day he flew back to England, and I went in to work and flashed my "I'm engaged" smile. My friends were happy but cautioned me to really search my heart; after all, he had let me down once before. All I knew was that this man wanted and desired me, offered me a life of security the likes of which I'd never known, and to him I was beautiful, desirable, lovely, and he spoiled me rotten! Always grateful, I never asked for anything more than his love, and clearly he proved he was willing to give that to me now.

The rest, as they say, is history. Married in May, I hopped on the plane with him to England, two suitcases in hand, years of memories left behind. Now, as I tried my best to adapt and adjust, I realized how lost I felt without my dogs, my music, and the things I had before I arrived. I loved being outdoors, and Michael had gone on some walks with me, but he preferred entertaining and being in London. And being left alone in this church for long stretches when he was away on business did little to ease my way comfortably into my new environment!

I needed Michael's love and understanding more than anything, but when I tried to approach him with my concerns about the strange things that were happening to me, he distanced himself. At first, he did acknowledge the initial activity in the church. He told me he felt it. He even opened up and shared with me an experience he had when he was younger—it seems he actually came in contact with a ghost dog while living in the Middle East. This dog came to him nightly and slept at the end of his bed. When he awoke in the morning, the only sign of the dog's presence was the warm indentation it left on his blankets.

Shortly afterward, though, I realized his need to be in control and, if anything was beyond his grasp of understanding, he shut it out and pretended all was normal in the church. He could be so romantic and attentive, but it always had to be on his terms. It also became clear that Michael disliked confrontation. In his world everything had to be perfect, simple, and never out of place. I could relate to this, as daily life had always seemed so out of control when I was young that I needed everything to be in order as a sort of safety net, a form of security. If I could make everything on the outside beautiful and keep it in its place, I figured I'd be accepted as good enough by others, though of course I never managed to live up to my father's high expectations.

Michael was a wonderful man who could be stubborn and pig headed until he got his way. It seemed that there were parts of me now that needed expression but I was not freely allowed to share unless it was on his terms entirely. Why could he not see I was completely out of my element? Why could he not understand that everything was so new and foreign to me here? I was beginning to sense that the more lost and out of place I felt, the more it drained him emotionally.

I knew on an intuitive level that if I could share with

my new mate more about the ghosts I seemed to be entertaining in my spare time, I would not be questioning my sanity to such a great degree. While the strings of insanity pulled at me tightly, I yearned for Michael's attention, both emotionally and physically, but I also knew just how much I could open up to him before he would shut down. This was not a good time to approach him, he would not understand...

Chapter 10

The next morning Michael announced he'd be away for two nights on a business trip and would return the third day after work. That night a blood curdling scream woke me with a start. My heart raced and tears streamed down my face as, alone in my four poster bed, I realized with a shock the scream had come from me!

I dreamed I walked among the dead where restless spirits re-enacted nightly the drama of their untimely deaths. The church and its adjoining field became a theater of intense traumatic energy, as outstretched arms reached from the damp earth through the swirling mist to grasp my bare legs, clasp my torso, and pull me down into the depths where they slept by day, only to be awakened at night to escape and wander the fields--hundred of souls searching, searching...for what?

I wasn't alone; standing next to my bed--her slight frame illuminated by the moonlight--was Catherine! How long had she been standing there staring at me? Or was she watching over me? I couldn't tell—I didn't know if I was dreaming, hallucinating, or going mad from all the energy that permeated this place!

"What do you want from me?"I asked, my voice nothing more than a hoarse whisper. Feverish and petrified from one nightmare, now I found myself stuck in another. *Wake up! Wake up! Please let me wake up!* It felt like a merry-go-round I couldn't get off...my eyes shut tightly, I counted to ten, hoping when I re-opened them all would be normal--just me in my bed awakening from some bad distorted dream. "One, two, three..." I whispered.

Instead I felt her touch me lightly, her delicate fingers wrapped around mine and tugged at me gently, urging me from the bed. Always when Catherine appeared something else would follow--a dark energy that remained hidden from view in the shadows. This darkness had a strong hold on Catherine's light, though I couldn't distinguish who or what it was. She seemed a prisoner perhaps, and I sensed a deep sadness that swirled about this beautiful young woman.

"What is it that you want from me, Catherine?"

She guided me down the spiral staircase, and her long blonde hair brushed against my tear-stained face. I had no choice but to follow as she led me outside. Both of us barefoot, I shivered from the damp cold as my feet sank into the soft grass of the graveyard. She released my hand and beckoned me to follow to her grave. Tears streamed from her emerald green eyes and her sadness cut deep.

"What is it Catherine?"

She pointed to the crumbling bricks and what appeared to be an open space partially covered in a stranglehold of ivy and lush fern. I hadn't noticed it before along the crypt. No way I was about to put my hands into that opening! I needed a flashlight--something more than the dim moonlight--to allow me to see. I stood up and brushed loose pebbles and dirt from my knees. Suddenly I realized Catherine was no longer there-- only the damned swirling mist brushing its bony fingers against my bare legs, and the distant hoot of a night owl that echoed softly from the woods.

No longer frightened, I rushed inside the church, grabbed a flashlight, and returned to the grave. I lay on the damp grass and brushed away the ivy and ferns, then braced myself for the possible unexpected as I thrust my hand into the opening. Jutting up from the damp chalky earth was a small rectangular box. I removed it carefully from its resting place and carried it back with me to the warmth and light inside the church. Nestled inside the rectangular box sat a leather book inscribed in delicate gold lettering *Aurum Nostrum Non Vulgi.* Below this, in smaller lettering, was inscribed *Al-Kimiya.*

Oh, great, I thought, *fine time for me to have to remember my high school Latin, if that's what this even is!* I had no clue how to read Latin or what those words might mean. However, I did recognize this as a great find. I held tangible proof of Catherine's existence—this was her diary, I just knew it! Yet I couldn't bring myself to open it up and read the first page. I stared down upon this fantastic book in my lap, but I knew it was not yet time. For weeks I'd been haunted, tormented, and virtually brought to my knees in anguish from the activity taking place here.

Now I felt isolated and alone in this place, and not quite ready to delve into the pages just yet. I needed Michael's love and understanding more than anything, but when I tried to approach him with my concerns and the strange things that were happening to me, he distanced himself—he wanted no part of it. But now I had proof! I held the book in my hands and, as much as I wanted to dive into those yellowed thinning pages, I wasn't ready. I placed it back into its wooden box, and slipped it into the farthest corner of my closet. I asked Catherine in a silent prayer to let me be until I was able to regain my strength and the confidence of my husband.

I'll help you Catherine, I communicated to her, *but please understand that you need to back off or I won't be any good to you...*

A little while later, settled back into my bed, just as I closed my eyes to drift into the realm of nothingness, I thought I heard the whimpering of a woman but dismissed it as the sound of owls that made their home in the old pine outside my bedroom window. The whirring, hooting sounds actually lulled me to sleep.

When I awoke again, it was the witching hour—somewhere between two a.m. and four a.m. This is the time when great power and magic marry themselves to darkness and light, and it's said that the soul leaves one's body sleeping while it explores the realms and mysteries of the astral plane. Some refer to this as a place of in-between. Others refer to it as a place of no-time, where spirits exist in more than one reality.

This can be a dangerous place for a soul to venture--even though the silver cord of life still remains attached to the sleeping body—because the chance of deception from those that want the light remain high. I knew that if I intended to help Catherine, I had to allow myself to be carried into the world of darkness as that was the only way we could both walk back into the safety of the light.

I found myself in a strange land, barren and void of life, watching those who had already crossed over drift aimlessly--their outstretched arms beckoning me toward their embrace. This was the lowest realm of the astral world, where souls lost all direction and purpose. They swirled about this place of testing where--their deep hollow eyes drained of any emotion--they chose to either enter the light or be completely swallowed into the depths and despair of utter darkness.

Be strong! I told myself, as I allowed the stream to carry me toward the light and it spiraled upward through spectacular colors, like a rainbow. I relaxed into this thrill ride, somehow knowing I was safe and protected. My soul began to merge with Catherine's. Her face appeared from out of the stream of colors. She took my hand as our spirits floated along the endless stream and we became one, both breathing the same air. We felt the same sensations as we saw through the eyes of one.

As soon as we made this connection the rancid smell of darkness that followed her descended upon me and sent me spiraling out of control. My arms and legs splayed outward and I tumbled through empty space. Without warning, I crashed down onto the hard oak floor next to the bed, my legs and arms tangled between the sheets, sweat pouring from my body. My hair was dripping wet as though I'd just stepped out of a shower.

"Dear God!" I screamed. "What's happening to me?"

Exhausted, and unable to grasp the truth behind what had occurred, I made my way to the shower to try to wash off the remnants of my experience. I burst into tears as the cleansing heat from the shower water cascaded over my body—it felt safe and familiar. My naked body, exposed and vulnerable, found safety smothered in a blanket of soap from head to toe; the little girl within me set free for the moment from the pain of the past. Free to discover hidden secrets that only Catherine could pry from the deepest recesses of my soul, yet still I sensed the presence of the heavy darkness that crept within the shadows of the church waiting for any opportunity to pounce when I was at my weakest.

The next day, curious about the bizarre nature of my dreams, as well as all that I'd experienced since moving into the church, I searched Google for anything that might enlighten me. Minimal research taught me that the plague, known as the "Black Death," was prevalent in England's distant past, and that the field behind our church had its share of history, and quite a disturbing one. This country had a bloody past and its ground was saturated with so much death and sorrow. When the "Black Death" arrived in England, so many people died that mass pits were dug into the earth and thousands of the dead and dying were dumped one on top of another without proper burial or headstones to mark their passing. According to the builders remodeling the church, a mass grave containing twenty-five hundred souls was buried several yards from where the church and the field conjoined!

Of course, I'd taken that bit of information with a grain of salt, and assumed they were a cheeky bunch of guys who'd do anything to scare the American lady! Now I recalled how, while walking through that section of the field previously, I'd come across several bones--one of them looked to be the pelvis of a small child! And remnants of leather shoes and clothing, along with colored glass bottles like those found in a chemist's shop, also littered the surface of this part of the field. The builders' words had managed to plant a sliver of dread in my heart and, unfortunately, what I read now served only to reinforce my dread.

Despite its darker periods, England had managed to retain its ancient beauty and lore just as a fine wine retains its taste with age, and the people here are survivors, proud of their heritage. I realized now that I lived in a country steeped in magic and mythical lore, a place where many still believed in natural magic and had not lost touch with their own gifts and powers.

I began to see how my tapping into the grimmer parts of its ancient past might explain some of my recent dreams, though I still intended to avoid that part of the field whenever I walked across to the woods. This information solved only part of the mystery for me, though.

I discovered through more in-depth research that there possibly existed a very powerful vortex that connected the church, its woods, and the surrounding villages to the earth's energy ley lines which extended as far away as Stonehenge and the green knolls of Glastonbury.

Next I came across a most helpful article and learned

that apparently some haunts are triggered by remodeling and construction. It was possible that, due to my sensitive nature, imprints from the past were playing out here within the church! The more I thought about it, the more I began to believe I was indeed being transported to another time and place—one that existed centuries ago! I had no way of controlling these visions and I hadn't a clue why I was having them. But something triggered this energy, and I figured I was up to the challenge of finding out what.

Despite the fact that I had builders at the house nearly eight hours a day, the sensation of being watched and touched by unseen forces was overpowering. Personal items such as jewelry and keys moved or became misplaced. Light bulbs flickered and flashed as though invisible hands controlled the switches, and without warning they'd shatter into explosive shards of flying glass. Once a piece of glass missed Michael by inches, as he sat working at his computer.

Leave it to Michael to find a logical explanation! He'd dismissed it as faulty wiring and contacted the electrician who investigated and found nothing wrong. We all had a good laugh over a cup of English tea and cakes; the electrician assured us everything would sort itself out and went on his way. Constantly replacing light bulbs--and the ones we replaced flickered and dimmed almost immediately—I knew better; everything was not okay.

Chapter 11

I actually welcomed the activity and noise when the builders arrived early the next morning ready to begin their next project: replacing the floor in the living room of the church. Their arrival brought with it a semblance of sanity to both the church and my life.

Hammering, drilling, banging and swearing—oh the joy of living in a construction zone! Not to mention the constant draft from the open door as the builders hauled in lumber for our new floor. The pot belly stove worked overtime just to keep the place warm. It was now moving into fall and I wanted our home to be complete by the upcoming holidays.

I left the builders to their work as I puttered away in the kitchen, making a special dinner for Michael when he arrived home. The remodeling of our quaint Italian kitchen was finally complete. Although Michael was an amazing cook, I desired to have one area of the church that reflected *my* style, a piece of *my* heritage, and I designed it after my grandmother Nona's kitchen in Sicily.

The floors were a deep, rich, black marble, and the cabinets a fine cherry wood with frosted glass panes. Michael insisted on a double stainless steel oven and stove. Our island was built of two hundred year old oak and dominated the central portion just beneath the oval balcony of the loft. Crystal wine glasses and dishes sparkled behind the frosted glass panes of the cabinets. An antique liquor cabinet displayed Michael's finest bottles of wine and rare Scotch whiskey on the north wall just below the spiral staircase.

Strands of garlic, dried red chilies, rosemary and sage hung above the island, adding warmth and old world Italian charm. Michael surprised me with an espresso machine and a baker's rack which I immediately filled with Italian coffee and an assortment of spices. Deep glass jars spilled over with dried pasta and risotto. Adding to the ambience was our ancient cast iron, pot bellied stove with clawed feet, which stood in a small alcove along the south wall. I'd fallen in love with it immediately and refused to let the builders haul it away. In addition to the ancient radiators that lined the walls in various areas of the church, the little stove added character and much needed warmth.

A duck roasted in the oven, champagne chilled in the fridge, and for dessert I was making bread and butter pudding to top with vanilla ice cream. Finally a good old fashioned home cooked meal! We'd spent more than four months eating breakfast at McDonald's, and dining in the evening at various pubs throughout the countryside. It was exciting at first, but eventually I longed for the time we'd dine--just the two of us-- in our own home. It felt good to finally feel a sense of peace and security after all the months of ongoing disturbances and wondering how I'd move forward in my new home

I planned to drive into town to research the inscription on Catherine's journal at the local library. I'd placed it far to the back of my closet, but still my curiosity wouldn't allow me to dismiss it completely. I promised Catherine I'd help her. I couldn't imagine anything happening out of the ordinary in a public place.

Basingstoke is the town nearest the tiny wooded hamlet of Winslade. In order to get there I had to drive along the narrow winding road I affectionately called "Hell's Highway." I learned upon my arrival that motorists drove extremely fast here, and I needed to keep up the pace or move out of the way if I wanted to live to see another day. So, still a bit weak from my recent paranormal experiences, I decided to call for cab to take me into town.

Why was it that whenever I left, the place appeared sad--almost lonely--as if it held its breath until I returned again? The sad-faced gargoyles perched along the edges of the gabled bell tower seemed to beckon me to stay as the dismal overcast gray sky sprinkled me with a slight misty rain. The old pine next to the bedroom window rocked and creaked, sending a small red squirrel darting along a barren branch. I watched him jump to the safety of the slanted roof of the church then quickly scurry away.

The loud honking of the cab as it pulled up the narrow graveled drive broke the silence and, pulling the collar of my leather jacket up tight to my neck, I hopped into the cab just before the onslaught of rain burst from the dark threatening heavens.

Basingstoke library is small and situated inside the Festival Place shopping center, a modern day mall that sticks out like a sore thumb from the rest of the centuries old cottages, cobbled streets, and quaint tiny shops. Trying to get to the library was a challenge as I found myself pushing and elbowing my way through a sea of bustling shoppers. Safely inside the library I began to search through rows of dusty old books for anything that would enlighten me about the meaning of the words written on Catherine's diary.

I sat for hours thumbing through the yellowed pages of dozens of books, until my back began to ache and my stomach growled with hunger. Beginning to think I was on a wild goose chase, I stood up to stretch my legs when I saw the aged little librarian approach me clutching a tiny book in her thin frail hand. Round bifocals perched carelessly on her narrow face and her pale blue eyes, magnified by the thick lenses, twinkled with excitement.

"This might be what you're looking for!" she said animatedly.

I'd shown her the inscriptions I found on the diary and asked if she would help me search them on micro film when I first arrived at the library. She agreed, and seemed genuinely excited after I gave her a bit of history on the church, and what was taking place there now.

"Al Kimiya," she said in a hushed tone, "translates as 'alchemy.'" She drew closer as though she was sharing a secret. "You know dear," she continued as she tapped me lightly on the shoulder, "don't open doors that can't be closed again." Then she slipped the book onto the desk in front of me, and turned to hurry away, glancing over her shoulder once as she winked before disappearing into a narrow row of books.

Totally intrigued, I felt the hairs on the back of my neck rise and the familiar chill of energy sweep over me as my body resonated with this exciting discovery. What exactly did she mean '"don't open doors that can't be closed again?" I brushed a stray lock of blonde hair from my face and settled in, hoping this tiny book would help me find some answers.

Alchemy is a science that centers on four very powerful elements—earth, wind, fire, and air. *Interesting,* I thought, as memories of high school chemistry surfaced. I dreaded going to that class, as it seemed my experiments always went wrong. If memory serves, I failed it...I read further...

According to this book, there are those who believe that if they could change simple lead into gold they'd obtain within their grasp the coveted philosopher's stone, a mythical stone said to contain great powers that enhance one's lifespan. Alchemy seemed steeped in mysticism and lore, and the book described in great detail how, in order to achieve immortality, one must obtain the blood of an innocent. But not just any innocent would do. It would have to be a rare individual, most likely from a family that had passed down this specific blood type for centuries. In other words, it was like looking for a needle in a haystack...

I continued reading and learned that, through the ancient path of spiritual purification, this initiate had to undergo a lengthy transformation to develop his or her insight and intuition by using sacred images. Supposedly, these initiates entered a system of eternal, dreamlike symbols that have the power to alter consciousness and connect the human soul to the divine.

You've got to be kidding! I wondered if what I witnessed in the woods that dark misty night was a type of alchemical practice. If so, it certainly did not resemble any form of the divine! What had they been trying to achieve? Did these people actually think sacrificing others would prolong their own mortality? Or was it the blood and the alchemical mixing of this stone that completed the magic? This was getting weirder by the moment!

The energy that night was dark, heavy, and sinister, and their actions seemed more like an occult ritual--a bloody sacrifice that left me disgusted and disturbed at the lengths to which others would go in order to obtain power. A young woman was murdered! In no way was this connected to the divine! This pack of hoodlums was nothing more than a band of fiends--a group of grisly ghouls lost in their own misguided illusions who crossed the boundary of sanity! Somehow, whether due to the trust they had in their leader, or for their own selfish gain, it appeared they'd bargained away their souls to the very devil himself! How many innocents had died for nothing because they were of the wrong lineage? *Madness!* I thought.

Is this what Catherine's diary is about? I wondered, growing anxious. If so, how was she connected to such deceptive company? And who was the man that wore the cross and conducted such an evil ritual in the woods that night? How had he been able to entice others to join his little coven of darkness? Certainly if this had anything to do with the divine it would have been practiced in daylight, not hidden in the shadowy bowels of night!

"I need a break," I mumbled under my breath. Pushing myself up from the tiny wooden desk hidden in the corner of the old library, I asked the be-speckled librarian if she'd set the book aside. I needed fresh air and a good strong cup of coffee!

The fresh air was liberating. I walked along the narrow cobbled streets and tried to organize my thoughts. I passed tiny boutiques, the post office, and a quaint little pub from which emanated the most delicious smell of fish and chips. Tempted to step inside, abandon my mission, and eat, I almost did just that until I noticed the most interesting shop of all up ahead.

Closer now, I saw the small rectangular sign hanging from the shop's window with delicate scripted gold lettering: **Psychic/Medium Here Today!** A musky smell of incense, thick and sweet, drew me to the shop's open door. I peeked in to see crystals of various sizes dangling from the shop's oval windows, sending out bright prisms of colorful light. I wasn't sure if I wanted to step inside. *Oh, what the hell,* I thought, *it couldn't hurt...*

"Bonjour!" I heard a woman's welcoming voice call out. "Come in, please!" Her soft French accent was warm and inviting, but I had no idea from where it was coming. The voice seemed to echo throughout the little shop until I saw a tall woman rise from behind the counter.

"Sorry, I hope I didn't scare you!" Her long auburn hair

fell past her slender shoulders, and she wore a colorful peasant dress complete with lace bustier out of which spilled her abundant cleavage. "What brings you to my shop?" She flashed a pleasant smile.

I couldn't take my eyes off of her. Her dark, almond shaped eyes were amazing, like a cat's eyes, and gold bracelets dangled from both her wrists. Several silver necklaces with a tiny golden cross hung from her long slender neck. "I'm Monique," she smiled.

I stared at this strangely beautiful woman. "I'm Evelyn," I replied finally.

"You, my dear, look as though you are on a mission!" she laughed. I stood there examining this small shop. Jars filled with some type of dark liquid lined one wall, while various herbs, sage, lavender, and rosemary hung from a display on the opposite one.

"What is it you're looking for exactly?" she asked. "Hmm--I think perhaps a reading?"

To my left was a small room, glowing with the light of a candle. A small, round table, complete with a crystal globe and tarot cards, sat in the center of the room. The floor was covered in thick lush carpets of reds, greens, and gold. Again, the thick sweet hypnotic scent of incense drew me in. This place seemed so familiar, though I'd never been here before.

"May I?" I asked, as I walked around the tiny room.

"Of course," she replied. "Come, sit." She gestured to the plush carpet. "I was just about to have a cup of my special herbal tea. Will you join me?" She left the room before I had a chance to reply. I'd planned on going for a strong coffee, but I couldn't resist this shop, this woman.

I sat down on the thick carpet and closed my eyes. Monique returned a few minutes later with hot refreshing tea containing a slight hint of orange, clove, and ginger. Its earthy aroma mingled with the incense that swirled around the tiny room. I took a sip and relaxed completely. This atmosphere, and the tea, made me sleepy.

"Give me your hand," she directed. Noticing my hesitation, she added "it's alright--I want to see your palm."

"You read palms?" I asked as I extended my open hand toward her.

"Something like that," she replied, as she winked and tossed back her hair. "Actually, I'm a witch! But don't worry," she added, leaning close, "I'm a good witch!"

She paused, then laughed, her eyes twinkling with delight. "I'm teasing, I'm a sensitive and healer just like you--I thought I'd better clarify that from the look on your face!"

I smiled weakly. "Hmmm," she continued, staring at my palm, "you see things, right?--Things that scare you--or perhaps puzzle you--and cause you to wonder about your purpose?" She looked up at me intently. "I don't need to read your palm--your energy tells me that. It seems your past has brought you here today."

"What do you mean my *past?*" I asked.

"I'm saying that you were guided here today--very unusual things have been taking place," she replied. "I must say, my little shop attracts a very interesting sort of clientele. No one comes in here unless they've been guided to do so, and by the look of things, you brought with you quite an entourage!"

"What entourage?" I was starting to get nervous.

"You have guests that led you here today," she informed me earnestly. "Catherine is here with you now—in fact, she brought you here today, and she needs you to tell her story!"

"Oh, my God!" I pulled away from her suddenly and stood up. "How did you know?" I felt as if bells and whistles were going off inside my head.

Monique stared up at me with her dark almond eyes. "Everything I am about to share with you is deeply centered within your--I can't stress this enough, Evie--your past."

I sat down again slowly. "I know this sounds crazy, but I-I think Catherine channels through me somehow." I waited quietly for Monique's response.

"You must give her a chance to tell her story, Evie, and that will help you open your heart to who you really are, "she said. "You are starting to awaken, you're in the process of becoming, and your destiny is here for the moment. You are in the transformational stage, which simply means you are changing, like the fuzzy little caterpillar that spins herself away into the darkness of her cocoon and waits," Monique continued. "She has the choice to emerge as the beautiful butterfly or to stay forever within the darkness of the cocoon-- just as you have that choice, Evelyn. There will always be the dark and the light. It's followed you since you were just a little girl."

Prickly chills of truth resonated through my body. Strange things had happened to me all my life since I was a child, but I dismissed much of it as imagination, and tried to put it behind me. At least I thought I had, until the dreams started up again. And then I met the church and all hell broke loose, as the floodgates of memories past opened abruptly.

"This world is filled with darkness and light, Evelyn," she continued. "Unfortunately, it's a bit off balance at the moment--*your* world is a bit off balance. We are all like actors and actresses on a stage playing our parts. We go through our daily motions, living our lives, and most of us never question our true purpose. Instead, we become numb and robotic, and try to convince ourselves that this is all there is." She paused, allowing her words time to sink in.

"Catherine will not allow you to have peace until you accept who you are--she can't, Evelyn. Haven't you figured that out yet?"

Monique was good. She seemed to know me better then I knew myself. I sat in silence considering everything she'd just said then nodded in agreement. No matter how hard I tried to dismiss the visions and visitations of Catherine, she seemed to have a hold on me that was undeniable. Monique's ability to see--or feel--her too, blew me away. Her validation was beginning to help me connect to the invisible forces that surrounded me.

"Catherine lived during a time when those who practiced natural magic were persecuted, even put to death," Monique continued. "You're a very strong woman, Evelyn. You intimidate the darkness, and it hates you for that. Listen very carefully to me," she said her voice suddenly very serious. "You are dealing with a very powerful enemy! He's been waiting for this."

This time I stood up so fast I nearly knocked over the tiny table. "What the hell are you talking about?"

She placed her hands on my shoulders. "Why did you come to my shop today, Evelyn?" she asked. "Do you think it was coincidence? You don't look like a fool to me! You look like a woman on a mission--very strong, very secure in your intentions and purpose--even if you haven't quite admitted it." She smiled a mesmerizing smile, and I knew her words rang true. Everything that had happened to me led me to this point. I was meant to discover this shop and this beautiful lady.

"The Coven of Nine are monsters!" she continued. "The ones who have forsaken the light for the coveted philosopher's stone, which they believe to be the key to eternal youth, have committed their lives to eternal darkness! Somewhere along the way they allowed their power to overtake them as they became hungry for more!" She held out her arm and revealed the tattooed snake coiled neatly around a small number nine extending up her forearm toward her elbow.

"The serpent you see tattooed here is the protector. *Aurum Nostrum Non Vulgi* when translated means '*our gold is not that of the common man.*' You and I and so many others around the world are the guardians of the light, and have been for millennia. The serpent is not to be feared--he is the symbol of strength and courage!"

She paused. "A group that calls themselves *Keepers of the Light* has existed since the beginning of time, and each generation brings with them a remnant of the life they left behind. You are a part of that group and are ready to fulfill that mission! You were unable to do that in the past--you needed to travel to England first." She sipped the remains of her tea, set the tiny cup aside, then grasped my hands tightly in hers. "Your marriage, I'm sorry to say, was never meant to last—it is nothing more than a means to an end."

What? I wanted to get up and run and never look back, but my body was glued to the spot. She seemed so confident, so sure of what she was telling me!

"Your marriage was only meant to bring you to England so you could release your past and heal, which in turn will release Catherine from centuries of abuse. But have no regrets! Be grateful for the time you've had in this relationship--if nothing else, it has made you stronger."

My heart sank as I listened to Monique because she was telling me things I didn't want to admit I knew were true. Her words struck many chords of truth within my soul. I felt the distance Michael had begun to put between us, and I sensed on many levels that he and I were not meant to be. I knew from the beginning our worlds were so different, and that I was searching for something Michael could not give me.

It made sense to me that my husband was the catalyst that had brought me here, and that I was here in order to fulfill a mission! In the past, I'd been betrayed by others, just as I sensed Catherine had been betrayed by whatever darkness kept her prisoner in the church...

"Respect the church and its residents; they are here to help you," advised Monique. "Catherine is here to help you... you won't be returning here again," she added, as if she'd read my mind. "My job was to share information that will help you with your purpose. A person comes into another's life for a day, perhaps a year, and sometimes forever. Mine was the time you spent here today." With that she released my hand, removed the tiny gold cross from her neck and placed it gently around mine.

"I can't accept this," I said, reaching to remove it from around my neck.

"You must--for luck," she smiled. She tucked her arm through mine and escorted me out of the little room and toward the front of her shop. "Now it's time for you to go--I have another customer," she said, just as the chimes on her shop door tinkled and in walked a tiny woman. I glanced at the woman as she brushed past me.

"Pardon me," I said, as I stepped aside to give her room to pass. "Don't I know you?"

The little woman made no reply, just stared up at me, her pale blue eyes sparkling mischievously behind thick bifocal glasses.

"I do--" I started to say, but was cut off by Monique as she moved me to the shop's door.

"Catherine needs your help," she whispered, "oh, and a word of warning." Monique hesitated before wrapping her arms gently around my shoulders. "Don't let the darkness absorb you. It's a trickster that comes in many forms. Believe in yourself Evie!"

With that, she shut the door, pulled down the blinds, and placed the closed sign in the tiny oval window. I watched as she peeked once through the blinds. Her dark almond eyes stared at me, intense and mysterious as she quietly mouthed the words "goodbye beautiful butterfly..."

I backed away from the shop into the gray English day. My mind swirled from all Monique had told me, and my head pounded with way too much information. I couldn't process it all right here, right now. I needed to get back to the library and retrieve the little book. I ran down the cobbled streets, the salty taste of tears streaming down my cheeks mingled with the pouring rain, only to find the library had closed for the day.

Chapter 12

The builders had gone, and Michael was busy basting the duck I'd left roasting in the oven when I arrived back at the church. Dusk approached, my favorite time of night.

"Mmm smells good!" I said. "I'm starving."

I couldn't imagine what I looked like--all puffy eyed and my hair damp and disheveled from the wind and rain. My mind reeled still from what I'd stumbled across earlier in the day. But knowing Michael, he'd be too involved in the cooking to really notice.

I sipped the red wine he poured, allowing its delicate flavor and warmth to spread slowly throughout my body. Candles adorned the island in the kitchen, and a lovely crystal vase filled with beautiful white lilies decorated the table. I took another sip of the delicious wine and relaxed into the moment, occasionally sneaking glances at him while he ate. Famished from the day, we sat in silence at the round marble table Michael had purchased when he was in Scotland. The popping and crackling of pine from the pot belly stove broke the silence.

"Here's to our six month anniversary," he smiled, raising his wine glass. His dark brown eyes stared into mine as he leaned close and kissed me deeply and tenderly. His thick mustache and beard tickled my lips but felt good, and I moved closer, savoring the moment.

Six months! It seemed as though I'd been here for an eternity with all that had taken place! Monique had to be wrong...Michael wouldn't be so affectionate if he was falling out of love with me! Though some days he was so unpredictable; there were times I felt so close to him and others when he was cold and distant. Sometimes I felt like one of his many collections, and that when he tired of me, I, too would be replaced by something new that caught his fancy.

I thought we had so much in common when we first met. I admired his love for other cultures and countries. He'd swept me off my feet with his charisma and charm, but since my move to England I sensed his underlying need to control me. I don't think he even realized it. Perhaps I depended too much on him, but he was the only one close enough to me now with whom I could really communicate.

Michael washed and I dried, and after the last dish he retired to the living space and settled in to read one of his favorite books. *He's in a good mood*, I thought, *maybe I can approach him with all that I've uncovered today. After all, he's such a good listener*. It came only as an afterthought that he was indeed an excellent listener when it came to his friends, but not so much when it came to me--the woman he purported to love. Accepting the truth of the realization that perhaps we were not really meant to be was too heartbreaking to consider and I wasn't about to give up just yet.

"Michael," I said, "we need to talk."

"Okay," he replied, as he rose, grabbed our wine glasses, and steered me towards the sofa. "What is it, darling? Can you make it quick, though--I see dessert's nearly ready."

Once I began speaking I found it difficult to stop, and blurted out everything that had transpired during the day. I told him how I found Catherine's diary, what I discovered at the library, and even mentioned all that had taken place at Monique's shop. I was exhausted but exhilarated by the time I finished. It had been a long time since I was able to open up and let it out instead of keeping it all bottled up inside. I even went so far as to mention the day I stumbled across David Hawksworth and his manor.

When I finished speaking, he sat there looking at me. You could have cut the silence with a knife. "Say something!" I cried.

"Damn it, Evie!" he exploded. "From the very beginning since we moved in here I've been dealing with your demons, specters, and ghosts! I thought once you finally settled in all of this would go away. Don't you realize how much you're cramping my style? Why can't you just let things be?"

"But it's all real!" I screamed at him. "I've got Catherine's diary to prove it!" I stomped upstairs to the loft to retrieve it. "See," I said, shaking the book in the air, as he stared up at me blankly from the sofa. "I have proof, I'm not going crazy!"

I plopped down exhausted as he grabbed his coat from the hook by the door. I didn't want to deal with him anymore. The door slammed and I heard the screech of tires as he drove off. So much for our six month anniversary! I buried my head beneath the pillows and prayed for sleep.

I awakened with a start to the smell of smoke. I reached out to wake up Michael but he wasn't there. Thick black smoke filled the air. Where was he? Where was the smoke coming from? I struggled from the sheets and saw Catherine's diary on the bed where I'd left it. I picked it up and rushed downstairs.

"Michael!" I screamed. "Michael!" Smoke was everywhere; the long slender flames licked the roof and slithered down the walls of the church. My eyes stung and my lungs felt like they were on fire. I couldn't breathe. I heard the sound of choking but I wasn't sure from where, I couldn't see...

I remember climbing back up the stairs. The sounds were coming from the bell tower. What in God's name was up there? I didn't like the energy of the tower, it was dark and damp, and I'd avoided it for so long. I reached up and slowly opened the trap door. Each step led me closer to the first level. Again I heard the choking sound--soft, muffled, and very faint--someone was gasping somewhere up there!

"Who's there?" I screamed, wiping away the stinging tears that clouded my eyes. The smoky haze began to clear and there, huddled in a corner chained to the wall, was a figure struggling to break free. Catherine! Her tormented face was filled with horror and rage.

"Catherine, what happened to you?" I screamed. "What kind of monster did this to you?" The smoke distorted my vision, and I remember screaming out Michael's name, then "damn!" as I dropped to my knees, wondering how I'd be able to set her free. My head felt as though it was going to explode. Everything seemed to be happening in slow motion. Suddenly the walls of the tower disappeared, Catherine disappeared, and I was once again transported to another place and time.

I found myself walking in the forest, near the aged oak that was becoming a familiar friend in these visions of mine. Two shadowy figures seemed to be arguing, though I couldn't be sure. The moon was barely a thin silver crescent in the evening sky.

I walked a little closer, hoping to get a better view. The sharp cracking of a whip and its snap against bare flesh assaulted my senses. A figure had fallen to the ground. Barely conscious, his skin ripped to shreds by the other's mastery of the whip, he lay face down in his own blood. As he begged for mercy, his words barely audible, the whip master reached down and grabbed him by his dark, blood-matted hair. "It's time to put you to rest permanently," he laughed.

"Uncle, I beg of you," whispered the dying man. "Show mercy. Please don't do this..."

"Mercy?" he snarled. "You've been nothing but a

burden to me! May you rest in peace!" he cried. His deep raspy laugh sent chills spiraling down my spine. Unprepared for what happened next I watched as the whip master drew a tiny dagger from beneath his dark cloak and ruthlessly sliced the man's throat. The assassin then let the dead man's head drop with a loud thud back into the thick pool of dirt and blood, his life force extinguished forever.

Although I could not see their faces through the shadows, I did see the golden cross that dangled from the whip master's neck as he heft up the dead man and threw him like a sack of potatoes into the roaring river below. He turned and stared at me. I drew back quickly into the shadows of the nearby brush, my heart quivering painfully. I realized he hadn't seen me--rather he'd *felt* me, sensed an invisible presence. He took one last look around, mounted his horse, and with a heavy handed whip sent his horse into a crazed gallop leaving only death and dust in his wake.

I ran to the ancient oak, so much pain and death it had seen, its long skeletal branches pointing me to the river. By the time I ran down the slight hill to the river's edge, what remained of the dead man had washed downstream without a trace. Who was he? Why had he come to such a fate as this? Who was the whip master besides a cruel murderer who seemed to take pleasure in destroying others? The dead man had called him "uncle." What had taken place here so many centuries ago? All I knew about him is that he wore a gold cross around his neck, and that I'd felt his dark negative energy in the church. I also knew that whoever—whatever--he was, his energy filled Catherine's heart with fear.

Chapter 13

Something wet and sticky dripped down my neck. *Oh my God, I'm covered in blood! Is it my blood?* I tried to move and a searing pain radiated through the back of my head.

"Evie! Open the door!" screamed Michael.

Door--what door? I realized I was lying on top of the trap door in the tower. I moved away slowly allowing Michael in. He picked me up and rushed me through our bedroom, down the spiral staircase, and out the church door. Smoke was everywhere. Flames licked and lapped voraciously at the slanted rooftop devouring the timbers along the eaves.

"I called nine-nine-nine!" Michael shouted above the sounds of the crackling flames. He sat me on Catherine's crypt and stared down at me. "I'm glad I came back," he said, "my God, if I hadn't..." He ran his hand through his hair.

Sirens pierced the night as fire trucks raced up the narrow graveled drive to the church. Within moments firemen sped back and forth to the church, ladders, hoses, and axes in hand. The next few hours were chaotic. When it was over, and all the flames had been put out, the fire chief told us we were extremely lucky. If we hadn't been home, we'd have lost everything. The only thing that might have survived was the tower, as it was not completely attached to the actual church and was built of stone.

Michael and I exchanged looks, but said nothing to the chief. It wouldn't have made sense to him anyway.

"Lucky you called when you did," the fire chief said. He

went on to tell us that the little pot belly stove was the likely culprit. It was old, and the chimney had separated from the wall somehow, allowing sparks to ignite along the eaves of the church. I couldn't help but wonder if something more sinister was at play. I couldn't prove it, of course, but we had used this little stove for many occasions without a problem. No, I refused to accept it! Something wanted me out of this place and was going to any lengths to keep me away! I was now all the more determined to stick it out and fight back.

"We placed plastic to keep out the cold and wind where the roof caved in," the fire chief explained to us. "You'll want to get it repaired as quickly as possible--this is just a temporary fix until you can do so. It won't keep out the weather for long. You folks going to be okay?"

We nodded our heads in unison. "Good," he replied. "Then I think we're done here. Bear in mind to re-attaching that chimney if you want to continue using that little stove."

"We will," replied Michael. We thanked them again, and watched as they drove off into the night.

"What were you doing up in the tower?" Michael asked. "You never go up there!"

I explained how I'd awakened to the smell of fire, and heard choking coming from the bell tower, but left out the part about my vision of the murder in the woods. We both agreed that if I hadn't climbed to the tower things might have been a lot worse. I knew that Catherine had saved me, but that didn't explain why she'd appeared chained to the wall. Apparently she tried to show me something, but I passed out from the smoke, bumped my head, and lost consciousness until I felt the sticky, wet blood trickle down my neck.

I wondered whether Catherine's chains were a metaphor—had they meant that she felt like a prisoner--or were they real? *Were you privy to the horrible murder I witnessed that night in my vision, Catherine? Is this what you needed me to see?* Or was the vision perhaps a warning to me to leave?

Chapter 14

"You're staying in bed today!" Michael shouted from the kitchen, on his way to deliver a cup of freshly brewed coffee to me in the loft. He placed it on the nightstand next to our bed and handed me Catherine's diary.

"You left it on Catherine's crypt," he said, in response to my puzzled look. "I didn't read it--whatever's going on is meant for you. I need to get to work, and to be honest with you Evie, I hope you figure it out before it ruins our marriage."

With that, he kissed me lightly on the cheek and left.

I sat there holding the diary and listening to the rain fall against the skylight above our bed. I sipped the coffee Michael had brought me. It was our favorite--an Italian blend we discovered at a small café out shopping one day in the tiny village of Odiham. We found it quite by accident as we gravitated in its direction--the tiniest little coffee shop covered in ivy and wisteria, hidden amongst the multi-colored houses and cobbled streets.

Filled with pastries and breads of various shapes and sizes and the endless list of coffees and liquors, the café made my head spin. Long bunches of red chili peppers and strands of garlic hung from the tiny café window. Various shelves displayed rows of olive oil, spices, teas, coffees, and baskets and samples of chocolates and cakes. Plump little waitresses offered fresh olives dipped with garlic and olive oil as we made our way slowly to the front of the line to place our order. Of course I couldn't resist a sample of chocolate!

For a moment I felt as though we'd been transported back to Rome, where Michael had taken me for Valentine's Day several months before we were married. It seemed like ages ago. I accused Michael of being a coffee snob. "That's funny," he responded. "I was going to say the exact same thing about you!" We laughed, knowing it was true--we were both coffee snobs, something we'd share together as husband and wife. There was so much to choose from, and we both agreed on the Italian blend. From that day forward no other coffee tasted the same.

I wiped a tear from my eye as I thought about my conversation with Monique, and how our married life might soon come to a close. Enough of that, I thought as I placed my coffee cup back onto the small table next to the bed. I opened up Catherine's diary to page one. *It's now or never,* I thought.

I'm not sure if anyone will ever read this journal, her story began, *but I feel it important to put down in words what became of me and why. I am Catherine Victoria Henry, and as I write this I know my life will soon be over. I've not much time left now, but I intend to return one day to make things right.*

My mother Isabella Catherine Henry nearly died giving birth to me. Never able to give my father a son to follow in his footsteps, great responsibility was placed on me to learn the craft which would forever guide my destiny and ultimately seal my fate.

My father, Sir Arthur Henry, a wonderful physician, was also a master alchemist and knowledgeable in the science of the metaphysical arts. His reputation for successfully attending many in our small village became well known to royalty, and eventually those in the High Court kept him away in London for months at a time. This left my mother and me in charge of our tiny shop while he was away. Father was very gifted and very powerful in the art of alchemy, but it was my mother who taught me about the secret world hidden within the woods and nature. Her gentle compassionate soul melted the hardest of hearts. Her gifts came naturally and she made it her mission to impart everything she knew to me.

She was a gifted healer who taught me how to gather herbs and natural plants from the forest, and the importance of how to use them to work with the hidden forces in order to maintain a balance between our world and theirs. She believed any upset to this delicate balance might allow powers of darkness to dominate, and made it very clear that this was already beginning to happen. She helped to heal many in our tiny hamlet of Winslade; our cottage was always filled with people who complained of ailments only she seemed able to cure.

She taught me how to listen to nature and to connect to the invisible world—the one most people cannot see. My powers became strong and I was sought out by many for my cures and insights to their past and future. At the young age of sixteen I became a midwife to many in our tiny village. In addition to the teachings of my father, my mother also instructed me about how to connect with the little people, elementals, and creatures of the night. She was a beautiful, intelligent woman. Father told me I'd inherited my gifts and beauty from her.

But it was father who I looked to for guidance and support. Yet it seemed he was always called away, which left me busy at our tiny shop. Although grateful that he trusted me with this duty, I felt an empty sadness when he was away. If I had been a son rather than a daughter perhaps he would have taken me on his journeys to London and the High Court. No matter, I knew the importance of his work and vowed to always do him the highest honor. I loved reading the many books he collected over the years, particularly the one called "Alchemy." He prized this book above all the others.

"This book," he told me "has magic." I never knew if he was serious or teasing me. He loved to tease me. "Catherine," he'd say "what lies within these pages could change the world one day. It works by listening to the hearts of others--whether pure or soiled with the mark of darkness--it shows no bias, but rather lives to serve its master. Never use its magic for selfish gain. Do you understand? Guard it well when I am away, and keep your heart pure so as to keep the book pure as well."

The night I introduced myself to that book it began to glow like the sun, and the heat that radiated from it nearly burned my hands. When I showed my father what had happened he placed the tiny book under lock and key and made me promise never to go near it again. He seemed angry and asked me not to question him again.

"One day when you are older," he said, "I will explain the significance of what has taken place. Swear to me, my little angel, you will never say anything to your mother!"

The look of sheer terror on his face—one I'd never seen before--when he mentioned my mother caused me to swear I certainly would not speak of it to her. I knew enough to heed his warning and respect his wishes, but I did not understand the need to keep anything from my mother. He left for England the next day and did not return for many months.

Many times I sneaked into his library hoping the book would be lying there on his desk. I knew better, of course, but couldn't resist the temptation to read what was within its pages. I spent hours searching for the key that would unlock his desk just so I might sneak a peek, but it was not to be. My father always took the key with him. He must have known me better than I wanted to admit! I resigned myself to making up all kinds of stories about what that little book held within, and how when my father returned I'd somehow manage to convince him I was ready for whatever it contained.

My mother made very clear the importance of never discussing our craft while we collected herbs and roots in the forest one day. She explained that even though what we practiced was for the greater good, many felt intimidated and would go to any lengths to turn our gifts toward an evil use. This made no sense to me, as I longed to help everyone with what I knew.

She warned that many individuals wanted to maintain control and power, and that they would always find a way to destroy the things they could not explain or see. Obsession with power was all that mattered to them, and anyone who dared break the rules would be punished or, worse yet, killed. This kept the poor in submission, afraid to question or break the rules of the wealthy, royalty, or the church. Magic--as they called it--was the mark of darkness! Again, this made no sense to me. Royalty starved the people through taxes and, if they could not pay, their land and livestock were taken away.

I began to lose all respect and trust in the ones who made the rules. They seemed to me to be the ones who practiced magic under the guise of authority and wealth. They were the ones who bore the mark of darkness, and their deceit and selfishness filled me with determination to keep the balance between darkness and light.

My mother cautioned me that my stubborn and headstrong nature made me vulnerable. "Your light is bright and your power strong--combined with your beauty you stick out like a beacon," she told me. "Be prudent if you do not want attract the powers of darkness! Remember, love, I will not always be here to protect you and to keep these forces at bay..."

Able to sense things before they happened, my mother was never wrong. She could detect the location of fresh water so villagers could dig their wells, and plants and animals thrived when she was near. The pregnant women of the village would come to her way before the birth of their children to find out the sex of the child.

The woods surrounding our village were magical, a wondrous place that became my sanctuary. I couldn't understand why others couldn't see what I could. Safe and complete when I walked and worked with nature, animals drew near and the spirits of the woods tagged behind watching always my every move. I caught them hiding amongst the shadows of lush ferns and tall oaks, their shy curiosity comical. Once befriended, they became my true allies against the darkness.

I took my mother's words to heart and practiced my true gifts out of sight of others. If knowledge and wisdom was power, then I'd perfect these traits in order to serve those in need and always for the greater good. But in the back of my mind I wondered about the little book hidden under lock and key within my father's desk.

What did my father fear? Was he afraid for the book or for me? I couldn't just waltz into his library and pry the book from the desk—he'd never forgive me or trust me again! My desire to hold it once again became increasingly strong until I found it unbearable to resist. I remember how I felt as though the book had come alive when it felt my touch. I'm sure others would dismiss this as nonsense, but I was convinced there was magic in its pages--almost as though the book had a soul...

My mother was taken ill the year of the great rains. I

remember sitting by her bedside begging her to stay. I could not understand why she was this very powerful healer and yet she couldn't heal herself; it was as if she refused to save herself. It doesn't work that way, she told me.

"Catherine," she said as she reached out to grasp my hand, "everyone has a season, and when that season has passed their soul will know and call them back home. Do not be fearful or sad—it's a great honor to be called back home... my time is over but, sweet child, yours is just beginning. Respect the darkness--it will always and forever be attracted to your beautiful light."

Then she asked me not to shed tears at her passing but to rejoice, knowing she'd always be there to comfort and assist me with my own journey until one day I, too, heard the call to return home. She kissed me lightly on the hand and closed her eyes as though she was only going to sleep. I felt her hand slowly release mine, and she was gone.

I stood by her graveside and honored her passing and sensed the invisible world honoring her as well. I also felt a great shudder of fear deep within the fabric of my being ripple through the forest that day as though some great imbalance had occurred within the woods. I looked down upon her lifeless body, now cradled within the depths of the earth, and vowed to protect the light--if not in this life time, then in a future one.

She told me this day would come and when it did I must be strong, but when she died a piece of me went with her. No one would ever know the great lengths she took to protect me, and without her I felt lost. I allowed her words to comfort me and tried to believe she'd always be there to watch over me and guide me along the way, though I didn't believe I had the necessary confidence to walk her path even though she'd taught me well.

How the heavens wept that day and the forest winds wreaked havoc with the ancient oaks and anyone else foolish enough to be out! Never had I witnessed a storm like this before! The woods and all its creatures seemed frightened, and I too felt the heavy presence that lingered there. My father escorted me from the woods back to our small cottage.

We ate in silence huddled around the small table next to the fireplace. I'd never seen my father cry but that night the tears came. It perplexed me that the world appeared so chaotic and cruel. The injustice of losing my mother broke my heart.

"No Catherine, please do not think this way..." I could hear her voice whispering throughout the cottage. "My soul called me back home; this is a day of great rejoicing. Remember, dear heart, how much I truly love you..."

"Did you hear her father?" I cried.

"Yes, little angel," he replied as he wiped away his tears.

He left that night for London, promising to return as quickly as he could. Business called him away. In the months that followed I started a movement to organize healing circles with the women of our village. Perhaps I was tempting fate, but my plan was for them to regain their inherit powers and strength. Forced to practice in the woods under the guise of darkness, I called it the "underground movement." I detested having to hide, but we had no choice. If discovered it could mean punishment, possibly even death. My father did not know, but even if he did, this was something I felt I had to do. Always in the back of my mind I heard my mother's soft voice saying "use your gifts wisely--only good can come of good, and darkness detests the light."

We called ourselves "Keepers of the Light," and as young girls would do we tattooed each other's bodies with a serpent coiled within the number nine--a reminder to always move forward with great courage and strength and to always share our light. And so I became a shop keeper by day, and a teacher, healer, and mistress of light by night, infuriated because what I had to offer should not be hidden from anyone, but rather free for all to enjoy....

Chapter 15

Keepers of the light! That's what Monique had said back in the tiny little shop in Basingstoke! I reached for my coffee cup and sipped the now cold brew. The church was silent, almost as if it held its breath waiting for me to read the next page of Catherine's diary. Even the insistent tapping of the rain on the skylight had stopped.

I pondered Catherine's strong commitment to healing, and realized that her gifts and talents allowed her to fear nothing; instead she fought for the cause of others, counseled, coached, and helped them heal—all without regard for her own welfare or safety.

I picked up Catherine's diary once again, anxious to learn more, and began to read:

I'll never forget the day he came into my father's shop. He was the most beautiful man I ever saw! His dark amber eyes were the color of honey and his long hair black, thick, and curly. I'm sure I looked the fool as I could not take my eyes away from his. It seemed he too had a problem unlocking his gaze from mine. We both burst into laughter at our awkwardness. He introduced himself as David Hawksworth of Hawksworth Manor.

David Hawksworth? I recognized the name, but no way could this be the David I met that day at the manor! Unless I'd been entertained by a ghost! *Impossible!* I thought. The English passed down their names generation after generation. The David I met that day had to be an heir. The thing that

99

bothered me is that he thought I looked like Catherine...I turned to the next page and read on.

He told me he was under the care and tutelage of his Uncle Sebastian until he was of age to take over the manor. He lost his father and mother in a horrible accident. They were out riding on a rare yet beautiful summer day and upon returning found their stable on fire. They tried to save the horses still in the stable and perished instead. I told him I lost someone very dear to me as well and understood his pain.

He came to my father's shop to purchase a salve. He'd heard of the shop and my father's special talent as a physician and hoped he could persuade him to take a look at his prize stallion, injured during a hunting trip through the woods. I told him my father was away at court, and had been for several months now. Disappointed, he told me many in the village had recommended my father as a wonderful physician.

"We have a special salve for animals when they are ill, but also I gladly offer you my own gifts."

"Lady, I'd be honored if you would assist me this day," he answered. *"I set out for the help of a physician, and find myself blessed to be assisted by his beautiful daughter instead! What more could a man wish for?" He bowed deeply and, extending his hand, escorted me out to where he had tethered his horse. We rode together toward his stable at Hawksworth Manor on this lovely English summer day.*

I love the smell of stables--the pungent odor of leather mixed with the natural smell of horses and straw. His horses were magnificent--rare and beautiful. He brought me to his horse, a lovely large bay stallion. I steadied him with my soft words and gentle touch then placed both hands on his injured leg. I held them there for several moments until I felt the warmth spread outward from my hands and into the injured bay's leg.

I looked up at David. "He should be fine now," I assured him.

"My God, your hands are glowing!" he exclaimed. "How is that possible?" He stared at me in wonderment.

"My healing comes from the warmth and energy radiated through my hands," I explained. I told him my mother said I was kissed by the angels themselves because I had this ability from a very young age. She told me not to question this gift, but rather to use it to assist others—something I'd been doing all my life.

"You are as talented as you are beautiful," he replied. "A rare and delicate fragile angel--one I think I would be lost without had I not met you this day!"

From that day forward we were inseparable. He came to my father's shop or I went to him at his manor. I taught him about nature and the connection with the divine, and about potions, cures, and medicines that helped heal the sick. We spent our days riding through the woods, David on his beautiful bay and I on a lovely chestnut he chose for me personally.

Being with him brought me so much joy--I couldn't imagine my life without him! We seemed destined for each other! I'm not sure if this was because we'd both lost those we loved so deeply. I'm certain this was a part of it, but our connection was deeper. Ours was an intense passion and overwhelming love that sprang from our hearts. He respected me and my gifts, supported me in my endeavors in our village, and seemed to enjoy assisting me at my father's shop. It was almost comical how the ladies of our village made themselves available whenever David was around. I didn't blame them. I, too, found myself lost in his deep set amber eyes and beguiling smile.

David spent a lot of time at my home because he hated the isolation and solitude of the manor. He said it was not the same after his parent's tragic death. The manor was an immense majestic place that seemed devoid of life without them, even though it bustled with servants always at his beck and call. He did not talk much about his uncle--only to say that he was often away in London attending to his duties as high counselor in the church.

I sensed a deep sadness when he spoke of his Uncle Sebastian. I knew better than to pressure him for details. I learned long ago that opening old wounds accomplished nothing but sorrow. Living in the past is a death sentence to the heart. I know this from experience as, after my mother's passing, my father seemed to distance himself from me and everything that reminded him of her. As a physician, it was expected he'd be away for long periods of time, but I rarely saw him anymore. I received an occasional letter, but they were few and far between. David was an answer to my prayers.

I fell in love with this man. Upon reflection, I think I gave him my heart the first day we met at father's shop! I know he feels the same. When not on long walks or rides in the woods, we made love for hours and listened to the sound of the pouring rain as we lay naked and warm in each other's embrace. He spent hours gazing at my body and the coiled serpent that I have tattooed along the length of my forearm. It seemed to mesmerize him.

He admired my courage and rebellious nature. Usually it was men and gypsies who adorned themselves with body art, he told me. He called me his "fragile angel with a gypsy's rebellious nature and an angel's pure and delicate heart." He said my beauty would still the heart of any man and that my gifts would be the envy of others. This made me vulnerable and delicate, he said. I assured him I could take care of myself.

The day finally arrived when I was to meet his Uncle Sebastian—I'd been invited to dine with David and his Uncle at the manor. I was not only nervous, I was petrified; he was a man of noble breeding who held a high position within the court.

Dressed in a beautiful gown of emerald green lace that David presented to me as a gift for the occasion—it has been his mother's--I entered the carriage he sent like a princess being escorted to the palace of my prince. My long blonde hair hung past my waist and the ruby necklace David had sent with the dress nestled snugly within my modest cleavage. As I stood admiring my reflection in the mirror I saw the briefest glimpse of my mother standing behind me. Her smile was most tender and reassuring.

I arrived at Hawksworth Manor just before dusk. The sky a beautiful golden azure laced with ribbons of pastel pinks, I loved this time of the evening when the nature spirits came out to play. I'd encountered a few when walking in the woods late at night. Always hesitant to greet me, they kept their distance within the thick mist. Aware that unknown entities relished the darkness, and that the dark was attracted to the light, I never failed to remember my legacy.

"You are the light which the darkness will always follow," my mother's words always echoed within the back of my mind. "Your beauty and your gifts will attract them like a moth to a flame."

"Lady, you are a vision!" David exclaimed as he opened the door. He kissed me gently on the cheek and took my gloved hand as he escorted me through the entry way and into the large living room. The lovely stone fireplace was lit and its warmth and golden glow invited me into the room. A

beautiful crystal chandelier hung from the ceiling and added its warm light to the room. So wrapped up was I in the beauty of the room I hadn't noticed the man partially hidden in shadow staring at me from across the room. Handsome and distinguished, he sat in a large red velvet chair smoking a pipe that hinted of cherry wood and cedar. He appeared to be in his early to mid-fifties.

He rose immediately to greet me. I was surprised at his height--he was well over six feet tall and very slender. Taking my hand, he kissed it gently and our eyes met and locked for just a moment, but in that moment I felt an uneasiness that shook me to my core. My mother taught me always to follow my instincts. Mine now told me to run...

"Uncle Sebastian, I'd like you to meet Lady Catherine," said David, his beautiful amber eyes twinkling as he touched me lightly on the shoulder.

Sebastian released his grasp but his dark eyes remained locked on mine.

"You are a rare gem, just as my nephew mentioned." His deep baritone set my nerves on edge. "Please come sit by the fire--you must be chilled from your journey." I heard my mother's voice whisper "run Catherine, run..."

After some lovely wine and small talk, I found myself escorted to the dining room by David's uncle. He wrapped his arm around my waist as though he owned me. David seemed not to notice. My uneasy feeling remained. I did not know this man, but I did not like him. His was a dark energy. His words sounded smooth like silk, but something deep and sinister prevailed.

David explained that his uncle attended the high court just as my father, but unlike my father who administered as a physician and scientist through his alchemical work, his role was that of counsel to the church. When David's uncle heard about my father he was most interested.

"I've always been very curious about the art of alchemy, even though I don't practice it," he told us, adding that alchemy was not welcome in some circles in the court, and definitely not in the church. "Some fear it to be a form of witchcraft and black magic, but I'm sure that's not the case with either your father or you." He smiled a sinister smile. "There are still those close-minded people who'd burn you at the stake if they learned of your special talents," he said as he poured more wine into our glasses. "Of course, you have the mark of high breeding, and I'm certain you'd never dabble in such foolish whimsical nonsense! It would be a pity if you were somehow to lose that lovely little head," he laughed. "A toast to the lovely Catherine!" He tapped his wine glass with a long slender finger.

Was Sebastian making a subtle threat toward me and my father? This I did not take kindly, though I did not let it show. I didn't want to upset David, as it seemed he was beginning to feel uncomfortable about his uncle's remarks. I could hardly wait until the night was over--I didn't want to spend another moment with this arrogant condescending man. The way he stared at me when David wasn't watching made my skin crawl. If I had been part of the menu that evening I felt he surely would have devoured me.

David insisted on escorting me home, and with my father away at court I invited him to stay. We made love until we were so exhausted neither one of us could move out of the other's arms. We seemed unable to get enough of each other. Being with him felt like heaven!

When I told him I thought I was with child, he drew me near and laughed in his husky voice that he hoped it to be true since he wanted me to be his wife. He placed his hand gently on my naked belly and tucked his head between my *bare breasts, and whispered "I love you Lady Catherine, my fragile, delicate, beautiful angel."*

"I wish my mother was alive, she would be so pleased," I said. David reached up to kiss me, assuring me she would be. "She's all around us," he said, "and always will be." The gentle patter of rain and wind against the thatched roof of the cottage lulled us both to sleep.

Catherine's pregnant, I thought, as I closed her diary and placed it on the night stand next to my bed. *Then why was she so sad? What happened to cause her to reach out to me with visions over which I have no control? Catherine, every time you come to me it puts more distance between me and Michael! These visions are pulling the two of us apart!*

I sat there wishing I had a love like David. *Stop feeling sorry for yourself--everyone makes mistakes in their marriage!* It seemed I had no control over my marriage, just as I had no control over the things that were happening in the church, and that I'd awakened spirits who had never been properly put to rest.

Chapter 16

Michael arrived home that evening and informed me he had to leave for India--his father was very ill and he felt he needed to be there. I remembered the first time I met his father. I wasn't sure what to expect, and in came this lovely, tall, elegant eighty year-old man, dressed in a suit and blue turban that matched the color of his twinkling eyes. He looked like a wise and kind sultan--something you'd see in tales from "A Thousand and One Arabian Nights"—and I was drawn to him immediately.

His English was not the best and I could tell he felt more comfortable speaking his native Hindi. When Michael and he conversed, it was like a tennis match--my head snapped back and forth as Michael translated.

"I'll be away for several weeks," said Michael. "Do you think you can manage without me?"

"I'll be fine," I replied. "You just be careful over there and give my love to your father."

We packed his bags and he was on his way--but before he reached the door, he held me close and kissed me deeply. "Stay out of trouble," he whispered.

"Always," I said, savoring his lips and his warm embrace.

I closed the old oak door behind me and pressed my shoulders up against its cold smooth surface. I thought of Michael's father in India and his home in the village of Juhlander, where we'd spent time with him for a week before our marriage. After surprising me with the trip to Rome on Valentine's Day, Michael then informed me he was taking me to meet his father in India! I think those were the happiest moments of my life. The smells, sounds, colors, and tastes were intoxicating, and quite a jolt to my system as I was not prepared for such major culture shock. My heart wept as I walked through streets littered with garbage and watched tiny children crawl through the stench looking for scraps of food. On the opposite sides of these narrow streets stood huge marble mansions surrounded by elaborate iron gates that protected the wealthy hidden within.

We ate fresh fruits and vegetables from the local markets, sweet mango and papaya, apples and melons that always left me returning for more. I awakened each morning to the delightful sound of street vendors, and braying of donkeys whose carts were so loaded down with goods it seemed almost comical to watch them as they trotted down the dusty streets to the central market place. It was odd to see cattle that roamed the streets like royalty, coming and going anywhere they pleased. They often brought traffic to a complete halt as these exalted beasts made their way across the busy intersection.

India's a mysterious, spiritual country that I'll never forget. I felt so blessed to have savored its beauty and diversity. Michael made love to me there every night with such passion. Every morning he'd pull me close and whisper that I was his angel. The short time we stayed there was magical and full of passion, abandonment, and sheer joy.

"Your marriage is coming to an end--it was never meant to be!" Monique's words kept echoing in my ears. "Michael is the catalyst that brought you to England, nothing more..."

Now I had several weeks to prove her wrong, however

bound and determined the spirits that resided in the church were to get me to agree with her. In fact, only hours after Michael left for the airport, the air in the church became thick and heavy with the presence of the dark energy I thought I'd banned to the outside. Clearly it had lingered there, waiting for any opportunity to invade my home once more.

I lit candles and placed them throughout the living room and kitchen. I even opened a bottle of red wine. I didn't usually drink without Michael, but tonight I felt the need to relax and unwind. I reached for the Italian crystal goblet that held the beautiful blood red wine, when the air in the church shifted suddenly and became so devastatingly cold I could see my breath. At first I thought the heater had stopped working, and I walked up the spiral staircase to the loft to check on our furnace. Within seconds, the candles I'd placed strategically throughout the church crashed to the floor and flew against the walls with such great force that I found myself momentarily paralyzed with fright.

"My God--what now?" I screamed as I rushed down the stairs and stood in the middle of the large living room waiting for the next attack. "I'm not your enemy!" I cried. "I didn't ask for this! I command you to leave my home--this is my place now!" I doubted I was very convincing, but I was the mistress of the church now, and tired of the ongoing battle between me and this unseen force.

The tears streaming down my face blocked me at first from noticing the shadow that lurked in the corner until it began to glide toward me--at first just a filmy black mist. As it swirled and grew, the outline of a very tall man began to emerge. Dressed in clothes from centuries past, a small golden cross dangled from around his neck.

"You!" he snarled. "Why couldn't you just stay away? My powers have grown since last we crossed paths--pity how it had to end when last we met! You do not belong here--how dare you invade my space!"

The shrill pitch of his voice shredded my spirit with distress and unease, like someone running their nails down a chalkboard. His presence oozed with evil malevolent energy and, as hard as I tried to run, I felt mired in quicksand and my legs would not budge. I stood there, grounded, my hands clenched tight, and waited.

His energy drifted close and the air became so heavy and thick I felt as though I'd been stuffed into a deep freeze. I struggled to breathe, and the heaviness upon my chest was unbearable. My heart pounded so hard it hurt--I thought it would burst from my chest! I remembered what Monique had told me. "We are of the keepers of the light." I felt Catherine's presence fill the church and knew she was all around me. It was as though her energy merged with mine.

Lightheaded now, everything in the church began to swirl around me as though I was about to pass out, but instead I felt an intense heat rise from the bottom of my feet and surge throughout my body until it burst forth from the top of my head, striking with powerful force the approaching darkness.

This energy swirled and encircled the man and, as I covered my ears to block out his loud piercing screams, this powerful force surrounded him like a mini-tornado and ripped him to shreds so quickly that his screams of pain and agony echoed throughout the church, but then subsided almost immediately. Soon there was nothing left but the echoing whisper of his screams--then total silence.

I stood there, unable to speak. I could still sense Catherine's presence, but it was not as strong as earlier. The lightheadedness I'd experienced was gone and now I felt drained and tired. All I wanted to do was sleep.

I heard whispers, voices echoing in unison throughout

the church. "It's not over--he's very powerful, even more so than in the past...he'll come at you again when you least expect it-- but this time you have allies Catherine did not have in the past..."

It seemed I'd been up against dark forces my whole life one way or another. I guess I couldn't expect it to be any different here! In fact I began to realize a very powerful vortex was beginning to open and its stage was that of this 13th century church. *Catherine, how are you and I connected?* I begged her to tell me.

I walked into the tiny bathroom and stared at myself in the oval mirror. My hazel eyes stared back at me—bright, but tired and stressed. They saw things others couldn't begin to understand. I continued to stare at myself, thinking of Catherine, and as I did my reflection began to shift and change. Deep emerald green eyes and full ruby red lips reflected back at me now. Surprised, I turned abruptly away. When I gathered the courage to look back, I saw two of us staring back at me from the tiny oval mirror.

"This isn't possible!" I whispered, as my body quivered with recognition. The truth began to burst forth into the light from deep down. Who in the world would believe that this woman--who haunted me persistently and tried so desperately to connect with me--was really *me* from a very distant past?

Unbelievable! What would Michael say when I told him about this? What would my friends back in the States say? Only a few pages were left in Catherine's diary and—almost as if she was not able to complete her life story--she was now telling it through me! My body shook uncontrollably as I picked up her diary and I began to read again. I was determined to finish it to the very last page no matter how much sadness it struck within my heart.

Chapter 17

David told me he'd be away on business in London, something he had to do for his Uncle Sebastian. Two weeks passed and I became worried that something terrible had happened to him. I planned to ride to the manor when I received an unexpected visit from Sebastian. I sensed his presence long before he walked into my father's shop. My senses--on high alert--told me to run.

"Lady Catherine, radiant as ever!" he oozed, bowing slightly. "My nephew tells me you are with child and that the two of you are to be married when he arrives home from London." He paused. "As much as I'd like to be the bearer of good news, unfortunately, I bring you sad news instead. My nephew was found murdered in the woods not far from here."

At first, his words did not register.

"David has no enemies!" I stammered, "no one who wants to harm him!" How was this possible?

"Apparently my nephew was murdered by a very skillful whip master," Sebastian explained, examining his nails nonchalantly, almost as if he was giving me the weather report! "His body, or what was left of it, was found in the river by a local woodsman. He was barely recognizable...I was informed when the townspeople found his horse roaming the fields and came to fetch me. Such a pity," he sighed, but when he finally looked directly at me, I thought I detected the faintest glimmer of a smile in his eyes.

I struggled to keep my tears at bay. I must not faint, I

thought, not now, be strong--do not give this man the satisfaction of seeing your vulnerability!

"Perhaps it was a highwayman looking for gold," he continued, shaking his head. "The nasty buggers are everywhere these days, too lazy for real work they'd rather murder the innocent and rob them of their riches."

My heart felt like it was being ripped from my body. "I don't believe you!" I screamed. I'd rather die than live without David, I thought, but as unbearable as life seemed without him, a new life had begun to grow inside of me.

"I've already seen to his burial," Sebastian replied. "It's over, there's nothing more to be done. I'm here to inform you it is my duty to see that you are brought to the manor until the child is born."

"I prefer to stay here!" I replied. "This is my home, I belong here. I don't want to go with you!"

"I've already spoken with your father, and he is in complete agreement with me," Sebastian replied undaunted. "It's already settled. An unwed mother—and one who claims to be a healer--will not go over well with the high courts. You'd be wise to consider my offer." He smiled a smarmy smile. "No more of this nonsense--you've been placed in my charge."

"My father would never have agreed to this!" I screamed. "You're lying! Get out of my shop!"

His face became red and contorted as he snarled "you have one week to reconsider! Then I'll be back to collect you and your belongings!" He slammed the tiny shop door behind him, and I watched as he rode away on David's beautiful bay stallion. I collapsed onto the shop's cold stone floor. What now? What happens now?

I awakened to the morning light as it filtered through the shop's windows. It was freezing. The embers in the *fireplace had long ago turned to lifeless gray ash. So this is it, I thought, my father has given me to another without my consent! How could he? Why would anyone want to hurt David? David, my beautiful David! My screams sent the owls nesting in the nearby tree into hastened flight.*

My stomach churned at Sebastian's description of the condition of David's body. His death would have been long and unbearably painful, and it was as if his uncle enjoyed every gory detail. Oh, first my mother and now the love of my life! Heaven help this child who grows within my belly! I beg of God not to forsake us!

True to his word, Sebastian arrived one week later. I rode in silence with him to the manor. I had no way of knowing what was ahead. He treated me civilly enough at first, but I often caught him lurking in the shadows staring at me with his intense black eyes just when I thought I was completely alone. He was so unlike David! I couldn't fathom how they'd ever been related. Also, I couldn't understand why my father would turn his back on me and entrust me into the hands of this stranger.

Sebastian presented me with a letter, penned by my father, that asked my forgiveness. He said that, since he was always away at court, he felt it would be in my best interest to be under the supervision and guidance of one held in such high esteem. After all, Sebastian was with the royal court and church. That was that, it was settled--I was to remain here at Hawksworth Manor until the birth of my child, who now grew large within the confines of my belly.

Sebastian kept a close watch on me and did not allow me outside. He said it was for my safety, but I did not believe him. I knew in my heart somehow I'd become his prisoner. Allowed access to the upper parts of the huge manor, I was forbidden to enter the lower levels that led to Sebastian's study.

Refusing to heed his words, I wandered through the great halls of his manor one afternoon when he was away on church business. All of the beauty I once admired about this place died with David. This was no longer a magical, beautiful manor--instead I began to feel I might surely die here.

I crept down the stairs quietly to avoid raising the curiosity of the servants busy with their household duties. I approached the great door of Sebastian's study and felt the first signs of fear. The possibility of being discovered caused me to hesitate, but I grasped the knob of the door and slowly pushed it open. I took in this study--filled with rows upon rows of books—and was surprised to see that my fears were unwarranted.

In the center of the room sat a large mahogany desk, and off to the corner a beautiful bay window allowed me a grand view of the manicured lawn and gardens. How wonderful the sunshine felt on my face! However, its warmth sent shivers down my spine. Why should this be?

I walked over to the huge stone fireplace and ran my hand across the cold smooth surface. On the floor in front of the fireplace was a beautiful Persian rug. Its velvety texture felt wonderful as I dug my bare feet into its soft plush thickness and my toes hit something hard that felt like a knob or a latch. I pushed the rug aside and to my surprise discovered a trap door! I reached down to open it and the rancid smell of death and decay assaulted my nostrils. I gathered my courage, held my breath, and pushed the door open wide.

It appeared I had to descend a staircase if I was to find out what lay beneath the study. I braced myself, and placed my foot on the first step. The stairwell was steep, and when I reached out to touch the walls, they felt cold and damp. The flickering of torches in their sconces provided me enough light to see my way. I didn't want to lose my footing and fall into the great void below.

The room was a great stone cavern. As my eyes began to focus, I realized there were symbols carved into the walls; symbols I did not recognize at first as the light was so dim. So distracted was I by the symbols, I did not realize I'd walked into the center of a huge pentagram etched on the cold stone floor. In front of the pentagram was an altar draped in black cloth, and on top of the altar sat a pewter goblet stained with blood. Lying next to it were silver and gold daggers and a very small black book.

I've seen that book before! Yes, of course, it's the same book my father had locked away in his library! I recognized the inscription "Al-Kimiya."What if it was the opposite of my father's? If I touched it, would it take my soul? I believed whoever owned the book became its master, but did the book become the possessor of their soul? I didn't care--I picked up the tiny book and clutched it to my chest. It did not burn me or strike me dead. However, I felt the tiniest surge of energy shoot through my fingers then quickly fade away.

Sebastian accuses my father of witchcraft, then hides away in the bowels of this cavern to practice the very thing that is unwelcomed in his holy church! I backed away from the pentagram and, as I turned to run up the stairs, spied shackles and chains hanging from the damp stone walls, beneath which lay scattered a pile of chalky white bones. Then I saw the beady-eyed rodents staring up at me. They bared bloodied and sharp teeth, and when they realized they were in no danger, began to feed voraciously on scraps of skin still clinging to the discarded bones.

I stumbled up the stairs back to the study sickened by

the sight, my stomach threatening to heave. I had to get out of there! I reached down to close the trap door and realized that, in my haste, I still carried with me the small black book. Too late, I wasn't going back down there! Hopefully he wouldn't miss it for a few days, and I could take it back. For now, I crept quietly back to my room and placed the tiny book next to my journal in the loose floor boards beneath my bed.

I could not sleep at night for fear I was being watched. One night, as I begged sleep to come, the dark form of Sebastian entered my room. Naked, he approached and I saw that his passion had risen between his slender yet muscular legs. I ordered him to leave my room, but he placed his fingers on his lips as if to silence me with such a gesture, and let me know that it didn't matter how loud I screamed, there was no one here to protect me.

I found myself lying face down on my bed, my belly full with child, pressed hard against the mattress as he entered me. The pain was excruciatingly unbearable! Just as I thought it might be over he pulled me over and entered me once again. I feared for my child's life--what if he injured the baby that now breathed within me? He seemed unconcerned with anything but his own pleasure as he grunted and groaned and spilled his seed inside of me.

"Forgive me David," I whispered, "forgive me..." I felt as though I was floating above my body looking down upon the unsightly scene. Finally spent, Sebastian rolled off of me.

"Now you are mine," he whispered tersely and pressed his lips against mine. "I will have you every night!" When I tried to pull my face away he grasped my jaw and looked deeply into my eyes.

"I rid myself of my nephew, as we no longer saw eye to eye--he left me no choice but to dispose of him--which I did with great pleasure!" he informed me with an evil grin. "I

loved the way the whip felt as it carved his flesh. It almost felt as good as being inside of you."

Disgusted, I turned away from him. He grasped my face and once again, forced me to look at him. "This is how it will be!" he growled. "You will give yourself over to me willingly in time...don't worry, my riding you each night will not harm the child--it's mine now, just as you are mine! You will teach me the gifts your mother bestowed on you--this is not a request!" he screamed then took me once more, his urges strong and painful.

"This child within you does serve a purpose," he said when he had finished. "You'll do as I say, otherwise I will take the child in your place! Either way the child has the proper bloodline and will serve her master well." He paused. "I thought I forbid you from entering my study--it seems you disobeyed me and now something is missing! I expect it back in my study come morning!"

With that, he left. Alone and afraid in the darkness, I cried out for David and cursed my father with every breath. "You will not have my child!" I sobbed. "I'd rather die first!"

But I took his warning seriously and returned the book to its proper place the next morning. In doing so, however, I knew I lost my only leverage to keep my child safe. I swear one day I'll destroy Sebastian--in this lifetime or another...

I couldn't believe what I was reading! The rape of Catherine and the intense control this man had over her! How many times must Catherine have submitted herself in order to protect her unborn child? I wondered if she'd actually been betrayed by her father, or if his consent had been a ploy by Sebastian to keep her at the manor. Her circumstances were unbearable--she was unable to stand up against such a man! How was I supposed to release her from such darkness and control? Depressed now, but determined, I picked up her diary once again.

He came to my room again, his passion raw, angry, and uncontrollable. Naked, around his neck dangled a small golden cross. This time he did not come alone. Four women and four men appeared from the corners of the room and joined in the orgy. He took me over and over as the others watched and chanted a language I could not understand.

The others were naked as well and danced and fondled one another, as the dim moonlight distorted their shapes and projected them--disfigured shadows, specters and ghosts— onto the walls. My only hope for survival was to pretend they were not real—this was the only way I could keep my sanity! He thrust hard within my body and the figures gathered close and continued to watch. The women grabbed my arms and tied them to the bed, while the men grasped my ankles to separate my legs, and held them so tightly I screamed in pain. When he was done, Sebastian removed the golden cross from around his neck and slashed it across my belly, drawing blood.

"No!" I sobbed. "My baby! Don't harm my baby!"

I don't remember what happened next. I awoke in the morning, the sound of wind and rain against the window panes. Bloodied and bruised, my wrists red and raw from where I'd been restrained, and I saw dried blood caked onto my belly. Oh my God--my child! My panic was unwarranted, as soon I felt a strong kick inside and knew my child was unharmed.

Servants came to my room to help me bathe and attend to my wounds. These emotionless little minions didn't speak to me or make eye contact; it was as if they were under a spell! They carried out the bidding of their master, and when they were done simply disappeared as if it had never happened.

I feel as though I've died! The constant kicking of the life I hold within my belly is the only thing that keeps me from going insane! It is not long before I will give birth! What's to become of my child? What's to become of me? Where are you father? All the months I have been locked away in this manor I've not received word from you! If you've sent word of my welfare then Sebastian has kept it from me. Do you know the things he does to me? I'm a prisoner here! He won't let me leave! But for how long and for what purpose?

Father, wherever you are, I need your help! David's uncle is not what he seems! Don't you know that he's deceived you as well? If you knew the truth about this man you'd never have placed me in his care! I know you will come to visit me shortly--you must realize the birth of your grandchild is to happen very soon...

I'm never allowed to leave the manor. I haven't felt the sun on my face or the soft dewy grass on my feet for so long! I've not been able to communicate with the forest or the creatures that live there. I've been cut off from everything and everyone I love. I hide my diary in the loose floor boards beneath my bed. If it were to be discovered, I fear he would kill me regardless of the child.

It's been several nights now and Sebastian has not come to me again. Yet I find myself unable to sleep for fear he will appear from the shadows, his specters at his side. Whoever or whatever they are, my baby seems to be of importance to them. Sebastian seems to have the same gifts as me, but he uses them for dark purposes. This makes him a very dangerous and unpredictable man! Whatever he's up to is for his own selfish reasons. I do know that if it comes down to my life or the child's, I will gladly give mine!

I understand now how my father feared that the book,

if left in the wrong hands, could become an intoxicating elixir, its magic fueling the promise of eternal life for those with greedy black hearts. It's clear this tiny book serves Sebastian's dark and warped desires, and that under his supervision he and this Coven of Nine have already lost their souls!

I wiped the tears from my eyes, and placed Catherine's diary on the coffee table. Reading it had drained me of all energy, and I felt an intense headache forming in the back of my head. It was as if my spirit experienced whatever she experienced, and I was living through her hell. My body grew tired from the endless abuse of the dense dark energy that always came when Catherine was around.

I thought about the Coven of Nine; Monique had first mentioned them to me, and now I understood more. That Sebastian had desired Catherine there was no doubt, but if he was connected to the Coven of Nine, he must have had more sinister plans for her and her unborn child. Catherine had a gift that Sebastian desired. It seemed he coveted this gift more than life itself. He murdered his nephew in order to gain control of the one person who carried the child that held the doorway to eternal life--at least this is what he hoped for. What I learned from Catherine's writing was something I could not even begin to comprehend!

I found myself thinking about David. The one and only man she truly loved had been murdered, removed from her life because of the lust and greed of another. But what of her father, why did he leave her to fend for herself? Was David's uncle that convincing? I had a hard time believing this.

Too tired to climb the stairs to the loft, I curled up on the sofa as sleep began to overtake me. I was awakened suddenly by a heavy pressure upon my chest. The air had shifted inside the church. The stone walls seemed to be closing in on me and I couldn't breathe. Was I dreaming? Caught up again in one of my visions? Distinguishing between present and past was becoming more difficult daily!

I tried to get up from the sofa but couldn't move-- invisible forces pinned down my arms and legs. I screamed, but had no voice. This presence climbed on top of me and slid its hands between my legs. *What in God's name is happening?*

I smelled the rancid warm breath of something upon my face and, as I tried to turn away, it grasped my head tightly. Panicked, I gazed around the church, but saw nothing. I could feel only this heavy thing pressing me down into the sofa.

Get away from me! I shouted inside my head repeatedly, until the words burst forth and my scream shattered the silence of the church. "Get out, whatever— whoever--you are! Get out!"

In response, it pressed harder upon my chest until I thought it would break my ribs. Instinctively, I began to recite the Lord' prayer. Not religious, this prayer nevertheless always seemed to bring me comfort. I repeated it over and over inside my head, faster and faster until the heaviness released and I felt it dissolve, then disappear.

The church was silent, except for my heavy breathing. Everything seemed normal and in its place. *Who am I kidding? Everything is far from normal! My world, my life, has gone way beyond normal, and I don't know if I can do this anymore! Why does this keep happening?*

I hopped up from the sofa, walked into the beautiful Italian kitchen that always brought me comfort and joy, and splashed cold water on my face. I sensed the slightest hint of another presence in the room with me.

"If it's you Catherine, go away! I can't handle the other's darkness anymore! It's too draining!"

She stood in the corner by the spiral staircase, her dark almond-shaped eyes the color of amber honey, her hair a tousled mess of dark brown curls that extended to her very tiny waist.

"Who are you?" I asked.

She reached out her tiny hand and beckoned me toward her, but as I approached she evaporated into a thin wispy mist. Bad enough I had the other energy to contend with, now someone, something, new had introduced itself to my space!

I glanced at the clock. It was nearly morning, and Michael would be back from India later today. I had time to go to the manor--I needed answers to so many questions! I felt perhaps David could help shed some light on Catherine's diary. He was connected to all of this somehow and I was determined to find out how.

Chapter 18

Warm sunshine greeted me as I stepped outside into the morning light and made my way toward the back of the church, dodging nettles and the occasional thorn bush that led to Trevor's field. Nothing, not even Trevor's wrath, could keep me from cutting across the field today! I walked across the empty field expecting the worst, but made it to the other side and climbed over the fence without incident.

I felt free as my feet made contact with the chalky surface of the narrow path. The familiar trees and distant screech of a red-tailed hawk seemed to welcome me along my way. It felt good to be out, as the fresh morning breeze brushed lightly against my face. An occasional rider on horseback greeted me as I pressed on toward the stables. I wasn't sure what I would say to David when I saw him again. We'd met only once and--awkward as that had been--I looked forward to seeing him again today.

It wasn't long before I came across the crumbled stables. I just needed to locate the hidden path that led to Hawksworth Manor. I recognized the beautiful fallen tree I'd rested on the first time I discovered the stables. I sat down on its smooth cool surface to catch my breath and organize my thoughts. The nettles, ferns, and ivy seemed denser and thicker here. Where was the path? *I'm sure it's here,* I thought, as I rose and began to rip away at the underbrush, the stinging nettles cutting into my hands.

"Damn!" I cried. "Where is it? Where's the path?" I felt

I was going in circles as I pushed and struggled my way through the thickets, my hands bloody and covered with red swollen welts from the angry bite of the nettles. Finally, I saw the clearing that led to the manor.

Thank God! I thought, *if I had to endure anymore my skin would surely be ripped to shreds!* The only thing I saw as I walked into the clearing was empty derelict buildings, scarred ghostly shells of centuries past. It appeared a wicked fire had roared through and devoured everything in its path. A hint of black charcoal mingled with the dusty chalky ground. Patches of bluebells and snowdrops sprouted up through the rubble. Thick tangles of ivy and delicate ferns wound themselves around the mounds of mortar and brick that had somehow escaped the fire.

This can't be, I must have made a wrong turn, I thought, confused. *What about that tree? I remember sitting on that very tree the first time I stumbled across the ruined stables.* I walked to the center of the clearing and hiked up the slight hill that overlooked the valley below. I could see the crumbled stables from here but no sight of the manor and its manicured lawns or rose gardens. *Where was the small fish pond with its tangled lily pads and multi-colored coy?* I wondered. *And what of the small chapel where I first encountered David?* Nothing here now but the damned ivy that inhabited everything!

Anger and sadness swelled inside of me. "No! This can't be happening!" I screamed, as I threw myself on the hard dusty ground, and began to rock myself like a baby. I started to weep, my knees drawn close to my chest, my head tucked down low, as wave upon wave of emotion buried so deep began rushing to the surface. I'm not sure how long I lay there; I knew only that I didn't have the strength to go back to the church just yet.

A slight breeze tickled my tear-stained face and the screeching of a hawk in the distance shook me out of my breakdown. I stood and gazed at my surroundings one last time, when suddenly I noticed a figure nearby on horseback. Nearly hidden within the cluster of oaks where the tiny chapel would have been, I wondered how long he'd been there...

Slowly he nudged his horse forward out of the cluster of trees. Still shrouded in shadow, I could not make out his face. The sound of soft hoof beats on the forest floor sent shivers down my spine. Again I found myself at the mercy of a stranger. He approached and I realized this was no stranger at all—he was David! I was sure of it! Sunlight glistened along the wicked scar etched across his angular face. His deep set honey amber eyes stared into mine. My heart raced, pounding wildly--not with fear but with anticipation.

"Not possible!" I said aloud, "I've gone mad!"

He drew near and his beautiful bay stallion softly shook his large head and snorted impatiently. "I can assure you that you're not mad, my lady," said David, his voice barely a whisper. "Come," he continued as he reached out his gloved hand toward mine.

I placed my hand in his, and the fangs of truth sank deep into my soul. This man was *real*. He pulled me up beside him on the large bay. The huge stallion's muscles quivered against my thighs.

"Hold on," he whispered, placing my arms tightly around his narrow waist. A light mist began swirling around us as if we were trapped within a whirlwind. I tucked my body close to his and held tight as his horse galloped through the forest at a furious pace. The trees and landscape disappeared, becoming nothing more than a blur. Suddenly, without warning, the huge bay came to an abrupt stop and almost sent me toppling to the ground.

"Oh my god!" I gasped as my heart pounded wildly. I couldn't believe what I saw-- in front of me, in all its magnificent glory, as Hawksworth manor! The sad-faced gargoyles peered down at me from their resting place and the delicate scent of purple lace wisteria tickled my nostrils. Everything was just as it had been the first time I stumbled across this place.

"How is this possible?" I asked as I slid from the large bay's back and welcomed the hard ground beneath my feet.

"It's real," replied David, dismounting from the beautiful bay. I'd forgotten how tall he was, and the closeness of his body next to mine sent all kinds of feelings racing through me.

"My uncle destroyed this manor, burnt it to the ground centuries ago" he continued. "You seem to have an innate ability to connect to its energy, and have brought it back to us like an artist would restore a beautiful painting. Evie--my beautiful Evie!--welcome to the other side of the veil--the very connection to your past!"

"This has to be another one of my visions, or I've really gone over the edge!" I cried. The sad-faced gargoyles seemed to nod their heads in agreement.

"It's true," they whispered. "You've gone mad!"

David stood there still. He didn't evaporate into a thin mist. I stared up at the manor, now hidden in shadow as the sun disappeared behind thick gray clouds.

"Okay, I give up," I said. I walked toward David and placed my small hand in his gloved one. "Show me what happened here."

In silence, we walked around the huge estate for nearly an hour. I felt the energy of the grounds and how it permeated deep within the surface of the soil we walked upon. I relaxed and allowed the very essence of David's energy to join with mine, and slowly--very slowly--began to see through honey amber-colored eyes.

It felt as though I was being pulled through a very narrow tunnel, which startled me at first and set my nerves on edge. *Had I made a mistake trusting this man?* I wondered. He must have sensed this and held me close. I gave up all fear and dove into the moment. *This is how Dorothy must have felt when she landed in Oz,* I thought. "We're not in Kansas anymore, Toto," I whispered.

There was David as a young boy, laughing and running across the green lush lawns of the estate. There seemed to be a celebration taking place. Laughter and music filled the air. It appeared to be near twilight, as the sun had not quite set beyond the horizon of the English countryside and the stars had not made their nightly debut within the crisp landscape of the evening sky.

"He wasn't always evil," whispered a distant voice.

David's soft baritone drew me in closer as I watched the celebration unfold before me. This time I was the specter, the invisible energy that some of the guests sensed that night but could not see. I was the cold breeze, or warm breath, they felt brush against their faces as they celebrated the festivities that evening.

I stood just inside the foyer, completely lost in the music, and watched the guests dancing and swirling within the open ballroom of the manor. The warm glow of the stone fireplace and brightly flickering candles enhanced the magic of the moment. I found myself stepping closer to get a better view when I noticed a beautiful raven-haired woman walking gracefully down the winding staircase that adjoined the narrow foyer.

Her dress, a red burgundy satin, clung tightly to her slender body as she glided effortlessly down the staircase. Her long black hair swirled delicately about her narrow shoulders, and her eyes were the color of midnight. Her skin, so pale and luminescent I thought at first another specter had come to join me, was alabaster white. She seemed to stare right through me as she made her way down the landing and placed her slender delicate feet upon the bare wooden floor.

"Raphaela--my beautiful wife!--such a vision and so enchanting you look tonight!" boomed a deep masculine voice from out of the shadows of the dimly lit foyer.

It was Sebastian! A much younger version, but clearly this was David's uncle.

"He adored her," whispered David. "In his eyes, she could do no wrong."

They embraced, his lips gently touching hers as he wrapped his arms snugly around her waist. "Come, let's join the party," he said. "We have so much to be grateful for!"

I saw the slightest hesitation in her dark eyes before she placed her hand in his and allowed him to escort her into the warmth of the ballroom and toward her admiring guests.

"What are they celebrating?" I asked.

"The birth of their son," David replied. "You see, my uncle wasn't always the man you think him to be. However, this night--this celebration--changed him forever."

And so David began to tell me his story:

"I was fortunately blessed to come into this world loved by my father and mother and, as the only child you would think me to be spoiled, but that was not the case. It's true my parents were wealthy, but I was taught to be humbled by our wealth. This manor you see was always filled with music and parties. My mother welcomed everyone here, no matter their station. She and my father devoted much of their time to the less fortunate, and when they died from the disastrous fire within the stables my Uncle Sebastian and Aunt Raphaela treated me like their own son.

"Raphaela longed for a child, to give her husband something of herself to raise and cherish, as they had me. She conceived several times, only to have God take away the stillborn and lifeless little bodies of her babies before they could take a breath within this world. Over time, her need for a child of her own consumed her every waking moment.

"My uncle was once a kind, loving husband--a man of his word and adored by everyone. He was high counselor to the church and held a very high position within the court. He begged Raphaela to forgive God for taking away their children and advised her to be happy about all with which she'd been blessed, but something burned so deep inside her.

"I remember the day she announced she was once again with child. I watched as she danced throughout the manor, at first causing much alarm amongst the servants--they feared she must be mad! My uncle seemed so pleased at first, but at night I heard them arguing behind the closed doors of their chamber.

"My aunt was older now, not the young girl she had once been, and my uncle feared for her welfare. He did not care if they had children. My uncle was afraid he might lose her--after losing five children already he feared this might be the one that would ultimately take her away.

They had me, after all. Even though I was not conceived from her womb, he argued that I was still their blood and they should be very grateful for that. He only wanted to continue the rest of his days in the loving arms of his beautiful Raphaela.

"She would have none of that, and requested he not enter their chamber again until after the birth of their child. My uncle was heartbroken. Of course, he didn't show it when I was watching, but I sensed the change in him. He stayed away at court, sometimes for days, even weeks at a time, until the birth of their child grew near.

"Of course, Raphaela had the best physicians who kept close watch as her time grew near. They urged her to stay in bed, and disallowed her any exercise or time outside her chambers, in order that she be well rested when the time to give birth arrived.

"I was given permission to enter her chamber occasionally, and I'd read to her and keep her company. I knew she had high hopes that God would not punish her this time. She told me he had no reason to, and that she was sure she hadn't conceived this time only to have her child taken away.

"Eventually, the strain this baby placed upon her body caused Rapheala to become anxious and depressed. I knew my aunt was not herself, but still thought her selfish for her lack of concern for my uncle, who tried everything to reassure her. I found myself angry with her as she hardly allowed him near her.

"The blessed day finally arrived, and I remember my uncle pacing nervously within the confines of his study and the soft creaking of the old wooden floor beneath his booted feet. I placed my ear against the oak door and heard him beg for the safety of his child and his beautiful wife. I listened to him say he'd never forgive himself if he lost her. I was so young, but my heart ached for them both. I'd never seen a man so in love with a woman, except for the way my father had loved my mother. I longed for the day I'd be blessed with such a love as this!

"To everyone's delight, Raphaela gave birth to a beautiful baby boy! His lungs strong, his cries echoed throughout the manor as he entered this world. Overwhelmed with joy and relief, Sebastian rushed to the chamber, only to once again be denied entrance. The physicians assured him all was well but that his wife refused anyone--even the nursemaid--entrance. Raphaela carried on this strange behavior for several weeks until she came to her senses and finally realized her actions were becoming detrimental to herself and her marriage.

"My uncle rejoiced that exile from his wife's chambers was finally over. Now allowed within his wife's chamber to hold his son and once again sleep within the arms of his beloved, Hawksworth Manor began to return to normal. Raphaela once again took long walks through the gardens as she had in the past. She loved to sit near the pond and watch the fish beg for crumbs from crusts of bread she tossed to them. Always, she had her son next to her; she never allowed him out of her sight. When the physicians assured her the baby was healthy, and nothing would happen to him, she agreed finally with my uncle to host a party. So proud, he wanted everyone to see the new addition to his family. I'd never seen him so happy.

"They threw a party like no other--grand and sophisticated—and perhaps a little over the top. It was a beautiful cloud-free night and the stars seemed brighter than ever before. Music, wine, dancing, and a feast fit for a king, the manor was alive and happy once again, as my guardians opened the manor to share their joy with others. Raphaela even allowed some of the guests to sneak a peek at the sleeping baby. She looked so lovely and alive as she danced around the ballroom with my uncle and the others. I remember the merriment and joy so very long ago."

David fell silent. I watched as tears streamed down his scarred face. He wiped them away and continued his story.

"The guests began to say their goodbyes and depart into the darkness of the night. I remember the loud chiming of the grandfather clock in the foyer as it struck the midnight hour. I retired to my chambers in order that my aunt and uncle could be alone. It was so long since they had this rare moment together.

"I thought at first I was dreaming, as I awakened to a terrifying sound that chilled me to the bone. The screaming seemed to last forever. I buried my head beneath the pillows to try to make the piercing wails go away. Then I heard my uncle shout orders to the servants to retrieve the physicians at once, and I knew something was terribly wrong with the baby. By the time the physicians arrived, it was too late--the baby was gone! There was no comprehensible reason for his death, but he lay there in his basinet so lifeless and cold. My aunt screamed and screamed to hold him in her arms as my uncle removed her from the chamber.

"Raphaela fell into a deep depression. She blamed my uncle for her son's death, said if he hadn't insisted on the party she would have been there to watch over him and he'd still be alive. Distraught, she jumped to her death from the bell tower of the small chapel shortly after and broke her neck.

"Never the same, my uncle became distant, secretive, and stayed away for long periods of time. Something dark and unholy took his place. He forbade me to go into his study, and kept it under lock and key. It had been such a favorite place of mine, and now I was forbidden entrance. The uncle I loved as a father became a stranger who shared only space with me in the manor."

I shook my head, unable to speak. I'd seen Sebastian as an evil presence in the church, a murderer! He defiled Catherine--I found it very difficult to see him as anything but a monster. I watched as tears continued to fall down David's handsome face, and could tell he loved his uncle still, and had even forgiven him.

"How is it possible you can still have feelings for him after what he did?" I cried. "He took your life! And he took great pleasure in abusing the only woman you ever loved! He kept her prisoner and still I'm not sure what became of her and her child!"

"Things are different on this side," David whispered softly. "Things are not always as they seem. My uncle is trapped and he keeps us here, his prisoners, and feeds upon our energy. His heart is black with vengeance, and he believes that by taking innocent lives he will somehow bring back what he lost so very long ago."

Suddenly I understood that Sebastian's position in the high court and church had become just a cover! If his real identity were discovered it would bring the walls of his life tumbling down! He had gained the trust and respect he needed so that he was able to practice his dark magic without being suspected or held accountable for the deeply disturbed individual he had become.

I saw how Catherine's innocence, beauty, and spirit had captured Sebastian's attention. When he gazed upon her, he felt as if she saw through his façade—as if she alone could see the true blackness of his soul after Raphaela's death. No one else was capable of knowing that truth, yet she saw it, and this disturbed and enraged him!

Mesmerized and unable to distance himself from Catherine's presence while in London, he drove himself into an uncontrollable rage, a dark moody frenzy that wasn't satisfied until he had her within his reach. Something deeper than her beauty stirred his passion and literally dug deep into his very soul. Her spirit conjured up a sheer madness that wrapped itself tightly around him, almost suffocating him, unleashing a deadly desire that nearly drove him insane--he had to have her, and he had to silence her...

I understood now that when he invaded her space, he invaded mine. Somehow he was able to link up in my dreams.

What in God's name was happening? How was I able to see and sense Catherine, and connect with energy as perverted and sinister as the Sebastian's? Where had my normal life gone and who would ever understand the complicated, intense, and unusual events unfolding in my life now?

"Until he is released," said David, "we are all unable to move forward into the light. You, my lady, were brought here to set us free."

"How the hell am I supposed to do that?" I asked.

"As you heal your past, you heal Catherine," he continued. "We won't be at rest until that happens. I never had the opportunity to live out my days with my beloved or my child. My uncle saw to that. But I tell you, lady, you are well protected and strong--he can't hurt you this time."

"What are you talking about?" I asked, surprised. "He can't hurt me this time?"

"You must have figured out who you are by now," he responded. "Why do you think we are so attracted to, and connected with, each other?"

"I don't like where this is going David, please take me back!"

I found myself sitting in the clearing surrounded by derelict buildings aged and weathered with decay. Off in the distance, enveloped in shadow and the cluster of oaks, he sat on horseback.

"Please help her, Evie," he implored.

The loud booming of thunder broke the trance. Streaks of silver lightening sliced thin ribbons through the grey cloudy sky as he galloped away into the swirling mist.

Chapter 19

It was a downpour by the time I made it back to Trevor's field. All was quiet, except for the sheep grazing lazily along the fence line. Michael was just driving up as I reached the middle of the field. The mournful honking of a lone goose drifted down to me from the gray overcast sky.

Perfect omen, I thought. Since geese represent fidelity, family, and a happy marriage. But this goose flew alone, as if he was lost. I knew how he felt. Yes, I totally empathized with him. My thoughts so involved in the plight of the lost goose, I nearly stepped on a rabbit that had ventured out from his burrow to lap up a bit of rain before bouncing off in search of fresh sprouts or some other delicacy. "If only life could be this easy," I whispered.

I waved to Michael but he didn't see me. Instead he disappeared from view inside the church. Away for nearly three weeks taking care of his father in India, I wasn't sure what to expect when I walked through the old wooden church door. As I entered through the dark foyer and into the warmth of the kitchen, he stepped into view and wrapped me tightly in his arms.

"I've missed you," he whispered as he kissed me on the lips, and this time it was he who lingered there. In fact, his body pressed tightly against mine and I felt the hardness rise within his trousers. But he didn't take it to the next level-- instead he gently released me from his embrace.

I helped him unpack from his long journey and, as he

showered, I made us a light dinner of Greek salad and red wine.

"I have something for you," he said. "I left it out in the car, I know how you like to rummage through my suitcases looking for little trinkets I may have brought back with me," he teased. He then presented me with a lovely pair of white and gold silk pajamas made especially for me, and my favorite perfume.

"Thank you," I said, as I leaned across the table to give him a quick kiss.

"Hmmm, your lips taste like wine," he whispered. "How about we take this upstairs?" He grasped my hand and led me to the loft where he threw me gently onto our four poster bed.

I awoke to the gentle tapping of rain on the skylight above our bed, restless but fulfilled from the lovemaking. Michael's soft snoring and the humming of the fridge downstairs were the only sounds inside the church--a total relief, as so much had transpired since he'd been away.

Thirsty as always after our romps in the bedroom, I wandered downstairs. After quenching my thirst I moved into the living room and sat on the sofa thinking about the night's pleasures. In the back of my mind I heard yet again Monique's bold statement: "Your marriage was just a catalyst to get you to England."

"Damn you," I whispered, as I relaxed into the softness of the sofa.

I awoke to Michael's handsome face staring down at me.

"Good morning, sleepy head! What are doing down here? I missed you when I woke up this morning."

"Sorry," I said, rubbing the sleep from my eyes. "I was restless last night--you know how I get after we make love," I said, teasing him with my cat has the canary grin.

"Thirsty," he replied, as he plopped down next to me. "How was it here while I was away?" he asked.

My mind raced as I tried to figure out what to say. I wondered if I should I tell him everything that had transpired. Could I trust him enough now to open up my heart and spill out the emotions aching to be set free? His usual M.O. was to walk away every time I tried to talk to him. Maybe this time, after being with his father in India, his heart had softened a bit.

"Michael," I began, "you know something weird's been happening to me ever since I arrived here at the church. You've never given me a chance to really share it with you. I know I'm not going crazy, and so do you."

"Continue," he said, as he reached for my hand and grasped it tightly. Surprised, I looked at him and saw the muscles of his face begin to relax.

"I know you share some of my beliefs," I went on, encouraged, "especially about past lives, and as much as I've been fighting it and as strange as it all sounds, I believe this church, our home, has become the center for some very traumatic energy from who knows how many centuries ago. When you and I moved in here, one of us--or maybe both of us--awakened something that's really never been properly put to rest."

I expected him to get up and walk away, to get in his car and drive away like all the other times I broached this subject, but he didn't.

"I know this sounds crazy," I continued, "but this church has been waiting for me for a very long time. I shared this with you before, but you didn't want to hear it, even though you've admitted that you felt the energy in here."

"What am I supposed to do, Evie?" he asked, a look of

concern on his face." I've invested a lot of money in this place. It's not like we can just up and walk away." He paused. "Maybe if you'd never come here the place would have remained peaceful. The energies of this church might not have been brought back to life." He paused again. "Perhaps my life might have been different--better if you'd stayed away."

"What's that supposed to mean, Michael?" His harsh words cut more deeply into my heart than if he'd physically slapped me across the face, and I couldn't hold back my tears-- they seemed to have a life of their own and blurred my vision as they streamed down my face.

"I'm sorry," he responded. "It's just that this situation is frustrating the hell out of me! I wanted us to be happy here-- I purchased this place specifically with you in mind."

"No, Michael," I replied. "You bought this place without asking me prior to our marriage, remember? I never said anything because your heart was dead set on it--I remember you saying it was 'your heaven on earth.' It was never my dream to live here! It's been hard adjusting and difficult living in a place that's always cold and damp and has been a building site for nearly a year now! You don't' see it, you're rarely ever here! I've tried making friends with whomever or whatever claims to own this place, but unfortunately it goes way beyond that! Apparently, this place and I were destined to meet--it was only a matter of time."

Michael released my hands.

"I didn't ask for this to be thrown on me!" I protested. "I fell deeply and madly in love with you, my prince charming, for lack of a better phrase! To be honest with you though, nothing I do is good enough! You seem always to do everything just a little bit better—like when I'm cooking and you push me away and take over! I mean, I love that you want to help, but it's like you always have to be in charge! Same thing when I do the laundry, you always step in and take it away..." Boy, was I on a roll! "Sometimes I think my *only* talent is this damned gift of medium-ship I share with Catherine and the rest of the spirits that haunt this place!"

Michael didn't say a word as he rose and walked out the door, slamming it behind him. I heard the crunch of gravel in the drive as he drove away. A few minutes later my phone rang.

"Don't bother waiting up for me," he said coldly. "I'll be sleeping at a friend's flat this evening."

"Of course you will! I retorted. "After all, our marriage is fine as long as it doesn't involve communication!"

I slammed the phone down and rushed outside. The fresh air assaulted my lungs as I gulped it in. I'd not rocked the boat this hard since our marriage for fear of losing my husband's love. Now, as I scrutinized the situation, I began to realize it never was much of a marriage— I thought about how he took some of my confidence away by taking away my independence. We used to read to one another, but I just couldn't do the voices of the characters as well as he--it was like he needed to hear his voice as the characters, and got bored when it was my turn to read. I felt a sense of loss, as though my input was not that important. I was beginning to feel like a past time for him until something better and more agreeable came along.

I knew if I called him to apologize it wouldn't accomplish anything. I learned early on that whenever I disagreed with him he held it against me. He wouldn't say anything, just chalk up another mark in his little black book of "things Evie has done to piss me off!" Then he'd pretend nothing out of the ordinary had ever taken place, when deep down I knew it was eating at him as much as it was me. After the dust settled he usually sent me an e-mail that pointed out the things I'd done to hurt him. I was never allowed to truly vent with him face-to-face.

I sat on Catherine's crypt and surrendered to its smooth cool surface. A thick mist began to swirl about me and I found myself welcoming its embrace. I thought about how I'd been facing the darkness, and everything it brought with it, alone and without guidance. How, when I tried sharing it with Michael, it made things within our marriage worse.

An idea began to form in my brain—I'd heard of people who helped clear houses of these kinds of energies. Perhaps it was time for me to enlist their services. I didn't know where to begin, so I decided a search on the internet would be my best bet. What should I search for-- ghost hunters? Got demons call us? Spirits be gone? Fortunately, my sense of humor helped me keep my sanity...

To my surprise, I found page upon page of listings! *This is ridiculous,* I thought. *I guess England's other pastime besides pubs and soccer is exorcising unwanted guests from houses!* Finally I stumbled across an interesting advertisement, but couldn't muster up the courage to make the call. All the "what if's" clawed their way to the surface of my mind. *What if they think I'm crazy, mad, or—worse yet-- insane? What if they think I'm making it all up? What if, what if, what if?*

"Just make the call," I whispered, willing my fingers toward the buttons on the phone.

"Housecleaners Inc!" boomed a woman's deep husky voice. "How may I help you?"

I couldn't speak at first. I felt foolish even approaching someone about what had been going on in the church.

"Hello? Is anyone there?" the voice boomed again. "I can hear you breathing!" She sounded a little annoyed. "Is this some kind of prank call?" Her voice was clipped with a strong

Scottish brogue.

"Yes, I'm here!" I replied. "I-I'm just not sure where to begin."

"At the beginning, lass," she replied. I could hear the amusement in her tone.

I proceeded to give her a rundown of what had happened, and she assured me they were more than qualified for this particular job. They'd seen their share of bizarre and unusual events, and she told me this should be a relatively easy clearing.

I arranged to meet with her and her husband the following week, which would give me enough time to break the news to Michael. I wasn't sure how he was going to react, but honestly I didn't care! If he wasn't willing to be there, I'd find someone who was able to relate to what was happening to me. I'd played the victim way too many times, and it didn't feel good anymore. I deserved better, and so did Catherine!

That day I also drove into the tiny village of Odiham, determined to keep moving forward now that I'd made that call. Suddenly I recognized how ironic it was that All Hallows Eve, the night of the dead, was the following week. It seemed appropriate that the mediums picked that particular night to release the church from the hold of its spirit tenants--I wasn't about to argue with the experts!

"Are you sure this will work?" I asked the woman from whom I purchased a sage stick hesitantly. I had read somewhere that smudging a house with sage sometimes released it from its haunting.

"Oh, indeed," she assured me, as I handed her my money. She stared at me with large owl eyes. "I've never had a disappointed customer," she winked. "Sounds like a simple enough haunting, but to be sure you might want to purchase a spirit board as well. You know, just in case you have a stubborn spirit or two! Tell you what, if you purchase the board, I'll throw in the sage as an added bonus!"

Quite the sales woman! I thought as I left her shop, both sage and spirit board in tow.

Michael wasn't too upset about what I arranged--in fact he seemed relieved. Of course, he made it quite clear he wouldn't be around during the purging of the church. His company was sending him to South Wales for three weeks. He arranged to have a cab pick him up that evening, and once he left I found myself alone in the church once more.

Three weeks to myself, I thought. *This ought to be fun.*

After lighting candles and placing them throughout the entire church, I proceeded to smudge it from top to bottom with the sage. I started in the tower, where I waved the burning sage torch—kind of like a big cigar--and worked my way down, focusing on allowing the savory smoke to inhabit every corner, window, and any entrance where dark energy seemed to reside. As I did so, I commanded the spirits to leave and asked for protection. I'd never done this before so I played it by ear. *What the heck,* I thought, *by the time I'm through I'll be surprised if the fire department doesn't show up!* Smoke was everywhere. Tempted to go outside to get fresh air, I hesitated, not sure of what I might invite in.

My next step was a little more intimidating--the spirit board. I had no idea if it would help or make matters worse. I'd always been under the impression they were dangerous and that playing with the board might unleash malevolent spirits. The shop owner had assured me it was only a tool to contact the dead and a way for them to communicate with the living--nothing more.

First I placed the board on the small marble table in the kitchen, took a deep breath, and released it slowly. Then I placed my fingertips on the small plachette on top of the board. Nothing! No surprise--I felt foolish sitting here in the first place! Just as I was about to lift my fingers from the tiny device, it began to move slowly across the board, sending the hairs on the back of my neck into a nervous frenzy.

"Who's here?" I cried. The tiny device proceeded to slowly spell out one small word. H- E- L-L. I waited patiently for more, but there was nothing.

"Did you mean hello?" I asked hopefully. The device didn't budge.

I asked again but received no reply. *Maybe I shouldn't press the issue,* I thought, and began to put the small board and device back in its box. I'd already smudged and blessed the house—hopefully that had been enough to send the spirits away.

My stomach complained loudly and I realized I hadn't eaten all day. I grilled fresh salmon, and sliced tomatoes and feta cheese and, after pouring myself a glass of chilled white wine, sat down to watch an old movie. I loved the classics and decided on *Rear Window* with James Stewart and Grace Kelly. *Just what I need--a thriller because my life isn't already thrilling enough! Really Evie, why not a comedy?* But I liked suspense and clicked on the TV as I slid the disc into the DVD player. I settled in and took a long sip of chilled chardonnay. *This is more like it,* I thought, as I savored the next sip of wine and relaxed into the movie. Suddenly I heard a loud crash that shook the church and jolted me from the sofa, spilling the much cherished wine everywhere.

"What the hell?" I screamed, uncertain whether I should run toward the sound or away from it. It sounded like something very large had crashed into the side of the church. Impossible! I rushed to the foyer where cold air greeted me and saw the door had been ripped from its hinges!

I stepped out into the night--not even a breeze rustled

144

the evening air! How could this be? I stood silently, as all kinds of thoughts raced through my mind. *What do I do now?* I didn't want to go back inside, but at the same time it seemed ridiculous to stand outside in the cold. *Get a hold of yourself, Evie,* I thought, as I rushed back inside. *What do I do? What do I do?* I panicked as I paced back and forth inside the tiny foyer.

I remembered John the builder had given me his number in case I needed anything while Michael was away. I grabbed my phone from the kitchen counter, found his number, and called, my hands shaking badly all the while. It seemed to take forever before anyone answered.

"Hello," a gruff voice said. "State your business."

"Oh thank God you're home!" I cried. "John, it's Evie! I need your help--can you come over right away?"

"Sure miss'us--are you okay?" I heard the concern in his voice, and relaxed a bit.

"I will be when you get here--there seems to be a problem with the door."

I decided to wait for John outside. Somehow I felt safer out there on Catherine's crypt then inside with whomever or whatever lurked there. Tiny shards of shattered glass lay scattered across the dark marble floor in the foyer. I recognized them as pieces of the beautiful charm the Bulgarian architect had given me to ward off the evil eye.

I made my way out to the crypt, and it wasn't long before I heard the popping and sputtering of John's old work truck announcing his arrival long before he pulled in the graveled drive. A few more spurts and sputters and all became quiet once again.

"Okay miss'us, show me what's been happening here," said John, as he exited his truck.

I took him to where the door once stood. I'd tried to sit

it against the side of the church so he'd be able to see the extent of the damage.

"What on God's green earth happened here?" he asked. "Are you sure you're not hurt?"

"I'm a little shaken, but fine--I thought the entire church was coming down when I heard all the noise. How did this happen?" I asked him earnestly.

"It's definitely been torn from the hinges and very odd if you look here," he said, pointing to the mangled hinges. "I don't believe someone was trying to get in, as much as it appears something or someone was trying to get out! What's going on here, miss'us?"

I didn't know where to begin, so I ended up telling him everything. He listened intently to my entire story, and didn't laugh, scoff, or walk away.

"Where are the tissues?" he asked when I was done speaking. I'd been so involved in telling my story I hadn't noticed the tears that now streamed down his wrinkled and worn face.

"Evie," he said, "you need to get out of this place--it's not safe!"

"That's the first time you've actually called me by my name," I said.

"Where you're concerned, I'm a softy," he smiled. "There's something evil that resides in here with you!"

"I've made arrangements to meet with a couple who claim to clear houses of unwanted guests. I plan to hang out until then. This is my home, after all. I don't have anywhere else to go at the moment, and I refuse to let some renegade ghost send me packing! What do you think, John? Do you think I'll come out of this alive?" I smiled.

"Evie!" he cried. "I hope you're joking!"

"I am, but it's the only way I've been able to survive!

And I'm not giving in this time!"

"This time?" asked John, concerned. "This happened before?"

"Yes," I replied, "long ago in the distant past."

His brow furrowed, and I sensed by the look on his face he struggled to comprehend the true meaning behind my answer.

Chapter 20

The husband and wife team arrived just before dusk. They seemed normal enough. I guess I expected them to come swooping in on broomsticks with a black furry cat as a mascot and a crystal ball tucked neatly away beneath long black capes.

Instead, they came in a dark green minivan, both dressed in snug fitting jeans and tees emblazoned boldly with "Housecleaners Inc.," their company logo. I had to admit it was catchy and showed a nice sense of humor. *Okay, so far, so good,* I thought as I greeted them at the front door.

"What happened here?" the man asked in amazement before even introducing himself. Of course he was referring to the old oak door, a bit scarred after last week's incident.

"Sorry," said the buxom redhead, "I'm Sheila!" She smiled a huge lipstick grin as she extended her slender freckled hand. "You'll have to excuse the manners of my mate--he gets carried away with places like this!"

"Hi, I'm Evie," I replied, shaking her hand.

"And this", said Sheila, pointing to her husband, "is Andrew."

"Sorry luv, very nice to meet you," said Andrew as he extended his large masculine hand. Wow, I could have gotten lost in those dark olive eyes--it seemed Shelia had quite a stud on her hands! As I said, they were not at all what I'd envisioned!

"Okay, let's get on with it then," said Andrew as he clapped his hands together and pushed his way through the entrance into the dark foyer. "Blimey!" he shouted, "we've got some strong energy going on in here! Sheila, come check this out!"

"My God," she gasped as she followed him, "what's been going on in here?" She focused her intense baby blues on me. I thought I detected a hint of fear trickle through before she composed herself. "Where's the bloody light?" she asked.

I flicked on the light, illuminating the foyer. The only thing I knew they'd see for sure was the luxury apartment suite of spiders who insisted on staying no matter how often I swept them away. Their webs crisscrossed the high ceiling and clung to the damp walls, exposing dead insects trapped within the sticky threads of their captors' nets.

"I sense most of the energy is coming from the tower," said Sheila as she walked into the warmth of my kitchen. "Lovely what you've done here, by the way," she added as she moved towards the spiral staircase. "Okay if I go up there?" She climbed the stairs before I had time to reply. I stood there, nodding my head.

Sure, go for it, I thought. *Better you than I—I hate that tower!*

She climbed the stairs, her husband close behind her. When they reached the trap door to the tower I heard Sheila scream and suddenly a loud crash reverberated through the church.

"Sheila, you all right?" screamed Andrew. "Darling-- you okay? Say something, please say something!"

"I'm fine," she moaned "just had the wind knocked out of me. I think something pushed me--something doesn't want me up in the tower, it grabbed my shoulders and pushed me!"

I ran upstairs to make sure they were okay.

"What happened?" I asked.

Sheila propped herself against the wall with Andrew's

assistance, and dusted herself off as she adjusted her tight fitting tee. "I'm fine, really. Stop fussing," she said as she pushed Andrew's hands away.

"Remember the time we were both in Scotland?" she asked, looking directly at her husband.

"Yeah luv, but I've tried to forget--bloody hell of a place that was!" He brushed his fingers through his dark wavy hair and lifted a thick lock from his furrowed brow. He shook his head as if trying to forget an unpleasant experience.

"You're right," Sheila replied. "Let's not go back down memory lane--that place belongs in the past." She turned her attention back to me and the present.

"What have you done here the past week or so?" she asked, gazing at me with her penetrating baby blues, her face a shade paler than when we'd first met.

"Nothing, why?"

"*Something's* riled up the spirits," she explained. "Are you sure? Nothing? Please think really hard."

"Well, I smudged the place with sage and attempted to make contact with a spirit board, but believe me it didn't work! It was a total waste of my time and money!"

"Trust me," she said, "it more than worked--you royally pissed somebody off!"

Annoyed, I assured them that whatever was here had been royally pissed off way before I ever set foot in this place! I told them they'd only tasted a very small sample of what the spirits here were capable of doing.

"You really resemble her," Sheila remarked as she reached out and touched my face. "She's truly exquisite and her light is blinding!"

"Who?" I asked.

"The young lady standing over there in the corner," she replied. "Andrew can you see her, sense her?"

"Not sure," Andrew replied "but there's something else lurking over there. I can totally sense his energy, and he's bloody wicked nasty!"

"Yes, I see him," replied Sheila. "Seems he's trying to hold her back, and he's *very* angry with both of you! You're presence here has made Catherine strong, and her boldness and strength is pissing him off!"

I shared everything with them over a cup of Earl Grey tea, but didn't mention the diary. I sensed Catherine needed me to discover for myself what had happened to her. I wasn't sure they'd believe me, anyway. The whole "Coven of Nine" and what it stood for seemed so out there.

"Unbelievable," commented Andrew.

"Truly," agreed Sheila, nodding her head.

"So what do I do?" I asked. "How do I get rid of the energy here and take back my home?"

"I'm not sure," Sheila replied. "Andrew and I have to put our heads together and research this. I've heard of the Coven of Nine, and if what you say is true, this runs deeper than a mere haunting of displaced spirits. However, you do have *that* going on out back in your field."

"I'm afraid if you just pack your bags and leave it's more than likely they'll follow," said Andrew. "Apparently it's not the church to which they're attached."

"Well, if not the church, then who?" I asked.

"Oh, you're so naïve luv," Sheila smiled. "They are attracted--and attached—to you!" she said gently.

"I don't believe this!" I jumped up and paced nervously back and forth along the marble floor in the kitchen. "How can this be happening? What am I supposed to do next? I just want to go back to the way things were before I came over to this place!"

"Unfortunately luv," Sheila said as she placed her

slender arm around my shoulders, "that will never happen. Cheer up lass, you've embarked on quite an extraordinary journey. Just based on what you've told us it's clear you seem to have awakened deep trauma from your past through Catherine. She has connected with you to help you. If I'm right--and I usually am--the two of you have crossed paths before...the big million dollar question is how and when?"

"You must realize," Andrew chimed in, "you are helping her as well. It's quite clear there is something holding her back, keeping her a prisoner--and without you she's stuck there with that bloody wicked energy."

"I never wanted any of this!" I shouted.

"Not consciously," replied Andrew, "but on a deeper level you agreed to come back and release Catherine from the grip of a very dark and distorted past."

"We admire you for this, Evie," Sheila noted. "You're allowing yourself to step into your light. Whether you want to admit it or not Sebastian has unfinished business with you, and your being of the living definitely gives you the upper hand. Do you know how she died?" she asked, turning her intense baby blues to gaze upon me once again. She looked almost angelic with that seriously pale face and those eyes!

"No, I'm sorry," I replied. "When Sebastian took her away she was with child."

"I believe this child may be the key to everything," said Andrew.

"Perhaps," I agreed, "but there's more to it than that. She speaks about a book she believes can actually command a person's soul. There's no way that could actually happen, right?"

"A book that traps people's souls?" repeated Andrew. "That would have to be some very powerful magic! Though anything's possible, luv. What's your take, Sheila?"

"Open up to the visions," Sheila advised. "Protect yourself, of course, but allow her to feel safe with you. If you react to any of this with fear it only fuels his energy and diminishes Catherine's."

"If this book actually existed, and I'm not saying it didn't, Catherine and Sebastian are battling for dominance of her child," Andrew added.

"I think you're right, Andrew..." Sheila looked at her mate. "The child is the key!" She turned to me. "You need to find out what happened to Catherine's child! I do believe what you have awakened here has followed you for lifetimes, but because you were not totally aware, they were forgotten."

As much as I wanted to shut down and refuse Catherine's requests, I had to agree that I couldn't turn my back on her. I realized months ago she was becoming a part of me, but didn't want to believe it. My heart had known all along, but my mind refused to accept it. There was no way she would allow me to forget her, because if I did, I'd be forgetting myself! And yes, what of the child? What became of the child?

"This time, my dear, you are very aware, which makes you a dangerous opponent for Sebastian," Sheila said. "We'll check back in a few days and see how you're managing," she concluded. I thanked them both, walked them to their minivan, and waved until they disappeared from view.

It was peaceful out here in the graveyard with the light mist swirling about my legs. The call of an owl echoed through the woods and off in the distance I thought I heard the faint reply of its mate. It was All Hallows Eve--only a few hours until midnight when the dead would awaken and rap on the old oak door begging to come in from the cold dampness of their ancient graves. Visions of Michael Jackson's "Thriller" flashed through my mind. *Odd,* I smiled to myself as I walked inside and closed the door softly behind me.

153

Chapter 21

"It'll be coming down from the highlands of Scotland and reach parts of North Hampshire before morning," the weather man announced as he predicted wicked winds and heavy rain for the next several hours. His voice sounded tinny and distant over the radio as it crackled and hissed with static from the approaching storm.

"Prepare for downed trees and power lines," he continued. "It'll be a rough one folks! Stand the ready!"

The old pine's branches scratched insistently against the window of the bedroom--the wind was already whipping through. That night the storm roared through the graveyard, sending several trees to their untimely demise. Minutes after I snuggled down on the sofa to read, I found myself without power and in the dark. The rain sounded like small pebbles slamming against the windows and I ran outside several times to rescue the trash bins I thought I'd tied down securely.

Thank God for the tiny pot belly stove and an ample supply of candles! The stove's golden glow danced eerily throughout the kitchen. Even without power I was able to make hot tea on the stove's flat top and was surprised at how much warmth it gave off. I placed several candles along the window seals of the church, illuminating the dark corners, and settled once again on the sofa.

Nothing out of the ordinary happened that evening. Maybe the presence of the two mediums had scared the spirits away. I doubted that, but on some level it made me feel better to think so. I didn't sleep much that night; the howling of the wind and the pelting rain unsettled me.

Never in a hurricane before, I discovered that one must have passed through when I ventured out in the morning to inspect the damage. Tree branches lay scattered everywhere. The bird feeders hanging in the trees had disappeared with the wind, and flower pots and small scrubs were overturned and broken. The large fern that grew near Catherine's crypt was tattered and torn. A large oak had fallen across the narrow graveled drive, its overgrown roots pointed up toward the gray sky. It looked like a giant mad man had stomped through and destroyed everything in its path.

Trevor must not have fared very well either. I heard the whining of a chain saw coming from the direction of his farm house. Still without power, I could see the lines that connected to the church were tangled in the branches of the old pine. I wasn't sure which was more unnerving-- the intense severity of Mother Nature's wrath, or the angry spirits that loitered within my home. I cleared up as much of the damage as possible and then decided to call the man of the hour, my dear friend John. Soon enough the sputtering and spitting of his old work truck alerted me to his arrival. I ran outside to greet him and what I saw surprised me--he'd brought his entire crew!

"I didn't expect this!" I said, barely able to contain the tears now flowing down my face.

"I asked them to help," said John "and at first they wouldn't volunteer. Then they found out they'd be helping you, and it was like magic--they appeared from out of nowhere within minutes!" he chuckled.

"It's so good to see you all again!" I cried. "If I had power I'd fix you up some breakfast!"

"No need," said John with a wink. "We stopped off at the local Mac's--figured you'd be hungry and somehow I knew you'd need a strong coffee. Not the Italian blend you like, so you'll have to make do." He placed the Styrofoam cup in my outstretched hand.

"I love you guys!" I smiled.

They looked at me and grinned sheepishly. I invited them all to sit around the tiny marble table in the kitchen. They shared stories of past storms as we ate our big Macs and sipped hot coffee. Then they immediately began to clear away the debris. A few hours later my power was restored and the churchyard cleared of any remains from the night before.

I thanked them again for saving the American lady in distress. Just as John tipped his hat to me, and he and his crew began to drive away, Michael pulled up

"Some storm!" Michael said as he wrapped his arms around my waist. "You okay?"

"I am now that you're home," I replied, snuggling deeper into his embrace.

"I've great news," he added. "I'm putting the church on the market!"

What? I couldn't believe what I was hearing! After all we'd been through in this church, now he was preparing to sell it? All this time spent living in a perpetual building site, not knowing what to expect daily, and sharing my home with the dead on top of that, *now* he springs this on me--and without consulting me first? Red hot anger rose inside of me.

"I thought we were a couple!" I shouted. "Did you not think this important enough to share with me first *before* you took it upon yourself to put it on the market?"

"That's what I do, Evie," he replied. "We were never going to live here forever!"

"That's not the point," I yelled. "It's the fact you didn't include me in the decision!"

I sensed his need to clam up and walk away just like

every other time things became heated between us. I wasn't about to give him the satisfaction. I pushed myself out of his embrace, let myself out, and found my way to the comfort of Catherine's crypt.

"Catherine, I'm not going to be here much longer," I whispered, gazing up at the gargoyles forever perched on the gabled bell tower. Their misshapen stone faces stared back at me--unfortunately they had nothing to say. Catherine's diary had ended abruptly, as if she hadn't had time to complete it. My mind began to race--where do I turn now?

"Sweetheart, come back inside—it's getting cold!" Michael called. I wasn't even aware he'd been standing there while I was lost in thought, begging Catherine to communicate with me.

"Coming!" I answered, as I pushed myself up from the crypt.

I took one last look at the gargoyles. "If only you could speak, I bet you'd have a lot to say," I told them, and could have sworn one of them winked at me. *Just a trick of the light,* I thought, as I looked away, and stepped out of the swirling mist and into the warmth of Michael's arms.

Chapter 22

She sat in a classroom hunched over a large wooden desk, engrossed in reading a tiny black book. Her dark auburn curls extended down toward her waist and highlighted her golden amber almond-shaped eyes, as she rested a slender arm against her heart shaped face. Never had I seen such alabaster skin--she appeared almost ethereal. I guessed she was no older than early teens, but couldn't be sure. She had a delicate feminine body and wore a tiny golden cross around her slender neck.

"Victoria!" boomed a loud baritone voice. "Are you finished with your studies?"

"Almost, father," she replied in a soft husky voice. She returned her attention once again to the tiny black book.

He walked into the classroom; he was tall and slender, but I couldn't see his face. I willed him to move closer to the light, but he remained with his back toward me.

"You must finish your studies," he said gently. "Remember their importance?"

"Yes, father, I remember," she said, looking up at him with her golden amber eyes--eyes that appeared very wise for a girl of such tender age. She resumed her reading and lost herself once again within the pages of the tiny book.

"That's my little angel," he said softly, patting her gently on her slender shoulder.

Turn around, God damn you, turn around! I tried willing him to face me, but he simply disappeared. Suddenly, I was running through a maze--how did I get here? It seemed endless. The faster I tried to run, the slower I became. My legs felt like rubber, unable to catch any speed, and it was like running in a pool of black molasses. He followed right behind me, a faceless demon in hot pursuit.

"Come on!" I shouted at my legs as I rounded a bend inside the maze. This direction seemed to be taking me deeper into the dark abyss. It was cold and I could see my breath as I struggled to keep distance between me and the demon pursuing me. I could smell his hot breath as it drifted toward me through the brittle air. He was catching up!

Oh God, I can't let him catch me! I thought. *Come on, pick up the pace!* The dense foliage in the maze grew thicker as small thorns sprouted along its branches. *My God, if I run into these I'm doomed!* The branches twisted and reached out to grasp at my ankles and bare legs. *Run Evie, run!* Just as a twisted withered branch began to wrap its thorny fingers around my ankle, she appeared. In her hands she held a tiny book.

"Shhh," she whispered, placing a tiny finger against her lips. "Follow me!"

I had to pick up my pace to catch up to her, she was quick. She stood in the narrow path waiting for me, then turned and ran, her long auburn hair flowing behind her.

"Hurry!" she yelled "or he'll find us!" She ducked into the shelter of an alcove and I climbed in beside her. Trapped, there was nowhere for us to go! I could hear his heavy breathing as he rounded the bend.

"What are we going to do?" I whispered.

"Hurry, place your hands on the book!" she ordered me.

I must have looked confused because she grabbed my hands, and placed them on the book with such force she nearly knocked me off my feet. Immediately the book began to glow and the heat radiating from it threatened to burn my hands.

"Don't let go--whatever you do hold tight to the book!" she screamed.

He stood there, right in front of us, but the light radiating from the book was so powerful he couldn't see us. I forced myself to hold on to it tightly, but wasn't sure how much more I could take. The heat burned through my skin, and the light grew brighter, illuminating the little alcove. Suddenly I was alone. Where was my rescuer? I no longer held the book but my hands continued to glow and emanate an intense heat that shot out toward my attacker.

The demon in pursuit hurled obscenities and seemed to be gaining ground! Just as I was afraid I'd lose the force emanating from the palms of my hands, the young woman stood there again, book in hand, her long auburn hair wrapped wildly around her slender shoulders. Her almond-shaped eyes held wisdom and knowledge for one so young. Her alabaster skin glowed iridescent, and she looked like an angel.

"Quiet," she whispered, her slender finger pressed tightly to her lips. "He's close, but hasn't figured out how to work it." She pointed to the book she held within her grasp. "It takes a trinity--the power of three. Remember this: It takes you, Catherine, and me!"

She was gone. "No, wait!" I screamed. "Please come back, Victoria! Wait!" I felt as though I was Alice in Wonderland, falling down the rabbit hole, twisting and turning along a dark tunnel and bumping and colliding against the roots and rocks of its burrow. "Please, Victoria, come back!"

"Evie, wake up!" I heard a man's voice say. He seemed so far away. "Sweetheart, wake up, you're dreaming."

No! I refused to open my eyes. If I did, I'd lose Victoria! I felt pressure on my shoulders and my entire body began to shake. "Damn it, darling, open your eyes!" There was that voice again.

It was Michael--had he been trapped in the maze too? Slowly I opened my eyes. At first his face was nothing more than a blur. A jackhammer pounded in my head. If this was a hangover, I prayed it would go away.

"Sweetheart, it was a dream, you're safe," Michael said as he pulled me close against his bare chest and began to rock me slowly back and forth. I couldn't speak. I allowed him to hold me, and listened to his soft voice reassuring me I was safe and that I'd be okay. The last thing I remember before drifting back to sleep is the memory of a tiny black book, intense heat, and the trinity of three.

Chapter 23

I took one last walk through the church and my footsteps echoed throughout the empty vastness. The moving van had left hours ago with all our belongings. I asked Michael to go without me--I wanted to take one last walk through the woods before I met him at our new place.

From the moment he placed it on the market, we had many potential buyers. However, just as the sale was about to close, for one reason or another, something would happen and the offer always fell through. I felt almost as though the church did not want us to leave. I knew if I mentioned this to Michael he'd think I was being ridiculous.

Clearly the church could not prevent us from leaving, yet the energy that day seemed solemn and bittersweet. I wanted to get to the woods--I sensed the deep depression settling in and needed to remove myself from its energy. Part of me had become deeply imbedded inside the church, and the very land itself...

The walk lifted my spirits, but as I crossed through the field one last time I noticed dark shadows shifting through the graveyard. Normally a peaceful place, it now seemed discontent and angry. I'm not sure how this was possible--it was something I felt within my heart and hard to explain to those who hadn't experienced it. I hadn't sensed Catherine for weeks, or for that matter the dark energy that always accompanied her. The church felt like an empty shell, soulless and without life. Even the tower that had formerly spilled over with nightly disturbances was quiet. I took once last look around before climbing into my car.

"Goodbye," I whispered. "Catherine, I hope you're finally at rest."

"Good riddance," squawked the rooks from their nests in the nearby trees. The gargoyles peered down from the gabled tower, sad-faced and menacing they challenged any intruders to stay away. The mistress of the household was abandoning ship; indeed it was a very sad day.

For me saying goodbye to a place that had turned my world upside down was bittersweet. It was here I'd awakened to something inside of me that I intended to hold onto. Despite the turmoil I sensed was still to come, I'd found a spirit of freedom and sense of direction that allowed me to establish a foundation of peace within my heart.

I thought back yet again to what Monique had said in the tiny little shop in Basingstoke: "Keepers of the light... you've been a part of this since you were a little girl. This is your destiny!"

Shortly after finding and reading Catherine's diary, I had stumbled across a group of women who referred to themselves as healers, and who advertised classes in energy work and Reiki in a local newspaper. Whether it had been fate, or whether something more powerful led me toward them, I don't know. I only know that I called that very day and made arrangements to meet with the two women who would-- unbeknownst to me at the time--place me on the track toward my true purpose.

I joined the women's Reiki group and became attuned to this very powerful energy. Amazed at how good I was at this healing modality, I advanced rapidly through levels one and two to a Reiki Master teacher, opened my own little shop, and offered classes and healing sessions. I finally found something that brought me passion and joy, and at the same time uplifted others and helped empower them to their greatest potential.

My client base grew and they loved the idea of coming to a 13th Century church for their sessions. I practiced in the church and gained nearly two hundred clients along the way. Several of them I attuned to Reiki and trained to become Reiki Masters as well, helping them to follow their inner guidance, awaken to their true gifts, and reacquaint themselves with their higher self and soul.

I continued to focus on my Reiki practice and knew that divine guidance had placed this so expertly into my lap. Introduced to powerful entities/guides that now assisted me in maneuvering my way through the church's intense energy, without Reiki and the healing I encountered, I believe I never would have remembered these gifts I'd been assigned way before I ever breathed my first breath from my mother's womb. I'd been nurtured and taught and guided from a young child, until I was told differently by my father. I volunteered and raised my hand and said "pick me!" to love this planet, "pick me!" to assist others and help them shine!

The night before I was attuned to this most amazing energy I had a very prophetic vision. I left Michael downstairs watching a movie and, as I climbed the spiral staircase to the loft, I saw a tiny Tibetan monk floating at the end of our four poster bed. No way could this be happening! But there he was, sitting in the lotus position hovering near my bed! For the first time since I lived in this church I was not afraid; I was at peace.

The tiny monk acknowledged my presence and pointed to his forehead. I watched as it began to pulsate and ripple, and within seconds a golden circle of light began to form in the center of his forehead and morph into another eye. I saw a tiny monk floating above my bed with three eyes blinking at me, and I wasn't afraid--I was mesmerized! He tapped the eye three times and disappeared.

The next day I discussed this vision with my Reiki Master, who told me I'd been assigned a very powerful teacher, and that the little monk was my guide, here to assist me with the opening of my third eye. He was the first of many guides that began to appear to me while I lived in England.

The night of my very profound attunement I dreamed of a golden temple built into the rocky face of a mountain in the Himalayas. Seated in the center of a room, lit only by the light of thousands of candles, I watched as the flames flickered and danced to the rhythmic music of chimes that echoed throughout this magnificent place. It seemed a ceremony of sorts was about to take place. I felt a tingling and rippling begin in the center of my forehead. Immediately, I placed my hand to my head and felt an opening, a soft spot, as if a thin membrane was beginning to form. *What's happening?* I wondered. My forehead felt moist and hot to the touch.

I remember trying to move but was frozen in place as the tingling and rippling became more intense and then stopped. I looked around the room--it was filled with dozens of monks, their foreheads encircled in a golden glow. They bowed, then walked toward me one by one and each presented me with a tiny scroll. One very young monk, no older than five or six, levitated toward me and, as he bowed, presented me with a key. He removed his hand slowly, but not before I noticed the tattooed number nine and tiny serpent spiraling along his wrist and ending at his small elbow.

"We are pleased that you have joined the order," he whispered. "You do us great honor...this key symbolizes freedom--it will release you from the prison of the mind and allow you to step into the power of the heart. This takes great courage, but will set you free." He tapped the middle of his forehead lightly, directing his other tiny hand towards his heart. "Your heart speaks to you through intuition, and inspires you to seek the truth, Catherine."

"I'm not Catherine!" I had protested, as I woke with a start and glanced around the darkened church. How long had I been sleeping? It felt like moments, but the clock on my nightstand begged to differ.

At the time, I did not connect the dots, but as I looked back now on the eve of my departure, I realized how similar my path had become to Catherine's. Somehow, some way, I'd sent out the call. And finally it had been answered. Or perhaps, finally I experienced enough heartache and pain and humiliation that I desired my heart to take the wheel, and the anchor of self doubt and not being good enough was slowly beginning to release its hold and I began to see the real me.

The energy within the church had shifted slowly. Once restless and alive with frantic, unsettled energy, it became calm and peaceful--almost serene. Michael pointed this out to me one day, but also told me that even though the inside of the church was cleared of negativity he felt the sinister darkness lingering outside, as if it watched and waited for any sign of weakness or vulnerability that might allow it the opportunity to seep back in.

I remember the words of a fortune teller back in the States who told me: "The powers of darkness will always be only one step behind you--due to your sensitive nature, they'll always want what is yours." Back then I was young and thought her to be a bit crazy. What did she know? She told fortunes for money! Now, as I looked back on my life and my many experiences and adventures, it seemed her words rang true...

Chapter 24

We found a home several miles away which also possessed an unnaturally disturbing history. At this point it was clear that Michael was attracted to the unique and bizarre, and our new home was no exception. He purchased a two-story townhouse on the outskirts of Basingstoke, surrounded by nearby woods and fields, which gave the feeling of country living but was much closer to the city center. However, this was no ordinary townhouse.

It had once been a mental hospital, and during World War II served also as a surgery center for wounded soldiers, mainly from Canada and the United States. In addition, back in the day and on the darker side of its history, it had housed young girls pregnant out of wedlock when their parents, ashamed and embarrassed, brought them to this hospital be locked away within the same space as the criminally insane.

These young girls and their children grew up and died here. The hospital became their home and their prison. As lovely as my new home was, I felt as though I'd leapt from the fire into the frying pan. The major difference was that this place was free from mold and the dampness that permeated everything in the church. An added bonus: There were no spiders setting up camp or marking their territory here!

Though bright and cheery, I felt an intense sadness boiling just beneath the surface. Even though it was Michael who wanted to sell the church, he seemed to become even more distant here than before. He'd quit his job in search of other pursuits and was now home twenty-four hours a day. It seemed we had nothing in common anymore; we were two people existing within the same space, going through the motions of husband and wife, but our hearts were no longer committed to one another. Michael was bored and longed for excitement, and I was on a fast track to discover my true purpose. Our paths had taken completely different directions.

It seemed no coincidence I ended up here, married to a man that really did not love me but was too afraid to let me know because he hated confrontation. Likewise, it was no coincidence that my path had crossed with an eight hundred year-old church brimming with the energy of a painful past. No matter how hard I tried to deny the events that had taken place, I knew I'd been brought here to England for a purpose far greater than a simple marriage where I was supposed to live happily ever after.

Over dinner one night Michael mentioned he'd visited the church. He didn't know why, there was something that pulled him there, he said. He admitted it wasn't the same. It had felt sad, almost lonely, like its life had been sucked away. He thought he'd seen movement inside by the large glass window, but said he dismissed it as his imagination.

"Evie, even the graveyard seemed lonely," he related. "It's unkempt and grown wild. The nettles and ivy have completely taken over. I know this sounds crazy, but it's as if it needed us there."

Odd that he'd opened up this topic of conversation, but I felt it allowed me to reveal something a local newspaper reporter from the Basingstoke Gazette had shared with me just prior to our departure.

"I'll be right back," I said excitedly. "I have something to show you!" I rushed up to our bedroom, taking the stairs two at a time. I fished out of my dresser drawer a clipping from the newspaper. I'd stuffed it into Catherine's diary and completely forgotten about it until this moment. The article was an interesting one about the church, but what I wanted Michael to see was the picture the reporter had snapped. It still took my breath away.

The young reporter had shown up out of the blue, and asked permission to walk around the grounds and snap a few photographs of the church and the graveyard. A few weeks later, he returned with some very unusual pictures.

"I'm not quite sure how to approach this," he'd stammered to me, "but have you had any strange disturbances or odd things happen here?"

"What do you mean by that?" I asked.

"Take a look at these photos!" he exclaimed, as he placed them in my hands. "My colleagues and I were skeptical at first about what I'd captured on my camera, but no matter how hard we try to rationalize it, we can't come up with any reasonable explanation as to what's on these photos!" He shook his head in disbelief. "Here, look for yourself," he said tapping the stack of photos I held in my hands.

I didn't see much of anything at first. He'd snapped trees and the surrounding graveyard, but as I looked closer I saw the misty apparition of a young woman with long blond hair standing off in the shadows underneath the old pine. Her tiny hands clasped tightly together, and her head bowed as if in prayer.

"Catherine," I whispered under my breath. She was barefoot and wore the same tattered dress I'd seen her in before. She leaned up against a tall gravestone, and when I saw what floated next to her my heart began to race. A face with skeletal-like features surrounded in a thin white vapor seemed to be materializing from the grave.

"Well?" he asked impatiently. "Do you see her--*it?*"

169

Like a little cherub, his round chubby face oozed with excitement. "Sorry," he said, "I just can't get over these photos!"

I couldn't deny he'd snapped some pretty awesome pictures. "Yes," I said nodding my head. "This is quite amazing--I see her and whatever it is standing next to her!"

"So you have had experiences here?" he asked. "I *knew* it!"

"Calm down, Sherlock," I said. "We've had our share of strange things going bump in the night," I laughed. "Just the usual settling in to an old church--it's bound to creak and make odd noises now and then." I didn't want him to think any of it bothered me.

"You're not very convincing," he replied skeptically. "I've done my research, as any reporter worth his salt would do. This church has some pretty dark history attached to it. I'd like to print this article--with your permission of course. I'll edit it to your liking if any of it makes you uncomfortable."

"It's a haunt like any other," I found myself saying. "Oh my God, I can't believe I just said that! Corny, right? What I mean is that we've had our share of nervous nights. This woman you see in the photo--her name is Catherine. She's buried over there in that crypt." I pointed to it. I shared only the bare minimum of her story with him—just enough for his article. I didn't want this place to become a hotbed for ghost hunters or the curious. I really wanted Catherine to rest in peace.

Now I handed the article to Michael. "Here, check this out!"

Michael shook his head in disbelief. "He captured her on film? It's quite amazing to see her standing there like that! Wow, I'm sorry I ever doubted you! Sure I felt the presence of something, but not like you did. Anyway, it's over now, the place is empty--as it should be--and I'm sure Catherine's at rest."

He handed me back the article and offered me a glass of wine, just like that, and it was dismissed, buried under the carpet, out of sight, out of mind. Michael's motto "see no evil, hear no evil, speak no evil," was basically to deny anything that didn't fit into his reality. *We've moved on to whatever it is one moves on to,* I thought. *End of discussion.*

I tucked the paper into my pocket quickly and reached for the wine he offered. *Fine,* I thought, gulping the wine with one swallow. I passed him the glass back and left him standing in the foyer as I walked up the stairs to our bedroom. I was tired, I was going to bed.

Chapter 25

"Do you think she sees us?" whispered the voices. A group of young children surrounded my bed holding hands, willing me to hear them, willing me to see them. I'd heard them hours before but refused to acknowledge their presence. If I did, they'd realize my gift and I'd never get rid of them. They'd latch on to me hoping I could help them.

I lay there pretending to sleep, and hoped they'd get bored and simply fade away. The sound of my closet door opening slowly set my nerves on edge, but I was bound and determined not to acknowledge their presence. Instead, I buried my head deeper beneath the covers, willing them to leave.

Just go! I thought. *Whoever you are, I can't help you!* I felt a soft touch on my shoulder. I held my breath and did not move. The touch became more insistent, as if dozens of little hands were trying to push me from my bed.

"Enough!" I shouted, tossing the covers off my head and looking around the bedroom. Everything was in its place but the closet door stood slightly ajar and my clothes were swaying gently back and forth on their hangers, as though they were being pushed by invisible hands.

"Stop it!" I shouted. "Just go away!"

My closet door slammed with a bang and nearly shattered the full length mirror that hung inside. I felt a rush of cold air brush past me, and heard tiny footsteps running frantically down the hall leading to the living room and kitchen downstairs. The pots and pans in the kitchen started banging, and the clinks and clangs of silverware being thrown to the floor got my attention.

"That's it, I've had it!" I shouted angrily, as I bounced out of bed and rushed down the stairs into the kitchen. It was total chaos! Pots, pans, and silverware lay scattered across the terracotta floor. Cereal boxes had been thrown across countertops, and the tap in the kitchen sink gushed wildly, sending water spraying everywhere. It looked like a temper tantrum of sorts and I wasn't about to let it get the best of me. Of course, my shouting at them only validated the fact that I could see them. It appeared they'd achieved their goal of getting me to acknowledge their presence!

I sensed young children at the center of this activity and my heart went out to them, but at the same time I didn't want to feed the energy that seemed to have awakened inside my new home. I couldn't help but wonder if these were spirits of the young mothers and their children abandoned here so long ago? I didn't feel negativity here, rather loss and sadness. This is the only home they'd ever known. How long had they waited for someone to recognize them and set them free? Apparently, I had my work cut out for me. Hopefully I'd left one spirit at rest back at the church. And now a dozen or so spirits were trying to enlist my services here. I began to feel like the girl from the TV series "Ghost Whisperer!"

I wasn't quite sure what they wanted from me--yet. Cleaning up the chaos they'd created in the kitchen was uppermost in my mind at the moment. The last thing I wanted was for Michael to walk into this mess. Tired of explaining to him what was happening, I knew it didn't matter anyway. The delicate threads of our marriage were fraying at an accelerated rate. I didn't expect him home for a few more days, so I wasn't sure why I was in such a hurry to clean up the mess. Perhaps I didn't want to admit that once again the weird and bizarre was all around me.

Michael was in Paris for a few weeks, which left me alone to entertain unwelcome quests. We didn't vacation together anymore. I sensed he was detaching his emotions from the marriage by distancing himself even further. He was still civil to me, but the closeness we used to share was gone.

Exhausted by the time I'd finished with the kitchen, I needed a good hot shower to wash away the grime and the events of the day. I made a silent request as I lay back against the shower tiles and allowed the hot water to splash against my body: please release me from this nightmare or at least help me figure out who I am!

The water went from hot to extremely cold. I exited the shower and found myself surrounded in hot misty steam. I barely found my towel and, as I wrapped myself snugly in the soft Egyptian cotton, I noticed it. On the small overall mirror above the sink was written the message: *Find Victoria!* The words jumped out in 3-D like a flashing neon sign that slowly slipped along the surface of the mirror, its tiny droplets evaporating into a thin mist.

This isn't happening! Had Catherine followed me from the church? I remembered the mediums had warned me that might happen. It seemed the only explanation! Who else would have left this message? A voice echoed in my ears: "Remember the trinity...it takes three--you, Catherine, and me."

"Victoria?"

After all the excitement of the day, I decided to treat myself to not one glass of Michael's delicious Amoroni, but to the entire bottle, which I drank slowly savoring every last drop. Tired and confused, I wanted nothing more than to sink into oblivion, and the wine was doing the trick. Somewhere around two or three o'clock in the morning I awoke to the loud chiming of the clock in the foyer as it announced the arrival of the witching hour.

All seemed normal except the jackhammer doing its jig inside my head. I had difficulty focusing my eyes, and everything was blurry. I realized I'd fallen asleep downstairs on the living room sofa. It was dark--the only light was the dim glow of the streetlight outside in the courtyard, and all around me dark shadows danced and played within the cobwebs of my mind. That bottle of wine had really done a number on my psyche!

Catherine stood next to the large bay window, her body illuminated by the light from the courtyard. In her hands she held a tiny black book. I sensed she was trying to speak from the urgency in her face. Something prevented her from doing so, or maybe I wasn't ready to hear her message. Her deep emerald eyes locked with mine and the intense heat of her gaze sent my heart racing at an outrageous pace.

"They took her from me!" she cried. "Because of this book, they used me to take away my daughter!"

I couldn't respond--if I did I'd be admitting I'd gone over the edge, way over the edge! The irony of acknowledging what was happening—that I was living in an old mental hospital and battling the extremes of dark and light--felt as though I might as well sell my soul to the devil. Why else would these things present themselves to me? Michael did not experience them, except when he allowed himself to tune in to them. I didn't have to tune in--they came without my permission and without invitation!

What was it that I was doing to attract this? I'd tried so hard to work my way out of the drama and victim mentality, and to replace it with focusing on my life purpose and spiritual growth. I noticed that when I began to focus on my internal growth and let go of the illusions of the outside world,

Catherine began to approach me. On a very deep level this made a lot of sense, as I was beginning to shed the darker layers of my personality and allow the light of my true self to shine. But how was I supposed to help Catherine move on?

She was struggling and would not allow herself to go into the light until her daughter was by her side. Victoria had unlocked the secret of the tiny black book, and kept the demon inside the classroom believing he was in control! She'd become the master of the book and the secrets held within its pages. I wasn't sure Catherine was prepared to see this, or if she did see it but the dark energy that kept her prisoner would not set her free. She was trapped between the world of the living and the world of the dead, and apparently so was I until I figured out how to put all the pieces of the puzzle together. I knew one thing--by connecting with her, we were very powerful. I had to keep that line of communication between us open otherwise we'd both be lost forever.

The crash of shattering glass in my upstairs bedroom brought me back to the present. "What now?" I shouted, glancing toward Catherine. She was gone! In her place stood darkness, his face distraught and shallow--his eyes black as coal and devoid of any emotion. The temperature had dropped twenty degrees, and I saw my breath swirl about me in the living room.

"Stay away from me!" I commanded, my voice strong and steady, completely taking me by surprise. I wasn't afraid, but rather amused that this specter thought he could intimidate me. "Not this time!" I whispered. "You may have had me in the past, and I'm pretty sure that you did, but how does it feel to know you can't hurt me this time? You're a coward that preys on innocent women and children!"

It was extremely cold now in the living room. Without warning, he threw a crystal goblet toward me from the coffee table. I managed to duck as it whirled past me and crashed into the wall behind me. Pieces of glass flew through the air and dropped to the floor, glittering in the dim light like a thousand tiny diamonds.

I sensed the presence of two standing beside me by the warmth that circulated slowly around my body. Then I realized I was mistaken--there were dozens standing beside me! The deep arctic blast remained, but I found myself encircled within a golden ball of light and shielded from the assault this specter aimed at me. The children of this home--*my home*--materialized and sent their love and compassion toward my heart!

At first this strength overwhelmed me, sending me to my knees, but as it grew stronger and their little hands remained locked within the circle they'd formed around me, I thought back to the vision I'd had when trapped in the dark alcove of the maze. My hands burned—they felt as though I'd placed them on a bed of hot coals.

"Allow the heat to become part of you and the pain will go away," whispered a familiar voice.

"Victoria?"

No reply, only the intense heat pulsating through my body as I focused on the specter gliding towards me. I refused to look within the deep hollows of his black eyes, but focused on radiating this heat towards him.

"You're not taking me, Sebastian!" I screamed, releasing the intense heat from the palms of my hands and sending him hurtling through the living room.

The room temperature changed--the arctic freeze was gone, but my body shivered still from the adrenaline pumping through me. There was nothing—it was as though he'd never been here. The children disappeared also and I was left standing alone and exhausted, as though nothing unusual had taken place and the clock in the foyer chimed the hour.

Just another day in paradise, I thought as I collapsed to the floor--*just another day in paradise.* It struck me as odd that I was no longer afraid. The bastard who called himself Sebastian had his work cut out for him; I'd be damned if he was going to take me to the depths of hell!

"Been there done that," I said aloud to no one in particular, unless of course the invisibles were within ear shot. If not, it was just me sitting on the floor, alone, exhausted, and happy knowing I'd sent the bastard back to hell--hopefully. My mind raced with thoughts of defeating such a powerful enemy, this demon who tormented Catherine! What of her daughter Victoria? My life had become more complicated and less simple than what I'd hoped for when I'd married Michael.

"Your marriage will not last," I heard Monique say.

"Quiet!" I covered my ears in a desperate attempt to drown out the lilt of her soft French accent. But I knew she was right--spot on, as the British would say...

Chapter 26

I wanted to get away for awhile—I needed some time away from Michael, and the house too, which seemed always to be crowded with the overpowering presence of the invisibles. I decided to visit Glastonbury, a place steeped in witchcraft, magik, and lore--a place that might shed some light on the Coven of Nine. Rumor had it that Merlin the magician once lived and practiced his magic there.

I looked forward to the drive--it would give me the opportunity to see the countryside and allow me to focus on what I was doing behind the wheel rather than on when or where the next paranormal attack would take place. *Total freedom,* I thought, as I drove along the winding road and all thoughts of darkness faded away, temporarily at least...

I approached the outskirts of Glastonbury and the first thing I noticed was the Tor, looming high atop a very steep hill. I sensed its energy miles before I actually saw it. The air swirled with the thick perfume of magic--it felt as though the Tor commanded this energy in some way. Some believed this was a place where ancient fertility rights had been practiced, while others said it was named after the Archangel Michael, and that his presence could be felt at the top of the spiraling giant towering five hundred feet over the villages below. The closer I drove to the city center, the more intense this energy became.

As I passed this magnificent monolith, memories of a distant past flashed through my mind. I dismissed these as imagination, and drove on. The Tor now behind me, I continued on my quest toward the bed and breakfast I'd rented for the week. On my list of things to do was climbing the Tor in hopes of experiencing its magic.

I arranged to stay at an inn a few blocks from the ancient Glastonbury Abbey, a place I also wanted to visit. Said to be the oldest above-ground church in the world dating back to Neolithic times, it was difficult for me to wrap my head around a church that existed still from the Stone Age! I felt a deep desire to investigate the abbey before I settled at the inn. Mid-morning, I had the entire day to unpack my bags and register. My urge to get to this ancient church was strong, and I found myself almost running to get there.

Amazing architecture--delicate carvings and intricate designs—greeted me as I walked around the carved archways and stood against the tall pillars of this relic. I sensed the presence of thousands of souls pass through me, perhaps the very stone masons themselves who'd labored so hard and given of their own lives to establish such a magnificent work. The place was haunting and exhilarating, to say the least. My imagination roamed free and I imagined Arthur and Merlin and all the gang walking through these hallowed grounds, along with so many others before them.

Interestingly enough, the abbey seemed to line up directly with the Tor that towered over the city on the steep hill several miles away. I'd heard there were powerful lei lines here, and the electric energy surged just beneath the surface of my feet as I continued to walk through what was left of the ancient church. As I glanced up at the Tor, the black stone giant seemed to acknowledge my presence. *I'll get to you another day,* I thought.

I sensed a calm peacefulness within the stone surroundings of Glastonbury Abbey. Perhaps that's what drew me here--the search for a semblance of balance to my spirit, which had been drained so these past few years. Behind the church was a pond filled with lily pads in full bloom. Two white swans swam lazily by, acknowledging my presence with a single glance before drifting slowly through the maze of tangled lilies. Trees of various shapes and sizes surrounded the pond and small benches placed strategically throughout the grounds, where one could sit and reflect, allowed me to savor the beauty and peace offered here.

I felt connected and whole, and allowed the guardians of this enchanting place to speak to me as I opened my heart to the sacred energy here. I didn't want to leave and hoped this feeling would stay with me long after I did. *Ciao for now,* I thought as I took one long last look before exiting the abbey. I made my way along the narrow streets toward the Merry Widow's Inn where I planned to stay for the next few days.

The inn was a quaint thatched roof cottage surrounded by a medley of flowers and vines. White and purple lace wisteria clung tightly, wrapping themselves along the eaves and open porch furnished with a small wicker table and chairs. Two aged willows greeted me as I opened the wrought iron gate. Its loud squeak announced my arrival. A pentagram flower bed uniquely displayed amongst the wild flowers and vines sat next to a lovely bird bath carved in stone with the face of the Green Man, legendary throughout this country. The smell of the flowers heady perfume, mingled with dense moss and ivy, made my head spin.

As I walked along the narrow cobbled path leading to the entrance of the inn, the soft tinkling of wind chimes hanging in the willows startled me. I turned around to open the door and there she stood in front of me, gazing at me with golden grey eyes, almost wolf-like in appearance.

"Geez!" I cried, as I jumped back, dropped my luggage,

and sent it scattering everywhere. The peace I'd experienced in the abbey was momentarily replaced by the rapid pounding of my heart.

"Hello dear," she said. "Did I startle you?" She extended her tapered hand toward mine. "I'm Agnes, but everyone here calls me Aggie. And this little menace is Oliver," she added, pointing to a very fat black cat weaving in and out between her ankles. He glanced up at me with large yellow eyes, meowed once, than dismissed me and returned his attention to his mistress.

"Hello," I replied, my voice shaky after being caught off guard. "My name is--"

"Evie," she finished. "Yes, I know who you are." She patted her silver hair and placed thin wispy strays back into place within her neatly wound bun. Then she smoothed the apron she wore over the white linen dress fitted snugly to her voluptuous figure that left nothing to the imagination.

"How did you know my--"

"Name?" she asked. "That's quite obvious, don't you think?" she replied, as she eyed me up and down with her large penetrating grey eyes.

"Excuse me?" I asked.

"I'm a witch dear, a very old witch," she said. "And Ollie here, well, he was my husband once until I got bored of him and turned him into a cat. Much better relationship now, if you ask me," she said with a wink and a mischievous smile that lit up her exquisite aged face.

"You're teasing me," I said, as I felt the anxiety release its tight grip on my chest.

"Dear," she replied, "you look as though you're carrying the weight of the entire world on those pretty slender shoulders and, before entering the threshold of my cottage, you will remove that weight, it stays out here!" She wrapped her plump arm around my waist as she opened the door to invite me in.

"What's that smell?" I asked as I entered the tiny hallway.

"Lamb stew, fresh baked bread, and peach cobbler," she replied. "I hope you have an appetite, you're very thin," she said eyeing me up and down once again with those mischievous grey eyes. "But lovely," she continued. "I guarantee my cooking will put some meat on those bones."

"I'm starving," I replied, as she led me up the narrow flight of stairs to my room.

"Well, this is it," she said, taking my luggage and placing it carefully in the corner next to a small bay window overlooking the garden. "You're more than welcome to open the window and let in some fresh air." Without waiting for a reply, she cracked the window open a few inches, glanced back at me, and winked.

"It's perfect, thank you," I replied.

"The bath is just down the hall, you'll have it all to yourself. You're my only guest this week. Funny how fate has ways of making things happen," she said. "Call me if you need anything--I'll be downstairs in the kitchen." She closed the door behind her and I collapsed onto the tiny bed. A few minutes later I heard light scratching on the door.

"Who is it?" I asked.

Nothing but silence greeted me. I guess I'd drifted off to sleep. It was probably Oliver checking out the new house guest. It couldn't have been more than a few minutes though, as the sun was still high in the sky, and even though the window was open the room had become quite warm. I walked over to the bay window and peered out, allowing the sun to soak through my body. Its warmth felt wonderful. Down below in the garden Oliver was in the process of stalking a hedgehog that had rolled himself up into a tight little ball no larger than a child's fist. He pawed at it for several minutes before becoming bored and pouncing off to other adventures in the lovely garden.

I heard the scratching sound again, muffled and faint. It sounded like it was coming from inside the walls. I placed my ear to the wall to try to distinguish its origin. Nothing...it stopped as quickly as it had begun. I moved away, and the scratching began again, soft and muffled but persistent-- almost frantic--in its urgency. What was trying to get out of these walls?

I freshened up in the small bathroom and as I gazed at myself in the mirror thought I looked quite amazing. I brushed the sun-streaked hair I'd let grow past my shoulders over the summer. My eyes sparkled--the intensity of the green took me by surprise. They reminded me of Catherine's. There was a glow about me, and I liked it.

I hadn't felt this way for quite a long time. I was dressed in vintage clothing I'd purchased from a tiny boutique I found while driving here—a white lace cami and a deep rich purple silk skirt cinched tight against my waist that pushed up my ample cleavage. I'd crimped my hair and let it hang wild about my shoulders, and wore the tiny cross Monique had given me.

"Ah, don't you look lovely!" exclaimed Aggie. "You look as though you belong here."

I jumped, bumping my elbow against the tiny sink in the bath. "You really have to stop doing that!" I laughed.

"You'll steal the hearts of the warlocks around here dressed like that," she said smiling. There are some lovely women in this city, but move over ladies, there's a new witch in town!" She patted me lightly on the shoulder and pointed me in the direction of the hallway.

"Hungry?" she asked.

"Famished," I replied, as I followed her downstairs and into the kitchen. "Oh, Aggie, I think you have mice or rats. I heard scratching coming from the walls in my room."

"Aye," she replied. "They're attracted to the garden, and when it gets cold they sneak in. I don't know how they end up within the walls. Poor things, they usually get trapped and eventually die. Sit down, eat," she said pointing to the grand spread on the kitchen table.

I pulled out a wicker chair to seat myself and noticed the small pentagram etched neatly on the wooden floor. Our eyes locked and she covered it quickly with a threadbare rug, as if it wasn't there.

Chapter 27

Exhausted by the time I reached the top of the steep hill leading to the Tor, I looked out over the city and the surrounding landscape. The view was breathtaking! I leaned against the blackish stones of this impressive monolith to catch my breath and instantly felt a slight rippling vibration, almost as though it was breathing and alive. On the opposite side was a labyrinth weaving its way to the bottom of the steep hill. The wind whipped through my hair, sending cold shivers down my spine. I was one of five people up here today. I'd noticed the others as they navigated their way through the tangled labyrinth below.

A light rain began to fall, forcing me to take shelter inside the Tor. I hadn't expected the weather to change so quickly, and I pressed close against the stone walls to shield myself from the whipping wind and rain. Again the tingling vibration surged through my body. I relaxed and sat down on the ground to wait out the storm. I heard the others in the labyrinth as they exited below, their shrill screams and laughter drifted up and carried by the wind. I was alone up here now, savoring the magic and power that surrounded this place.

I closed my eyes for what seemed only moments. Had I fallen asleep up here, lulled by the soft vibration and safety of the Tor? It was pitch black, and I heard a deep humming from somewhere. What was making that droning noise? Thunder rumbled through the sky, and bursts of bright lightening fingered its way through the darkness, illuminating the labyrinth. I thought I saw movement. Who on earth would be venturing out during such a powerful storm? The humming grew louder. It sounded like a hive of angry bees. Another sharp blast of thunder and waves of lighting shattered the sky, providing me a glimpse of dark hooded figures weaving their way through the tangled maze below.

They seemed to be the source of the humming, their deep monotone voices blended with the rumbling thunder. From where I stood it sounded like a symphony carefully orchestrated by unknown forces. Who were these hooded creatures of the night? I needed to get down there for a better look! I felt as though I was a part of them and that I belonged in the labyrinth.

The closer I got to the maze, the louder the humming became until it completely took me over, pulling me in. I don't know how I knew I belonged here, but something primal tugged at my heart. I'd been here before and shared an intimacy with this group that now roamed the corridors of the tangled thickets. It seemed as though they were a part of nature itself as they moved and blended with the trees.

They formed a circle in the labyrinth that night under a black moonless sky void of stars. Lighting their way with torches, they began an enchanting ritual of song and dance. I stood outside a circle of ancient stones that marked their hallowed ground and excitedly watched the worship of druids. I listened to their leader read from a small black book, and grew even more excited.

He was its master and, as he read, the words drew me in closer until I found myself in the center of the circle beside him. The deep rich green of his eyes held me captive, and the low monotone of his voice lulled me into a trance. I felt as though I'd left my body and was watching myself move to the rhythm of his voice and the others who swayed slowly from side to side. Even the trees moved in rhythm with him.

I realized I'd seen that book he held before! He signaled me to place my hands upon it, and the intensity of the heat it ignited thrilled me and sparked immediate recognition. It was the Book of Souls! Somehow I was unable to escape it--but what was its significance in my life? I swayed to the hypnotic melody of his voice and something very primal and urgent responded within me. I *knew* this man. He was a druid priest I'd encountered many lifetimes ago. How was this possible unless I'd lived in Glastonbury? Why else would I have been drawn to come here?

He removed his dark robe and let it fall onto the damp mossy ground. As he pulled me close his deep penetrating gaze never left mine. His naked body gleamed against the flickering torchlight and awakened a restless raw passion inside of me. Something reckless and wild I hadn't realized existed until now stirred, yearning to break free. Intense desire coursed through my body like a fire igniting and unleashing long ago memories. I needed this man to sweep me up in his embrace--to feel his naked body press close against mine. I desired—no, hungered--for him to be deep inside me.

The members of the group drew closer and tenderly removed my clothing as though they'd read my mind, then withdrew back into the shadows and watched as this man lay me to the ground and tenderly but urgently entered me. The groans of his pleasure sent me writhing in wild ecstasy. His urgency grew until I thought I wouldn't be able to bear the intensity much longer. Flashbacks of this man's love and life reeled through my mind--I'd been with him before just like this, in this exact place! My God, who was he? Who was I?

"My seed now grows within your belly," he whispered. "She'll be very powerful and her gifts will awaken many, but not in our lifetime, my love." His passion spent, he removed himself from my weak and sated body. He pulled me close and tenderly wiped away the dirt and debris that clung to my naked body. He wrapped my clothes gently around me as his lips pressed tightly against mine. His taste was sweet and I savored it. Brief visions of our lives together sprinted through my mind. He'd been a powerful and honorable man. A devoted guardian of nature and all she stood for when the earth had been balanced and all lived as one.

"Remember me," he whispered. The others had left the labyrinth. Intent in our lovemaking, I hadn't realized when.

"The Book of Souls," he whispered, "is who you are, your lineage. To preserve order in this world from the chaos to come, never forget who you are," he said, pointing to his heart then mine. "You have, and always will, walk with the shadows because you are of the light. Just as Catherine is of the light, by remembering this moment you will begin to set her and yourself free."

"I don't understand," I said, as I reached out toward him. His embrace was strong and reassuring, and I didn't want to lose this feeling of safety, protection, and the all-consuming intenseness of an everlasting love.

"The book is who you are," he repeated. "We came here a long time ago in order to set balance for generations to come. But it's not the book itself that has the power. It's the one who possesses the book and the purity of their heart." He pressed my hand lightly against his chest and the rapid beat of his heart thumped against my open palm. Then he was gone.

"Wait!" I screamed. "You can't leave--I need answers!" My clothes were tangled about my ankles pinning me down. I was unable to move. "Please!" I sobbed, trying to cover my nakedness. Somewhere off in the distance I could hear a loud tapping--where was it coming from? The tapping was urgent.

"Evie dear, are you okay?" It was a woman's voice. Had she been in the labyrinth the entire time?

"Evie, I'm coming in!"

Coming in? I thought. "Who are you?" I asked. "Where is he?" I hadn't realized my eyes were closed the entire time. I forced them open, but they felt heavy and listless and it took all of my effort to steady my vision. Everything around me was spinning. The blurriness slowly went away and as I focused I saw a woman standing in a doorway. I realized I lay in the tiny bed at the inn, tangled between moist sheets, my hair and body drenched, my heart pounding wildly. I reached quickly for the sheets, pulled them over me, and began to wipe the tears from my face.

"That must have been one hell of a dream, dear," said Aggie.

Chapter 28

We sat huddled at the kitchen table drinking Aggies's special tea as I relived the events that took place within the labyrinth at the Tor. A part of me still felt as though I was up there, lost in the maze with the druid priest. Just the thought of him sent shivers up my spine.

"This was much more than a dream," I said. "Dreams do not feel that real!"

"Aye, that's the magic of the Tor," said Aggie as she sipped her tea. "It's a magical place full of mysterious secrets. Many people leave this place transformed. I experienced it myself and knew immediately I was meant to stay."

"What are you saying?"

"There are vortexes up on the Tor that can literally take you back in time. It sounds as though, while up there, you passed through one of the thin membranes within the veil and experienced a life you've lived before. Of course it didn't happen at that actual moment in time--you must have brought it through your dreams. The labyrinth was the catalyst that set the stage for you to tap into that past life you had with the druid priest."

"It happened up there, Aggie!" I protested. "Since the moment I landed in England strange things have been happening to me! I thought if I got away and came here I'd be able to figure it all out!"

"Now, now, dear," said Aggie as she poured me another cup of tea. "I know just the thing to calm you down." She reached into a small cupboard and pulled out two small crystal decanters. "Apricot or peach?" she asked with a wink.

"Oh, Aggie, I really don't want any. The tea is fine."

"I'll not take no for an answer," she replied, placing the bottles on the kitchen table. "Pick one, my favorite's the apricot. It'll warm the cockles of your heart and other things," she teased. "But by the looks of you and that glow you have about you, I'd guess the other things have already been taken care of!"

"Aggie!" I said, as I felt the heat of a blush rush to my face. "Okay, apricot!" I took a swig of the brandy she poured into a tiny shot glass. "Wow, that's strong!" I could just imagine the face I was pulling about now.

"I take it you like it," she laughed. "I make it myself, my own special witch's brew." She offered me another swig.

"Sure, why not? I'm not driving!" The golden liquid began to work its magic, and as I relaxed slowly and succumbed to its warmth, I began to tell her all that had happened since my arrival in England. I sensed she would understand and didn't feel judged, I just let it flow out of me naturally—my marriage to Michael, the strange experiences at the church upon my arrival and afterward, my Reiki healing practice, everything! She listened quietly, pausing only now and then to pour us each another cup of tea.

"What happens now, Aggie?" I asked, suddenly tired. "Where do I go from here?"

"Listen to your heart--it led you here, didn't it? No one can give you the answers you seek but yourself, lass." She returned the decanters to the safety of the cupboard. "You're welcome to join me at my Wicca's circle tonight if you'd like, it might cheer you up."

"What happens at a Wicca's circle?" I asked.

"It's where a bunch of old witches get together and

shoot the breeze," she laughed.

"Come on, be serious! I've been through hell and back, Aggie! Will this help me or not?"

"Oh sweetie, I'm sorry, it's just that you need to lighten up and not take things so seriously. You've been through a lot, more than most, I'll give you that, but maybe you should be grateful for that."

"Grateful?" I sputtered. "What do you know about grateful?" Who was she to tell me how to feel or act? I could feel the red hot anger boiling up to the surface--it took all I had to hold it in.

"You chose my inn out of all the other places you could have stayed--do you think that was coincidence?" Aggie shot back. "You listen to me, lass. The reason you attract what you attract is because you're tired of the merry go round and you're ready to get off! Now, I don't know you from a hill of beans. Until you arrived the other day, you were a complete stranger! But let me tell you something--I like you Evie! You have a special gift, and all you've done since you got here was try to hide it. You don't have to do that this lifetime, dear. What you have you need to share with the world! Open their eyes and light their way!"

I turned away. I wanted to run--get away from here as fast and as far as possible. But wasn't that something I'd done all my life? What would it accomplish? What she said was true, and it infuriated me that someone I hardly knew could read me so well. I had tried to hide the real me from everyone my entire life by pretending I was somebody else to appease others. She was right, I wanted off the damn merry go round! Weary of the fight, I no longer wanted to be something and someone that somebody else wanted me to be!

Why they tried to shut me down from expressing myself had always puzzled me, but in order to protect myself I allowed others to dominate and control me through the many stages of my life; escaping at times to live a solitary existence until I became bored and found myself climbing back on the merry go round because others expected that of me.

"Okay Aggie," I said. "You're right--I'm tired of the damned merry go round! I've struggled with it all my life until recently. I've discovered so many things about myself, yet strangers have been the ones who have had to point them out to really make me begin to see."

I felt a sense of peace wash over me as I breathed in long soothing breaths and allowed the words I spoke to really sink in. I needed to release years of old beliefs and emotions— and the apricot brandy's magic was a good start!

"You have to ask yourself, what motivates you, lass?" Aggie advised, giving me a warm gentle squeeze. "You're an amazing woman, can't you see that? Stop and think about all the times others have been assisted by your words and the way you've communicated to them. Why is it you've been able to do that for others but not for yourself?" she asked.

"I'm not really sure, Aggie. But I know this much--it goes back to my childhood days." I sighed. "I've always allowed men to intimidate me and walk over me. Sometimes they did it in such subtle unassuming ways that I justified it as love. But it was never unconditional. When I reflect on this, my heart hurts because it's true. Perhaps that's why Catherine contacted me--she was also abused by others. I've tried so hard to dismiss the connection between the two of us from the very beginning by dragging my feet in denial, knowing all along my spirit needed her to push me in order to discover the truth about who I really am."

"Pretty powerful stuff, dear," replied Aggie. "It'd make for some very interesting reading if you ever decide to write a book," she winked. "Join me at the circle tonight. It'll do you good, I promise. I need to tend to my garden now," she said brushing a stray lock of silver hair from her face.

"Come on Ollie, make yourself useful and earn your keep--there are plenty of mice that need the life scared out of them!" I watched as she walked down the narrow hallway with Ollie leading the way, occasionally stopping to glance back at his mistress before bounding out the door into the warm sunshine.

Chapter 29

I wasn't sure what to expect when I decided to join Aggie at the Wicca's circle that evening. Wild thoughts raced through my head--perhaps I'd see cloaked creatures prancing around an open fire pit, daggers in hand, as they slaughtered an innocent virgin! *God, I really need to get a life!* I admonished myself.

When we arrived, I was surprised to see that everyone there appeared normal, at least within the boundaries of the woods under the light of a full moon. They formed a circle and held hands, chanting softly and melodically. Their beautiful voices encouraged me, and immediately I felt a strong desire to join my voice with theirs. Again I felt as though I belonged here, and overwhelming emotion washed over me. It was as though this group of women became one with nature, blending into its very fabric.

I sensed the strength of the bond of sisterhood within the circle, and welcomed it as they invited me to participate in their sacred dance performance and ritual by pulling me in and clasping my hands. I felt very much alive as I weaved in and out among the others, their graceful elegance softly seductive and liberating. I felt safe and able to lose myself within this group of women, which allowed me to dive deeper into the rhythm of this intoxicating dance. As I did so, I saw her standing just outside the circle.

Barefoot and wearing the same tattered wisp of a dress, her emerald eyes locked instantly with mine. This had to be a hallucination! Her long blonde hair cascaded wildly around her slender shoulders, as I tried to convince myself I was seeing things! She stood watching us prance about in the circle, a bewildered look upon her beautiful delicate face.

My God, how was it possible for her to find me here? I wondered. As my mind raced I felt a wave of emotion wash over me, and I beckoned her to join us in the circle. She approached, and I discovered she hadn't come alone. The sick smell of death and decay hit me like a ton of bricks, forcing me to drop hands and break the circle.

"*No*--don't break the circle!" she screamed. I looked around quickly to see if the others were aware of what was happening. Aggies's golden grey eyes met mine, and I felt as if she had read my mind.

"I see her!" Aggie yelled, and signaled for everyone to grasp hands and hold tight. "Stand strong!" she commanded, her words barely audible above a wind that seemed to appear from nowhere, as the smell of death and decay slithered its way toward Catherine and me.

"Oh my God, he's strong!" one of the women screamed as they all huddled together tightly in the circle. I sensed the smallest vibration of fear ripple through me. *Please don't leave,* I implored them silently. They didn't budge; it was clear their sense of loyalty held the circle strong. The wind intensified its howling and threatened to pull us apart.

Sebastian's angry growls and screams boomed out in the darkness. I felt the familiar pain of the jackhammer as it rattled through my head.

"Not now!" I screamed, placing my hands tightly against my head. Suddenly, blackness surrounded me as I drifted away slowly, carried once again down the rabbit hole. I sensed I was not alone...

She lay in a pool of her own blood. The smell of rusty

copper, thick and sweet, lingered in the air around her. Tears streamed down her beautiful face as she reached out her delicate hand, her voice barely a whisper.

"Give me back my child!" she cried weakly. Fragile and very weak, she needed someone to help her before she bled to death. I realized I was standing in her chamber--the one she'd been held prisoner in for so many months. I could hear angry voices in the background behind me. *Can they see me? Can she see me?* She seemed to look right through me as she reached out, begging for her child.

"Catherine, what have they done to you?" I cried, trying to push my way toward her. Something held me back. I couldn't move.

"She's served her purpose!" boomed a loud baritone voice. "Get rid of her body. Better yet," screamed the voice, "put her out of her misery!"

That voice! I knew it well! I could barely contain my anger and fear.

"Sebastian!" I whispered tersely. I looked about the room unable to focus my eyes--everything was foggy except Catherine, who lay weak and near death on the bed before me. I felt so helpless! Brought back in time to be a witness and nothing more? It killed me to see her this way!

My vision cleared, and I saw him standing in the corner, a newborn clutched tightly in his grasp. He withdrew a small dagger from beneath his dark cloak.

"Oh my God!" I screamed. "Don't you dare harm that baby, you evil bastard!" My words drifted silently through the air. I knew it was useless--they could neither see me nor hear me. I watched helplessly as he threw the dagger--it seemed to twist and spin in slow motion through the stagnant air--to one of his minions standing quietly in the shadows.

I stood mesmerized, as a large cloaked figure suddenly

intercepted it and sent it spiraling out of control. It landed on the wooden floor with a loud thud.

"You overstep your bounds, Sebastian!" thundered an unfamiliar voice.

Who in the hell is that? I wondered. I squinted to get a better view. He towered over Sebastian and was cloaked from head to toe. I couldn't make out his face.

"Give me the child!" the voice commanded. "Do not make me ask twice!"

Who was this? And why was I unable to move? I needed to see who belonged to the disembodied voice, but felt surrounded by an invisible protective shield preventing me from participating in the events. Whoever it was commanded respect and seemed to hold more authority than Sebastian. Clearly this was a tug of war over the baby.

"The child belongs to me now!" Sebastian retorted.

"Remember your place!" the voice responded sternly. "I promised you the baby--I kept my end of the bargain!"

"Don't pretend remorse!" shouted Sebastian. "It's a little bit late for that now, don't you think? You wanted this just as much as I! You didn't think twice when you found out the secrets held within the pages of that book!"

"Do not tell me how I feel!" the cloaked man barked at him. "The book was in my care long before you crawled out from beneath your rock and slithered your way into our lives! Be very careful of what you speak next or I'll send you straight back to hell!"

"Forgive me," replied Sebastian, a bit more timidly now. "I misspoke. But no power--not even yours!--can undo that."

"Give me the child!" His voice shook the very walls.

"Very well!" Sebastian acquiesced.

I wasn't sure how much longer Catherine could hold

on. I sensed she'd given up already, but the strong will to hold her baby wouldn't allow her to slip away completely. Not yet.

My vision cleared and I watched in silence as the tall cloaked man in black leaned over Catherine and gently placed the child against her breasts. The baby wriggled and cooed, reaching out its tiny hands toward her pale tear-stained face.

"Promise me one thing," she whispered as she gazed upon the tiny bundle, before turning her attention to the figure standing next to her bed.

"What is it, child?"

I watched her try to raise herself up to speak, so pale and weak it seemed the angel of death must be hovering frightfully near and allowing her one last short reprieve before siphoning the life from her weakened body.

She gazed up at the cloaked figure that stood beside her. "Promise me that you'll call her Victoria, father..."

The cloaked figure nodded his head before he replied. "She'll be well protected and provided for. Forgive me, Catherine."

The shallow swelling of her chest stopped and she stared off into space. Tiny tears began to pool against her cheeks before sliding onto the bloody sheets. She was gone; the tiny infant slept soundly within her lifeless embrace.

Chapter 30

I awoke to find myself surrounded by twelve women staring at me with concern. At first I thought I'd died and wasn't sure if I had managed to make it to heaven. Weak, drained, and unable to move, my lips felt parched and dry and my entire body ached.

"Am I dead?" I asked, looking up at the beautiful faces peering back at me. "Are you angels?"

"Oh, my goodness, no!" one of the angels replied.

"We thought you were a goner for sure!" chimed in another, as she stared down at me with piercing golden gray eyes. "You've been in and out with fever for several days now." I recognized Aggie's voice—as she spoke to me, the dense fog in my head began to clear.

"What?" I asked, struggling to raise myself from the tiny bed. It was no use--I could barely lift my head above the pillows and fell back, exhausted.

"Rest," said Aggie. "You're out of the woods now... Margaret, go fetch a cup of my special tea," she directed a raven-haired sprite seemingly unable to take her eyes from me. "Margaret!" Aggie repeated, loudly enough to wake the dead. "She'll still be here when you get back!"

"Sorry," Margaret replied as she jumped up to carry out Aggie's order. I heard her dainty footsteps on the stairs as she rushed down to the kitchen below.

"Wow, you sure know how to bring excitement to a party!" laughed Aggie, patting my hand and wiping damp strands of hair from my forehead.

"What do you mean?" I asked. "What party?"

"You don't remember the Wicca's circle and everything that happened that night, do you?" she asked.

"No..." I hesitated, trying to remember. "I'm not sure, everything's so fuzzy."

"Don't trouble yourself, lass," said Aggie as she handed me the tea Margaret had fetched from the kitchen. "When the time's right, it'll all come rushing in and we'll be here to help you. It's important you remember that night, Evie, but for right now let's focus on getting you back on your feet--okay, everyone out!" she then demanded. "Let Evie rest--the worst is over, thank God and all who watched over us that wicked night!"

"We're so glad you've come back to us," the women said almost in unison as they slowly exited the room looking back at me sympathetically.

"I'll be back to check on you in a bit," Aggie reassured me. "Rest now, lass, you're safe." She took the empty cup from my hands and closed the door softly behind her. A few seconds later, she peeked back in. "I forgot to mention Ollie's by your feet--he hasn't left your side since we brought you back." She winked and disappeared. I managed to sit up long enough to see the fat black cat curled up in a ball at the foot of my bed.

"Well," I said. "Look at you, my protector!" Exhausted, I fell back into a dreamless sleep. I'm not sure how long I was asleep, but the smell of fried bacon drifted up to my room, tempting me from the comfort of my bed. A bit shaky, I placed my feet on the cold wooden floor and stood still for a moment to allow the spinning of the room to stop and my eyes to focus. Then I made my way slowly down the stairs and into the kitchen.

"Good morning, lass, I hope I didn't wake you!" Aggie

cried cheerfully as she slid bacon from a hot griddle delicately onto a white china plate.

"Good morning, Aggie, no you didn't wake me, but your cooking did," I smiled as I reached for a slice of bacon. I savored the salty morsel. "I think I remember what happened now, though I haven't pieced it all together yet. I've been getting flashes but they fade away quickly before I can really grasp them and put them together. I feel like I'm going crazy."

"Shush, now, lass," Maggie responded. "If you're going crazy, then we all are."

"What do you mean?"

"We saw what you saw," she replied, now animated at the memory. "I would never have believed it if I hadn't witnessed it for myself! Somehow you dragged us all with you to the seventeenth century! My head still hurts trying to figure out how you managed it!"

"What are you talking about?" I asked.

"You broke the circle screaming about the pounding in your head," Aggie explained. "The minute the circle was broken, whatever evil was being held back walked in, and you and everyone in that circle were transported back in time. I wish I could say it was a thrill ride, but that would be an understatement. It literally blew my socks off!" she said, shaking her head.

It was coming back to me now. "I felt her pain, Aggie--how could anyone be so cruel? What was so important about the child that Catherine's own father would betray her like that? He let her die! What did she do to deserve such a fate?"

"We're all capable of evil, lass," she sighed. "He allowed the secrets of that book to completely consume him. His obsession with its promises--which were really his own misguided fantasies--led him to the betrayal and ultimate death of his daughter."

"What's so important about that damn book?"

"The Book of Souls does not judge--it allows free will to anyone who tries to possess it," Aggie explained. "It is the person herself who touches it that is evil or pure, and it responds to their energy. It thrives on that person's weaknesses or strengths, and gives them what it sees in their hearts. Catherine's father lost his humanity when Isabella died. Sebastian lost his when Raphaela took her life after the untimely death of her son. These two men shared the same fantasy--they desired immortality and lost themselves in the pursuit of unnatural practices in order to obtain their desire!"

"What about the baby--Victoria?" I asked.

"It appears this child of Catherine's could possibly open a vortex, which would allow the Coven of Nine to move between the many dimensions of time without the knowledge of others," Aggie replied. "This child would be that powerful...if I'm correct—and I think I am--Sebastian intended to make this child his for the purpose of conceiving a child of his own when the time was right, therefore making the blood line pure. What purpose this would serve, I'm not quite sure; however, after you dragged me back several centuries, I've begun to believe anything is possible!"

"So, you're saying that, although David didn't inherit the same dark attributes of his uncle, he did carry the blood of the Coven of Nine within him--and when Catherine became pregnant this sealed the fate of her unborn child?"

"Yes! Seems the instant she conceived the seed within her belly, this new life was empowered by the blood of the coven as well as the gifts she'd inherited from her grandmother Isabella!" Aggie said excitedly. "This powerful combination was what Sebastian needed in order to obtain the promise of eternal life, the fabled gift of the philosophers' stone! The blood of their love and the birth of this child would ignite the beginning of a time for darkness to harness the light, if left in the hands of this powerful and very dangerous man..."

I looked at her quizzically. "Yes, but what does that have to do with me?"

"This is where it gets weird..." Aggie said hesitantly. "I've had several discussions with the rest of the coven, and we all came to the same conclusion." She stared at me for what seemed like an eternity.

"Well?" I asked. "You're making me uncomfortable! What did you all figure out?"

"You told me you thought the reason Catherine connected with you is because you knew each other from a past lifetime--I agree with you, but not for the reason you think."

"I *was* Catherine in a past life--everyone I've been contacted by has called me Catherine!" I replied. "But that's stating the obvious, don't you think?"

"Ah, but you *weren't* Catherine," she said softly. "And before you get your knickers in a bunch, I want to ask you a question and I want you to be completely honest with me--*and with yourself!*"

I could feel the hot flash of anger rise to the surface. Who did she think she was--telling me I wasn't Catherine? From the very beginning Catherine had sought me out, haunted me! I'd endured night after night of torment and frustration trying to help this ghost put her past to rest! I defended my life against Sebastian who, for whatever reason, believed I betrayed him, *and* I lost the love and respect of my husband! I could barely contain the volcano threatening to blow within! Yet somehow I did, and the anger dissipated slowly.

"Ask me anything--at this point my life is an open book," I sighed.

"Have you ever been betrayed by someone you loved

with all your heart?"

"What kind of question is that?" I shot back. "Have *you?*"

"We're not talking about me right now--the focus is on you! Who betrayed you in the past?" she continued, relentless.

I sat there glaring at her. I felt the volcano inside begin to grow until I could no longer contain it.

"My father betrayed me in the past!" I screamed. *"There,* are you satisfied?" Hot angry tears burst forth and rushed down my face. I couldn't stop the flow. By the time I finished I was exhausted, relieved, and felt like a fool.

"Are you happy now?" I asked, as I wiped the remaining tears from my face.

She didn't reply for some time, and sat in silence allowing me to let the words I'd spoken really sink in. Slowly, I began to speak:

"I adored my father and looked up to him until I turned twelve, when I started to realize he couldn't be trusted. He'd been seeing other women on the side, and I saw how much this broke my mother's heart--to the point where she tried to commit suicide." I didn't look at Aggie; instead I fixed my gaze on the pattern of leaves that adorned the sugar bowl on her table.

"When she took the pills something deep inside of me became very, very afraid. I didn't know how to handle it. I started making excuses not to attend school because I was afraid she'd do it again." Suddenly I remembered how I'd felt the need to protect her, how anxiety and fear dogged me daily whenever I was away at school or out with my friends.

"Luckily, she never attempted suicide again," I continued. "Instead, she just up and left in the middle of the night--no note, no goodbyes, nothing!" I looked up at Aggie briefly. Her expression was one of kindness and sympathy.

206

"I was devastated beyond anything words could express--I believed she no longer loved me!" Tears sprang to my eyes again. "Hurt and betrayed after she left us in the night, a part of me curled up and died that day--it felt like my passion for life and what I stood for locked itself away inside my heart in a tiny box. She'd been my anchor and my light, and it seemed as though when she walked out, she cast me out of her heart as well! To this day, I don't know why she up and left in the night."

Aggie reached for my hand and covered it with hers. The warmth and pressure of it soothed me as I continued:

"I never saw my mother angry, but I witnessed her when she was down or sad. She believed in psychics and loved the tarot and astrology, but when it came to my gifts she seemed to shy away--I'm not sure if it was out of fear, or if my father's influence prevented her from promoting that part of who I am. I know she had some kind of fear when it came to my father. She would always want me to grab the mail before he arrived home from work. She seemed very insistent. Didn't want him to see the bills, maybe? I don't know.

"We did not lack for money--he made a very good living. We went camping, hiking, boating, water skiing, and sledding every year. My father was big on the outdoors and sports and he excelled in everything. Yet, and I don't understand why, he intimidated me for as long as I can remember. My girlfriends thought he was drop dead gorgeous, and that he looked like Dean Martin to the 'T.'

"When mom was around I felt safe. There was security, organization, peace, and--even though she never verbalized it--love. When she left, it broke my heart. My sense of peace and security, and the calmness that surrounded her were gone. She left all the furniture, did not take one thing, just her clothes and she was gone. My father never sat us down to explain, it was as though she'd never existed!" Aggie squeezed my hand.

"Anyway, after mom left suddenly all the household responsibilities were dumped on me. My father worked long hours and I was automatically put in charge of my younger sister Nickie, and brother, Seth. Laundry, cleaning--you name it--became my jobs overnight. Dad gave us money and most of the time we'd go to the closest hamburger joint for our meals. When he was home he cooked--he was an awesome cook when he had the time...

"I continued with my piano lessons and recitals, and lived in that house though I hated being alone in it. I felt like I was always being watched and I knew something else lived there too—it was almost like that house pushed my mom out! My brother and sister didn't pick up on it, and dad was totally oblivious.

"We spent a lot of time on our own, and my routine was housework, school, and studies. After school I rode my bike two miles to my grandparent's farm where I kept my horses. Mom had understood my love for horses and was the one who went out and purchased my first beautiful palomino, Chiquita. She encouraged me to barrel race and ride whenever I had the chance. Horses and nature were just a part of who I was and she seemed to respect that. After she left, I escaped as often as I could to exercise the horses. It's where I found solace and peace--with my four-legged beauties." I smiled at the memory.

"My father started to become furious at my always tending to them--I didn't get it, couldn't understand his frustration with me, or why he had such a problem with me being at my grandparent's and with the horses! One day I came home from riding--he was already home from work and sitting in the kitchen—and the minute I walked in the door I knew something wasn't right.

"He shouted at me 'you smell disgusting--like the horse

stable! Not only that—you look like those damn horses you're always tending to—horse face and all! Get the hell upstairs and take a bath so I don't have to smell you or look at you anymore!' Then, as if his words hadn't been hurtful enough, he slapped me across the face!

"I stood there stunned, while he turned his back on me dismissively. I didn't know why he said those things, but his cruel words stuck with me." I began to sob, but caught myself and continued through my tears. "It took years before I liked the way I looked and dressed, and stopped worrying about what others thought of me! Previously he'd told me I wasn't good enough, called me a disappointment, said I wasn't perfect, and was too sensitive for my own good!"

I took a deep breath. "The only way I knew to protect myself at the time was to always obey--the word 'no' never entered my vocabulary! Shortly after that incident, he insisted I take a bath every night the minute he arrived home from work. This made no sense to me until I discovered a peephole in our attic, conveniently located over the bathroom fan. Anyone--even my father--could spy on someone in that room!

"One night I pretended to take a bath. I prepared the bath water but didn't undress. Instead, I placed my ear next to the bathroom door and heard my father climb the stairs leading to the attic. I waited in the bathroom until I heard him come back down. After he closed the door I could hear his heavy breathing as he stood in the hallway."

I glanced at Aggie. "How could my father do such a thing? I wanted to tell others what he'd done, but I felt ashamed and honestly didn't think anyone would believe me! After all, he was the dad--what dad does that?"

Aggie reached out, gathered me in her arms, and hugged me tightly. I cried softly and relaxed into her embrace. We remained like that for a few moments until I gathered my composure and sat up again facing her.

"My father knew I discovered his secret and never approached me again. When my sister took a bath I made sure he was downstairs and I guarded the bathroom like a hawk. I never discussed with her the times my dad peeked on me while I was in the bath.

"After that I found it hard to trust others. I tried, but figured if someone I loved and admired as much as my father could deceive me and hurt me in such a way, then others could too--it took me years to admit that the man I looked up to, trusted, admired, and who was supposed to protect me and keep me safe, had betrayed me!"

Aggie leaned forward. "Have you figured out who you are yet?" she asked gently. The meaning behind her question suddenly became clear, and I stared at her in wide-eyed disbelief.

"There is absolutely no way I could have been *her!*" I cried. *"She's* the one that rescued me from the demon in the maze! *She* led me to the alcove! *She* showed me the true power of the little black book! You're crazy if you think I'm *her!*" I couldn't even say her name! Words escaped me--that line of thinking was completely crazy!

"Everyone called you Catherine because that's what you wanted to hear," Aggie persisted softly. "It was easier than hearing the truth, so you blocked it out, and when Catherine contacted you I believe you already knew who you were--you blocked the memory to avoid reliving the pain. You were bound and determined to help Catherine, but she was also bound and determined to get you to face the truth. Why do you think Sebastian hates you?"

"Enough!" I screamed.

"Hear me out, lass!" Aggie continued. "You must have been very young when you figured out who he was and what he'd done to your mother. That's why you could not see his face when you had your vision of Victoria in the classroom. You blocked the memory in order to protect yourself from the demon that chased you through the maze."

"Stop it," I screamed. *"Get out!"*

"I'm sorry, Evie, but you needed to hear the truth!" Aggie rose from her chair and walked out of the tiny kitchen. I waited until her footsteps faded and I heard the front door close.

"Damn you!" I screamed. "Damn you to hell, Catherine! *Why?"*

Chapter 31

I calmed down slowly as I sat in Aggie's homey kitchen and focused the betrayal of my father yet again. I reviewed also the events of many relationships that had ended in betrayal and confusion. A pattern began to emerge that I hadn't wanted to see, but that now brought clarity to why something very deep within my psyche had feared my father and why I'd left him at such an early age...

The truth is, I thought, *the day I discovered my father spying on me while bathing was the day I walked out of a secure life and into the unknown, unstable life of struggle and insecurity--not knowing whether I'd have food to eat, or a roof over my head. It was then I vowed never to let another soul hurt me, and promised myself I'd find a job, finish school, and make it on my own!*

I did just that, but along the way I made lots of mistakes, hooked up with the wrong kind of guys--married too young and a mother before I was really ready, I gave up my entire life trying to find something or somebody that wouldn't hurt or betray me. To say I was attracted to the wrong kind of guy would be an understatement! I picked bad boys and tough guys because I didn't feel deserving of anything else. My father's words--that I was ugly, stupid, and had the face of a horse--always haunted me...

My first marriage, which lasted ten years, came to mind. Though he cheated on me, it ended amicably. Now I saw how I internalized the deep betrayal I felt as my fault for not being good enough, attractive enough. A fairly gifted artist, I used to draw these amazing pictures for my daughter's rooms, but I gave this up when their father made fun of them and ripped them from the walls. *The blessing in all of this is my two beautiful daughters, who I raised by myself,* I thought.

As I recalled the types of men I'd allowed into my life, I came to the sudden realization that it wasn't as simple as my father's betrayal of my trust--they'd all been replacements for my father! I picked men who were broken to prove to my father I could fix them--that I could do things right and be perceived as good enough! What a screwed up way to think! These relationships usually ended when I finally realized I couldn't stay around and be abused or treated badly...

Through the years, I worked so hard to accomplish what I had and to dig myself out from under the hold of my father. I bought my own home, raised my daughters alone, earned my own income--a good income--and worked my way up the corporate ladder, all before I even met Michael! I earned the respect and admiration of my co-workers and gained many friends, all on my own merits. These are things I vowed never to let my father take away. And yet, always, his unkind words and actions seeped through whenever I entered into a relationship.

If what Aggie said was true, how had I not seen it from the very beginning? Confused and angry--to think I'd been denied my true identity by hiding behind another's—it finally all began to make perfect sense. I remembered the incident in the shower when I discovered the message written on the mirror: "Find Victoria."

Catherine tried to get me to see who I really was and how we were connected—only she couldn't come right out and tell me--she needed me to discover it for myself! I could see why Sebastian hated me--if it was true then I managed to

213

outsmart him on so many levels, and it pissed him off that I returned once and for all to set the record straight...if—I hesitated to even think it—if I am to accept that I was Catherine's daughter, it would make perfect sense that I botched so many relationships in this current lifetime!

So lost in thought I hadn't noticed Oliver, who'd curled himself up into a tight ball on my lap, and who's deep throaty purr brought me back to the present.

"Ollie, you little minx, I forgot you were here," I laughed as I stroked his head. "Tell me something Ollie, just between you and me; she didn't change you into a cat *really*, did she?" He looked up at me with his golden yellow eyes and I swear he winked. "Never mind," I said. "Pretend I didn't ask!" He hopped from my lap and stretched his plump furry body lazily from side to side before disappearing from the room.

Sebastian has his hands full this time around! I thought, as I exited the comfort and warmth of the kitchen. I owed Aggie an apology. She could see things I wasn't able to see and she definitely struck a chord, otherwise I wouldn't have lashed out at her like that. *Damn my stubborn pride!* I thought, as I made my way outside to find her.

She was sitting in the cool shade of the willows sipping tea. I wasn't sure how to approach her or what to say. In the little time I'd known her, I considered her a friend. What if I'd ruined that?

"Aggie, I'm so sorry! I don't know what came over me in there!" I felt a fool standing there, as though my words were not enough. She'd taken me in, watched over me, listened to my story with genuine concern, and I'd lashed out at her with little provocation on her part.

"Sit down, lass," She said reaching out to me with her long tapered hands.

I welcomed their warmth and sat next to her in silence

as she sipped her tea. I'm not sure how long we sat there, the silence broken finally only by the tingling of the chimes hanging from the old willow. Its long slender branches swayed gently from side to side teased by a light breeze.

"I have to go back home tomorrow and I don't know what I'll find there," I sighed.

"Whatever you find will be the right thing," she replied. She looked at me with her penetrating golden grey eyes and smiled.

"Why now--after all these years?" I asked.

She didn't reply for some time, just sipped her tea quietly, pausing occasionally to look at me before losing herself in thought once more. Not a very patient woman, I understood the situation called for patience. She'd speak when she was ready. I stared into space, waiting for that moment to arrive. It wasn't long before she cleared her throat, a signal she was ready to share something very private and personal with me.

"Okay, lass, I've punished you enough," she winked, then smiled.

"Really, do you enjoy teasing me Aggie?"

"I have to admit, it's fun," she laughed. "You're not a very patient woman, lass. It was fun to watch you squirm."

"You're a wicked woman, you know that, right?" I laughed. "Please share with me whatever you have to say. I promise I'll behave."

She sat back, sipped the last dregs of her tea, and placed the empty glass next to her on the damp grass. As she turned to stare at me with her unusually captivating eyes, she reminded me of a she-wolf in human form. Wise and elegant, her hypnotic eyes drew me in as she began to speak softly.

"I came here from Scotland, planning only a short visit, and now--forty years later--I call this my home," she began. "It's as if destiny called me here for a purpose. I didn't plan it

215

that way. I was perfectly happy the way my life was--at least that's what I thought at the time, until I came here and discovered the magic that surrounds this blessed place.

"My young husband passed of cancer and left me a widow at thirty-five. I was devastated and beyond angry if there is such a thing. We'd planned on having a large family-- that wasn't meant to be. I'd lost our one and only, stillborn. He never took a breath, just came out cold and lifeless. I didn't blame this on God, I figured he had a reason for taking away my child--but when my husband died I was furious and turned my back on everything! My heart guided me here and I've never looked back."

"I'm so sorry, Aggie."

"I'm not telling you this for sympathy," she said. "I'm sharing because we all have our stories, and baggage we carry with us that we use to define who we are. But it's not who we really are, Evie. Consider this a blessing what's happening to you. Most people go to their grave never figuring it out. You decided on some level to accept the challenge--be grateful that you did, lass."

I watched as she wiped the tears from her face. It must have been hard for her to relive that part of her past, and I felt she'd shared this story with only a select few. She was a powerful witch--I'd felt her energy and the magic that surrounded her the first day we met, and I began now to understand the real role she played in my life.

"Who are you really?" I asked.

"Your friend," she replied, "as long as you need me."

"I believe you're more than that," I pressed her. "I believe I knew you many lifetimes ago, and that's why I'm here. If Catherine was my mother, then Isabella would have been my grandmother--that would place you at about her age!" The words sounded foreign as I spoke them, yet my heart

216

resonated deeply with what I was saying.

"Poppycock!" she said winking at me. "Who'd believe such a fantastical story?"

"Are you--"

"Teasing you, lass?" she said, finishing my sentence. "I expected you to show up one day. I've known it for a very long time now. You've almost come full circle, but I must warn you, you have a few more speed bumps to maneuver before you're in the clear."

"I'm not sure I follow you."

"When you took us back in time, you opened a portal and, whether you realized it at the time or not--you agreed to heal many lifetimes of trauma and abuse."

"This is where I get lost," I said shaking my head in frustration.

"I'm not allowed to say much except that you agreed to get off the merry go round this lifetime and break the pattern of abuse. When you held the Book of Souls it reacted to the pureness of your heart and exposed Sebastian for what he really is. He's held on to you for so long through your many relationships and something deep inside of you finally said 'enough!' When you close this chapter of your life, Sebastian will lose his control and that scares you!"

"*What?* No, you're wrong!" I protested. "Do you think I've enjoyed being tormented by an angry sadistic maniacal ghost?"

"No, of course not," she replied. "But anything else would mean that you'd have to step out of your comfort zone. You never felt like you were good enough to stand on your own. You've moved way beyond victim mentality and you know it, but that sense of normalcy and freedom feels worse in a sense because you've never experienced it before."

"You're killing me Aggie!" I moaned. "But I get it--I

really get it! My God, I've never connected the dots quite as profoundly as you." I paused, then confided "the men I attracted into my life were controlling and--as I become more honest with myself—I see how they all reminded me of my father. I placed him on a pedestal--thought he could do no wrong--and I put the men in my life on that pedestal as well. I allowed myself to lose *me* in my relationships because I didn't want to disappoint them or lose their love, as I'd lost my father's so long ago!

"All my life I've searched for someone to love me for me, no strings attached--for honesty, integrity, and someone I could trust. I've searched for the one who wouldn't abandon me, judge me, or abuse me physically or emotionally. I thought if I could make things better for someone else, even at the expense of my own happiness, it would make me *good enough*. If I could be the best mom, best employee, best lover, and wife--even if that meant giving up my own identity--then I would be *good enough*—but good enough for whom?" I paused. "I tried to be good enough in the eyes of my mother and father, but it seemed I continually made the wrong choices!"

And what about Michael, I wondered silently. Had I lost his love as well because once again I tried to prove I could *fix* the man in my life, and therefore be *good enough? What do I do now?* So many questions remained unanswered--I felt as though I'd barely chipped away at the many layers that presented themselves to me on a daily basis. I realized I was becoming a different woman altogether. I was discovering an inner strength I hadn't realized until Aggie made me look deep within and dig for things I'd tried to bury! I wasn't sure what I was afraid of--I only knew that I could feel my fear growing weaker and my courage much stronger...

I looked at Aggie in surprise as even more light began

to dawn...

"My God, Catherine's been teaching me how to begin to love myself, to honor my own truth, and learn how not to betray myself! She's been trying to bring me out of my shell-- unlocking a part of me I had forgotten even existed!"

Aggie smiled and nodded enthusiastically.

"Through all the hell I've endured since coming to this place, I'm beginning to see the blessing! Through Catherine's constant visitations I've been forced to face my inner demons and gain the courage and conviction necessary to battle the unseen forces that haunted me in the church!" I looked at Aggie. "I can't lie to you--the thought of this fills me with fear, but I'm beginning to understand I'm being asked to stand my ground and fight back! I see now I'm beginning to develop a powerful inner strength!"

Exhausted and weak, I wondered how much trauma and stress I unloaded by acknowledging the truths Aggie had spoken earlier? The liberation of it felt great!

"You're on the last leg of your journey here, lass." Aggie smiled a bittersweet smile. "When I look at you I feel only love and I'm blessed to finally know you in the flesh, instead of you always showing up in my dreams," she winked. "That became quite annoying at times--you were frustrating as hell in them too!"

"What!?"

"Yes, it's true--just as Catherine contacted you back in the States, you were connecting with me here in England on some level." She laughed. "Wild, don't you think? At one point, just like you, I really thought I'd gone over the deep end! And now, look--here you are helping me as much as I'm helping you! I love you, lass, I really do!" She placed her arms around me and hugged me tightly. "Come on girl, it's your last night here--let's say we throw one hell of a party!"

Chapter 32

I hate goodbyes, but knew in my heart I'd see her again in this lifetime. The haunting cry of the mourning doves that nested within the eaves of Aggie's cottage reminded me of the bittersweet moment when I'd said goodbye to the church. Now I felt that emotion wash over me once again.

I took one last look around the tiny room that, in a sense, had become my home. I made the tiny quaint bed, tucked the quilted comforter in one last time, and closed the door behind me. I dragged my luggage through the hallway to the kitchen below and found her waiting for me. She was joined by twelve other guests—the close knit sisterhood of Wicca's—who had befriended me and who I was proud to call my sisters.

"I'm going to miss you all!" I cried, reaching out my arms to encircle every one of them in one last group hug.

"You'll be back to us one day!" they replied. "You're a part of us now, Evie! We'll be with you always--if not in person, within your heart!"

We said our goodbyes and Aggie walked me to my car.

"I packed a lunch for you, lass," she mentioned. "Put in an extra helping of peach cobbler. You still have a few pounds to put on them lovely bones!" She brushed the tears away from her eyes. "Damn allergies," she laughed. "I'm gonna miss you, lass!"

One last hug and she walked away. She glanced back once, and gave a quick wave before disappearing from view.

"I'll miss you too, Aggie" I said as I climbed into the car. I began the long drive home, not sure what awaited me there, but I felt as though a great weight had been lifted from my shoulders. I knew I could face almost anything now.

Michael always seemed to be under the impression that I hated England. He was wrong. I hated the weather, and complained about it a lot, but so did the British themselves, and this was their home! I drove along the narrow country road and remembered the first time I stepped foot on English soil. It was raining, no surprise there--but as Michael drove through the rolling hills to our new home I was most impressed by the green lushness of the countryside.

I felt as though I'd landed in a garden in paradise, though it would have been almost perfect if someone would turn off the faucets every now and then! Such was the perfection of this magical place, and the topic of conversation in almost every pub!

The closer I got to home the more anxious I became. It felt as though a troop of boy scouts were tying slip knots in my stomach. The way they were going about it, I'd give them the honor badge just to get them to stop! Aggie said I'd be fine. That whatever I found would be the right thing. Okay, I could accept that, but it didn't mean I wasn't petrified.

Halfway through the journey I realized I was starving and decided to stop at the White Horse Inn. I'd already devoured what Aggie had packed for me--double helping of peach cobbler and all! *Shoot me,* I thought, *sometimes when I get nervous, I eat...*

The White Horse had quite a reputation. Apparently, it was named after the petrographs that dotted several hills along the rolling countryside, which by the way seemed to be connected to the many crop circles that drew thousands of visitors to this part of the country every year. If I had the time I

221

would've stopped to investigate, but my life was already oozing with paranormal activity. *One mystery at a time Nancy Drew,* I thought.

I decided to stay the night. After placing my luggage in the upstairs lodging I wandered downstairs to the pub for a light meal and pear cider. I watched the other guests as they dined, chatted amongst themselves and made toasts, clinking their glasses. I seemed to be the only one on my own that evening, but was at peace just the same. I signaled for the waiter to bring me one last cider before retiring to my room. I had a long drive ahead of me in the morning and I wanted to be rested. I didn't know what I'd find when I arrived back home.

My head had barely hit the pillow before I drifted off to sleep. Startled awake from a very deep sleep by a guttural rasping noise, I saw it, sitting on the armchair in the corner, watching me with intense golden eyes.

"Who the hell are you?" I asked.

"Don't you recognize me?" it asked, leaning forward from the armchair into the dim moonlight that filtered into the room through the window. "I watched over you at Aggie's when you were with fever, curled up at the end of your bed, keeping you safe."

I couldn't see anything but blackness and intense golden eyes as it pushed itself up from the armchair and walked toward me. It stood tall and lithe, blending in with the shadows, and stared at me with what I could only describe as feline-like eyes.

"Think back," it said, still hidden in the shadows.

"Did she send you here?" I asked.

I wasn't sure what the response would be. I convinced myself this was some bizarre dream induced by too much pear cider and the combination of double peach cobbler and all the other food I'd consumed earlier in the day. On top of that, my anxiety had built to an alarming crescendo as I'd debated earlier how to best approach my husband when I returned home. So I was surprised when the catlike figure responded in kind.

"That's what she does when she cares for someone," it replied. "She had me follow you to make sure you'd be okay."

I swear it almost purred. "I don't mean to be rude, but you're just a figment of my imagination, brought on by too much—"

"Booz?" it replied. "You can believe what you want, but that won't change the fact that I'm here. Of course, I'll be gone in the morning and you'll dismiss this as just another paranormal experience. So why not enjoy our time together? Lighten up!"

I stepped from the bed and walked toward the dark shadow. The closer I got, the colder it became until the air was so frigid I could see my breath.

"Come closer," it purred, as it stepped from the shadows, its arms outstretched and inviting. I stepped closer, and that's when the overpowering smell of decay swooped down on me like a rabid vulture. I couldn't speak or move--I tried to scream, but the words stuck in my throat as I gasped for air.

"What's the matter?" it asked. "Cat got your tongue?" The feline features began to morph into a hideous face, grotesque and angry. He snarled at me, cursing my name. As he reached out to grasp me, I stepped quickly away dodging the sharp bite of his energy and leaving him grasping at nothing but air.

"Get out, Sebastian!" I screamed. "You almost had me fooled, but your disgusting smell gave you away!"

"Stop fighting who you really are!" he growled. "Let me

show you the powers of the book--just like old times, hmmm?"

The deep dark intensity of his eyes pulled me in and I almost felt myself let go as he swirled closer, beckoning me with open arms to enter his embrace. What was it about that book? For a moment I found myself entertaining the thought of discovering its powers and the secrets it held within.

"Come child," he cooed. "Come home, where you belong."

Had he been able read my thoughts? For a moment I pictured what it would be like if I lost myself. If I just surrendered and let go. What would be the harm? His promises were almost convincing. I wondered momentarily if I belonged to the other side. I moved slowly toward him, and that's when I saw her face! She lay in her bed chamber, holding her child for the last time. Then she faded slowly away.

Snap out of it, Evie! thundered through my head. *Oh God!* The jackhammer had awakened!

"Come," the cooing voice repeated. "You're so close to being mine again." The black mist swirled and danced all around me.

"No!" I screamed, as I stepped back out of reach of his cold embrace. I wasn't about to get lured into his trap! I realized it was I who had the upper hand now and quickly repositioned my thinking.

"Now that I know who and what you really are, your presence doesn't intimidate me!" I cried. "You're a coward, Sebastian!" I screamed at him. "I find you weak and pathetic! Get out!"

I hoped I wasn't pressing my luck, but I had to appear confident even though deep down I felt like a bundle of raw nerves barely holding it together. I was determined to stand my ground! If I showed any sign of fear I knew in my heart I wouldn't live to see another day. This dead thing that stood before me had absolutely no power over me unless I allowed it!

I never had that in the past because I never believed in myself. Too much had transpired to doubt my capabilities now! Catherine never had this opportunity--she'd been deceived by not one, but two very powerful men, and I owed it to her to set things straight. Sebastian preyed on an innocent young woman and held her captive by threatening her and her unborn child. He deserved to be sent straight to hell! I remembered I still wore the tiny golden cross Monique had given to me. "For luck," she'd said. I fingered its smooth surface, then quickly ripped it from my neck and threw it at the darkness.

His loud tortured screams threatened to burst my ear drums, but I didn't flinch. I remained still, sending him thoughts of love and forgiveness. I needed to put out the fire, not feed it, and anger would only fuel his energy. I needed to defuse it. For the life of me, it took everything I had to conjure up such emotions, but I knew that's what I had to do. He was once a human before he'd turned to the dark side.

"What about your wife Raphaela, and your son?" I asked. "It wasn't your fault she killed herself! She was sick and distraught by the loss of another child!" I couldn't tell if what I said made any difference to something that appeared to have lost all of its humanity. I began to feel Catherine and Victoria both around me, and the presence of the powerful trinity as I concentrated on somehow getting through to his heart. I felt them coming through--it was as if we had merged into one.

It was a battle of wills, but as I continued to stand my ground I sensed his power beginning to dissipate. He'd been my teacher, Victoria's teacher, many lifetimes ago, and he'd taught me well. The lessons I learned then backfired on him now, and he was pissed! He underestimated the power of the trinity, and the fact that the light of Catherine, Victoria, and me--when connected--was so immensely powerful he couldn't break through.

The Book of Souls did not judge--I knew it was like a karmic barometer that remained neutral, feeding off other's energy by what it felt within their hearts, and Victoria's was pure. The book amplified her light out into the world, shielding her from Sebastian's countless attempts to draw her into the darkness under his apprenticeship.

Unfortunately, the book fed from the evil it found within his heart and mirrored back to him the darkness that dwelled there. She was very wise for one so young and had discovered the truth. He hadn't factored that into the equation when took her from Catherine's death bed to raise her as his own. It seemed his only mission was to draw upon his niece's innocence, so he thought, in his insane attempt to seek immortality by using her and the power of the book.

He hadn't counted on being counterattacked by a karmic boomerang. The three of us were strong. It was as if we merged and became one, which protected us from his psychic attacks. Slowly the rancid smell of death and decay left the room, and his shrill screams of anger and surprise along with it. I was left standing alone in the middle of the tiny room to live another day once again. I hadn't realized I'd been holding my breath, and now I lunged toward the open window and gulped in fresh air, almost passing out as it stung my lungs.

I might have won the battle, but I wasn't sure about the war. Needless to say, I slept the rest of what remained of the night with the lights on, tucked snugly beneath the warmth of the heavy comforter and prayed for daylight.

Chapter 33

The remainder of my drive was relatively quiet, not much to tell. I slipped an audio tape into the CD player--"Along Came a Spider" by James Patterson, one of my favorite authors. I enjoyed his writing style, short quick chapters that remained crisp and entertaining, page turners to the end.

I found it difficult to picture myself back at home again. It felt like I'd been away for years--so much had transpired the week or so I was gone. I'd grown and changed so much in that time--from the timid caterpillar to a beautiful butterfly-- though I was still a bit wet behind my wings! There was so much more I needed to discover about myself!

My experiences living here had introduced me to an entirely new Evie--one I enjoyed being around! She was gusty, passionate, and strong! Felt good to finally become my own best friend! Something quite profound had shifted inside of me and I wasn't afraid anymore. I devised my new motto: What you see is what you get, accept me as I am!

"Thank you, Catherine!" I shouted at the top of my lungs, momentarily drowning out the voice on the CD as I zipped through the countryside. It wasn't long before I reached the Basingstoke exit, veered off the motorway, and entered the roundabout that pointed me in the direction of home. Whoever wrote "home is where the heart is" knew exactly what they were talking about! It isn't a physical location, it's the feeling you get when you're completely at peace within your heart. It doesn't matter where you are or where you go, you can experience it anywhere. I felt it in Glastonbury, and a part of me was still there...

I entered the narrow drive, parked the car, and immediately noticed there were no lights on to greet me. Michael's car was not in its designated spot. The house was exactly as I had left it a few weeks ago, everything in its place, just the way I liked it. The only thing missing was Michael.

I hadn't told him exactly when I'd return, only given him a general "about two weeks." Knowing Michael, he probably got bored waiting around for me and ventured out in search of stimulating conversation with friends or in search of new acquaintances--probably the latter. He had no problem attracting new people into his wide circle of interesting collectables. I used to feel very insecure about that but, as I walked upstairs to empty my luggage the only thing on my mind was how much I wanted to take a long hot bath.

I sank deeply into the tub and allowed the lavender-scented bubbles to surround me. It felt good; I was safe. I lit candles, placed my head against the rolled towel behind my neck, and closed my eyes as my body responded to the soothing warmth of the water. I stayed until the water grew cold, then withdrew my body from the tub's embrace and stepped out dripping wet to reach for the towel. It was then I noticed the envelope sitting on the vanity, my name scrolled boldly across it in black ink.

My hands shook as I picked it up. *This can't be good,* I thought, as I ripped open the envelope and slumped onto the bath mat in the middle of the floor.

"Christ, Michael--*really!*"I said to myself as I eyed the letter, not actually able to focus on the words as the tears began to well. I was afraid to read what it said.

Michael had written me a "Dear John" letter! Turns out

he hadn't the courage to speak to me face to face, and instead typed this letter on his computer, printed it off, and stuffed it into an envelope. Then he left, knowing I'd find it eventually. In a nutshell, he'd retreated to Paris for four weeks and said he wanted me out before his return! He purchased a one way ticket back to the States and left it tucked neatly inside the envelope with this goodbye letter. As far as he was concerned, our marriage was over! He said he thought it best to end it this way--he was tired and worn out, could no longer cope with the responsibility of a wife!

That's just perfect, Michael! I fumed inwardly. *Don't give me the opportunity to fight for us, or try to fix whatever was broken!* My sense of betrayal was immense; so many emotions flooded to the surface--it was as if I'd been blindsided by a tsunami and never knew what hit me! I know I should have expected this, yet somewhere in the back of mind I always thought things would work themselves out.

I finished reading the letter, ripped it into a thousand little pieces, and tossed them into the wastebasket. I exited the bathroom, still wrapped in my towel. Weak, now my heart hurt —as though a huge vise was squeezing the life out of me. The last time I felt this kind of pain was when my mother passed away. She left me once when I was a young girl, then a second time forever when I became a young mother.

I left home when I was fourteen--told my father I wanted to be with my mom. I discovered she'd moved to a small apartment, where unfortunately she didn't have room for me. She told me she'd come for me when she moved into her house and, once she moved again, I was allowed to be there with her, but she wasn't the same mom I'd known from the past.

We never talked about the first time she took off in the middle of the night when I was twelve. In fact, the few times I brought it up she turned away and withdrew. I knew if I wanted to keep her friendship, I could never bring it up or I might lose her forever.

She had a boyfriend ten years younger than her who was a sloppy, deadbeat drunk. He wasn't living with her when I moved in at first, but I hated him from the first moment I met him! He was someone I just knew I couldn't and shouldn't trust--there was something scary about him! I shuddered at the memory.

I *know* he abused my mother, but she denied it. The day I witnessed him push her, slap her, and knock her down, I stepped in immediately. I inserted myself between the two of them and didn't budge! He balled up his fists as if he were going to slug me, and I told him if he laid a hand on me or my mom, he'd regret it for the rest of his life! He packed his bags and walked out, though eventually mom let him come back. That's when I left home—again--at age sixteen.

I got myself a job at a local A&W restaurant, rented a small basement apartment, and finished school. I'd visit mom when the bastard boyfriend--now her husband--wasn't around. I wasn't really allowed to be there when he was home, anyway.

I always wondered how my mom could choose somebody like him--she didn't drink, and now she had alcohol in the house; she seemed depressed, and wasn't at all the woman I'd known in the past! She helped me with groceries, and as much as she could while I was on my own, but everything I learned about female stuff--like my period, and about bras and all those feminine things my mother should have taught me, I figured out on my own.

My sister came to live with me for a while, but eventually it just became too hard for us. My grandparents took her in and continued to raise her until she turned eighteen. When things got too tough and I couldn't afford to pay my bills, I moved back in with mom for a time. Things had calmed down somewhat--her husband had a job, although he still drank too much, and they seemed almost happy.

I didn't have my own room, so they set up a cot for me in the storage area near the furnace in the basement. At least it was a place to sleep! I have this one memory that haunts me: One night as I lay there in the dark, on that cot in that tiny room in the basement, I felt uneasy--very uneasy. Later I woke up, startled to see my stepfather standing over me! He just stood there, staring down at me! I pretended I was asleep--I didn't move, I barely breathed--and eventually he went away. I told my mom about it, but she didn't believe me. At that point I worked two jobs, and when I put enough in the bank, I moved away.

I thought now about how my mother was murdered on my birthday--the same day I found out I was pregnant with my youngest daughter, Angie. Mom always remembered my birthday and made a big deal of it. We'd meet for lunch and just hang out together and catch up. She was still alive for the birth of her first granddaughter, my eldest Jennifer Nicoline, and adored her.

Mom came over the eve of my birthday and asked me if I'd do a tarot reading for her. I saw the death of this beautiful woman in the cards, but assumed it was a friend of hers having a marital issue with an abusive husband and brushed it off-- but there was something depressing around her that I could not put my finger on that day. Four minutes to midnight on the same day I found out I was pregnant with my second child I received a call that I needed to get to the emergency room stat!

When I arrived at the hospital I was given the news my mother had been shot! Despite the attempts of the physicians on call--including open heart surgery to remove the bullet-- they did not succeed in saving her. What upsets me most is that the last memory I have of her is seeing her split open from sternum to mid-section, laying naked on a cold steel gurney. I remember covering her and leaving the hospital in a fog. Since then I refuse to celebrate my birthday on the day of, and I hate Thanksgiving because my birthday and that holiday are so closely connected.

To this day I'm convinced her husband did it, but the police said there was no proof and closed the case almost immediately. I attended her funeral and watched her be laid to rest. I shed so many tears I could literally have filled the Mississippi. That was the one and only time I visited her grave. I said my goodbyes and never went back. Something inside of me detached--if I had not, I wouldn't have been able to move forward in my own life.

I hated her at first. And I told her that every day after she passed. I needed her! I needed her guidance and support and I wanted my daughters to have a grandmother! I missed her perfume and the way she laughed. I missed her cooking and baking--there were always these amazing chocolate chip cookies she'd be pulling from the oven, or apple pie, and when it came to the holidays she went all out. Those were the good times, the qualities she passed onto me and that I shared with my children.

I had nightmares for months after she passed--dreams of being at her home but not being able to find her. I'd search every room of her house in tears, calling out her name. The house is eerie and darkness is everywhere, and I'd wake up in a cold sweat, tears streaming down my face. These dreams wore me out because I couldn't understand what they were trying to convey.

There were times I sensed her around me. I'd get a hint of her perfume, just subtle enough to catch my attention. I'd see things that reminded me of her, more signs she was around me. After her death, my stepfather literally bulldozed her house with everything in it. I only desired one thing when she passed--a beautiful quilt I'd made one year for a Christmas present for her. I devoted a lot of time and love to that beautiful blanket, and to have that because I knew she cherished it would have meant the world to me. But it wasn't meant to be...Mom gave me life and shared part of that life with me and then she went away...

The letter from Michael elicited the same kind of pain and cut deep, slicing through to the very essence of my soul. I swear I felt it shudder as I threw myself on the bed in the master bedroom where I stayed for three days, refusing to eat or drink. I wanted to escape and the best way to do that was to bury my head beneath the covers and sleep...

I woke up at midnight on the third day--I think--to the loud chiming of the grandfather clock downstairs in the hallway. I actually thanked God that the annoying sound stirred me from my depression. Divine intervention, perhaps? All I knew was that I needed to get my act together. Drowning my sorrow in a sleeping stupor was not my style. When I finally opened my eyes, I realized I was not alone. The young spirits that resided here stood by my bed, weeping. When they realized I'd seen them, they evaporated into a thin mist and swirled off into the darkness.

Enough of this! I thought, as I pushed myself to a sitting position on the bed. My legs felt like liquid rubber, shaky and weak. I tried to stand and immediately fell back onto bed. The room--and everything in it--was spinning out of control! As soon as everything stopped I tried again, but this time I took it very slowly, allowing myself to get my land legs before trying to walk.

The first thing I needed was a shower. I didn't smell so good. I also needed to eat otherwise I knew I wouldn't have enough strength to get me through what I needed to do. I could hear Abbie's soft Scottish brogue echoing throughout my bedroom:

"What you find will be the right thing." I could hear Monique's thick French lilt: "Your marriage was the catalyst to get you to England--nothing more, little butterfly..."

I recognized that if I hadn't had met Michael I'd never have come to England, but finally acknowledged that I'd never felt at home with him. I really loved him though--Michael had offered me an escape from what I thought was a boring life. I was tired of the same routine, same job, same everything. Lost relationships, lost dreams...my children grown and on their own, living and excelling in their own lives, didn't need me anymore. I wanted, desired, a change of scenery.

Michael offered me a life that I'd only dreamed of, or read about in books. I travelled the world with him; he thought I was beautiful! But Michael knew nothing about my father or mother--nothing about the loss...to a point, he took away the pain or hole in my heart, but somehow he also emphasized the emptiness I felt inside.

When Michael came into my life I thought finally for once I'd made a perfect choice. This time my father could not be disappointed in me! Now I saw how I was always a possession--something to look at, but not someone who could have her own opinion or an independent mind. Unfortunately, to him I was a knick knack, something pretty to prance about to others. He did not see the real me. Just like my father...

Often I felt as though I had to walk on egg shells around him, afraid to really let my hair down and be me, because if I did, he might lose interest in me. He bought rare paintings, grew tired of them and set them aside, and then purchased something else. I kind of felt like that, as if I was a rare painting and his interest was beginning to fade.

234

Sometimes it was as if Michael had two different personalities. He was more surface and yet not. He loved to show others what he acquired and could be ostentatious, yet he was also humble. He showered me with gifts, but after a while that grew old. I needed his emotional side, not just his material side, to shine through. He never understood that I needed him to hear me, and how he shut me down whenever I tried to share my emotions. Had I ended up here married to a man that really did not love me but was too afraid to let me know because he hated confrontation?

I saw now also that it was no coincidence my path had crossed with that of an eight hundred year-old church brimming with the energy of a painful past. Perhaps no matter how hard I'd tried to deny it, the events taking place here served a far greater purpose than a simple marriage in which I was supposed to live happily ever after--that seemed now more like a cliché than reality...

I stepped from the shower fresh and alert. The house was quiet but I wasn't alone. I sensed the energy of the young spirits all around me. They were sending me their courage and strength just as they had the night I'd been attacked by Sebastian in the living room, which seemed like ages ago now. There was no darkness here, only love and support from the young mothers and their children imprisoned here years ago.

I'd nearly given up--almost allowed myself to lose hope! But in doing so I realized I was stronger than that, and if I allowed myself to walk down that path everything I accomplished while here would be lost forever.

It would be a few weeks before I boarded that plane to the States, and I intended to make the best of it! I stuffed as many of my belongings as possible into the same two suitcases with which I'd arrived—seemed rather fitting to leave the same way I came in. In reality though, I was leaving with so much more. I left the packed bags in the hallway. I'd be back to collect them before I left. I thanked the spirits for watching over me, then closed and locked the door, and walked out into the pouring rain toward my car.

Chapter 34

I headed down "Hells Highway," destination the abandoned church. It had been taken off the market several months ago--seems too much red tape and legal hoops to jump through caused potential buyers to eventually lose interest. Bad for them, good for me! I couldn't help but wonder if there wasn't more to it. Perhaps it was the intense heaviness and disturbing atmosphere of the place that kept buyers away.

I drove the narrow road at top speed, over my fear of suicidal motorists. Besides, it was late and there was not much to come by except the occasional rabbit stopped dead in its tracks by the bright beam of my headlights as I rounded the curves at breakneck speed. I braked to avoid a brave one as he hopped into the tall grass beside the road, then continued on. I rounded a few more bends before slowing down once more.

If memory served me correctly I was nearing the hidden drive. I forgot how easy it was to zip on past if I didn't pay attention. I parked at the end of the narrow graveled drive and walked the rest of the way. I'm not going to lie--it was creepy...the graves were illuminated by a half moon, hidden briefly by billowy clouds that caused the stone markers to appear as if they had released their dead tenants, who swirled and danced through the thick mist.

I couldn't see the guardians, but I knew they were perched on the gabled tower. It was silent--too silent. Not even the screech of a night owl or the rustling of a badger foraging for food. I reached into my bag and pulled out a flashlight. I needed to shine some light on this place. I hit the high beam and scoped out my surroundings. The place looked sad, if that was possible. Perhaps I picked up on all the old energy, which was so thick and you could literally cut it with a knife.

I couldn't see much, but what I did see looked overgrown and wild. I passed Catherine's crypt, and the familiar energy of our connection shot through me. I traveled back in time for just an instant to when I'd witnessed her death.

"Catherine," I whispered, as I continued toward the old oak door. We had locked up the place before we left and turned the keys over to the solicitors, but fortunately I kept one of the large skeleton keys as a souvenir, and quickly tugged it from my jacket pocket. I could probably get busted for trespassing, but I highly doubted it. This place was just another derelict building, abandoned and forgotten.

I turned the key, releasing the rusty tumblers within the chamber of the lock as I slowly pushed the heavy oak door open. The familiar scent of dampness and mold filled my nostrils. It was freezing inside the narrow foyer, and I clutched my jacket closer as I carefully made my way through to the Italian kitchen.

"Hello old friend," I whispered, as I closed my eyes and imagined when it had been filled with the intoxicating aromas of Michael's cooking and the laughter of our guests. I shined the flashlight through to the living room and was shocked to see it hadn't taken long for the spiders to take over! Cobwebs glistened along the high rafters and dust bunnies accumulated on the bare marble floors. I felt as though I was home, but also that the home had forgotten about me. The pot belly stove no longer stood in the little alcove by the south wall. It had finally managed to escape the confines of the church.

"Well good for you!" I laughed.

The energy was oppressively heavy and I had to force myself to climb the spiral staircase to the loft. Once a bedroom filled with romance, now an empty shell littered with scraps of shredded cloth and feathers--possibly a nest the rats had made to escape the bitter cold. I hesitated as I walked through the low brick archway that separated the bedroom from the tower. I'd made up my mind to face the demon that dwelled there, as we still had unfinished business. I wanted to exorcise the darkness so I could return home, but not until the break of day when the demons slept. Then I would manage to summon up enough courage to go up there.

I stepped out of the archway and turned my back on the tower, and felt once again the unmistakable feeling of being watched. A heavy oppressive weight seemed to bare down on me, and for an instant I sensed the jackhammer within my head begin to rumble. *Not now!* I thought. *I'm not up for any visions!* So intense was the feeling, I nearly broke my neck as I darted from the loft and ran down the staircase two steps at a time. Once I made it back to the living room the jackhammer released its grip and I relaxed.

I brought a sleeping bag, and some food and drink, and proceeded to spread it out in the center of the living room. I ate then quickly tucked myself in between the sleeping bag's thick quilted layers. I watched in silence as thin streams of moonlight filtered through the large window near the pew. If anything evil resided here, it remained hidden within the dark corners of the church and tower.

Here in the living room, surrounded in soft moonlight, I felt peaceful and safe. I could hear the owls that nested in the old pine as they rustled in the branches and prepared for their nightly hunt through the misty woods. It seemed the perfect night to be here, welcomed once again within the church's embrace. I lay my head on the pillow and instantly fell asleep, only to be awakened the next morning by the warmth of the sunshine filtering through the large window.

Chapter 35

The sun cast intricate shadows across the walls and the high beamed ceiling, making it appear less formidable. In a way, I felt this had always been my home and that I belonged here. Perhaps I'd *always* walked between two worlds--the living and the dead--and hadn't realized it until I came here! The intense energy that bled from every crack and crevice within this place certainly challenged me, and I thought I coped very well actually, considering the circumstances...

Unfortunately, in the process of discovering who I really am, I managed to lose a husband. But, looking back now, I realized I never stayed in a relationship for long; I seemed always to be searching. No matter how much I focused on my relationships my heart seemed to yearn for more, as though something was always missing. I didn't understand what until Catherine came into my life, although she managed to pull me on a journey that even now still seemed beyond comprehension.

Two weeks remained for me to figure out how to move forward on my quest. I still hadn't set things right with the darkness that surrounded me. Until I put it to rest, a part of me would always be looking over my shoulder--waiting for the next attack. I still hadn't figured out what message breathes life into the Book of Souls--not completely. Victoria figured it out and gave me a taste of its immense power when she rescued me from the maze. Who had it now? Had it evolved into a living entity of its own, rebalancing the karmic deeds of others by its mere presence alone?

So lost in thought, I hadn't registered the light tapping on the old wooden door. It grew louder and more persistent as it echoed throughout the empty shell of the church. Had I been discovered? After all, the church did not belong to me anymore. Maybe if I remained quiet whoever it was would give up and go away.

"Are you there, dear?"

It was a woman's voice, but who was it and to whom was she talking?

Tap, tap, tap.

"Dear, are you in there?"

Great, I thought. *I can't hide in here forever!* I managed to make my way to the dark narrow foyer, and hesitated for a brief moment as I took in a long deep breath. I grasped the cold brass handle and opened the door. I think my heart might have stopped for a brief moment as I stared down at the tiny frail figure looking up at me with bifocal glasses that magnified the intensity of her pale blue eyes.

"Well, there you are!" she said, smiling up at me. She grasped my hand.

"What are you doing here?" I asked as I stepped out into the bright sunshine.

"Oh," she replied. "I have people here I visit on special occasions." She gazed about the unkempt graveyard before turning her intense blue eyes back in my direction.

"Have you seen her yet?" she asked, patting my hand lightly. "Have you found what you're looking for? Did you decipher the book?"

She fired her questions at me so rapidly that at first I couldn't answer. I was still trying to get over the shock of her being here. I walked over to Catherine's crypt and immediately sat down in order to regain my voice and to jump start my heart into beating once more.

"Forgive me," I said, "but I'm a little confused."

"Well," she continued, "you never made it back to the library for the book, so I assumed you must have given up. Then I spoke with my niece Monique, who shared everything with me. Of course, I knew all along you wouldn't take my advice! I recognized the rebel in you when we first met." She tilted her head back and released a small giggle. Her eyes continued to engage mine. Something passed through me as she continued to stare. I sensed she felt it too. It was a sense of familiarity. I'm not sure why that bothered me, but it did.

"What advice?" I asked. She really had me stumped.

She gazed about the graveyard for what seemed like an eternity before setting her sights on me once again. She plopped her tiny body next to mine on Catherine's grave, and ran her hand along the smooth cool surface of the stone.

"It seems," she said, smiling brightly, "that you opened up doors that can't be closed again."

"Oh my God!" What she was saying slowly began to register.

"It was *you* I saw that day in the crystal shop! Monique is your niece?"

She avoided my question, and lifted herself from the crypt to walk toward the entrance of the church.

"I see you've planted guardians at your threshold," she said, stooping to break off a sprig of lavender and place the delicate purple bloom gently to her nose. She took a long sniff, and tucked it into her pocket.

I couldn't figure her out--was she purposely avoiding my question? She could be a bit senile, considering her age! Or was there more to this interrogation?

"I'm sorry," I said. "Did you say guardians?"

"You must have known you'd be surrounded in

darkness from the moment you moved in here," she answered. "Why else would you have planted the guardians so strategically?"

"I'm not following," I replied. I felt stupid--where the hell was this conversation going?

"When lavender, sage, and rosemary are planted near a threshold, it sends out a warning to the darkness that it doesn't belong." She walked around the thick lush rosemary and sage, and tenderly stroked it between her nimble fingers. "These guardians have very powerful magic and only those with witches' knowledge are aware of this."

"I'm not a witch," I said. "I just happen to like these particular plants."

"And yet," she continued, "you just happened to choose three very powerful ones which, when combined--as you've done here--create a very potent magic! They send a message to the darkness and prevent harm to the mistress that plants them. Have you been injured or harmed in any way since you've lived here?" she asked. "Tell the truth," she winked. "I'll know if you're lying!"

How was I supposed to respond to that? I could say honestly I hadn't been harmed physically--but emotionally and mentally was another story altogether! Yet through all that had taken place here I'd never been harmed. Something had always stood in the way of that darkness--a barrier that kept it at bay.

"Okay, I'll give you that," I conceded. "But that still doesn't tell me why you're here."

"Protection," she said. "You needed me and now I'm here. I see you no longer wear the amulet my niece gave to you. I gather it must have served its purpose when you needed it the most?"

I thought back to the night the cat-like creature attacked me. Yes, that amulet had served me well as it had revealed Sebastian's true nature! Unfortunately, it did not have the power to send him back to hell.

"What makes you think that I need you?" I asked.

"You've almost come full circle here in England, and you'll be leaving very soon," she replied. "But Catherine is still very restless, even though I sense she hasn't come to you for a while. Living in the present and the distant past, as you do, can be wearing," she said.

"That's putting it mildly, don't you think?" I said.

"But you are doing it," she said, "and with such courage and conviction!"

"I have no other choice!" I responded. "They needed me. And as much as I hate to admit it, I needed them."

"Not many people will believe your story," she said, "but I can tell you here and now that it is true. You've been called upon to awaken and cleanse the souls of those from your past and--as crazy as that sounds--it's very real! Monique and others just like me were assigned to you many lifetimes ago to assist you on your journey. The darkness managed to take over everything at one point and consumed much of your family, raping them of their inheritance--not of money, but of something much more precious. Its purpose was to own their very souls.

"Catherine knew this, and passed this wisdom on to her daughter, who's been trying to convey this to you. The wealth and strength that resides within you took lifetimes to germinate, and now that it has awakened, the darkness fears you. As you and Catherine began to connect more deeply, your strength and determination set the wheels in motion and began to turn the tide of darkness and usher in the light. It will fight you tooth and nail! You're clearing generations of abuse and trauma, child."

"Okay, stop right there!" I said, exasperated. "This all

sounds like a bunch of mumbo jumbo! Who in their right minds will ever believe me—believe my story?"

She peered at me through her thick bifocals. Her intense pale blue eyes shimmered with tears. "Those who love you, those who have come before you, and those who will come after you've left this worldly plane. You know," she continued, wrapping her frail arm about my waist, "I've never told you my name. Come, let's sit next to Catherine and soak up the sunshine, it's so rare here in England." She moved toward the crypt and sat down in the thick lush carpet of grass beside it.

"Come," she said, and patted the ground signaling me to join her. I sat down next to her and closed my eyes and lay my head against her slender shoulder. "My name is Hope," she whispered, as she stroked the long locks of my blond hair and brushed them carefully off my forehead. I felt the tiniest flash of a headache. Just a slight niggling before it faded away.

"Hope is a lovely name," I whispered and opened my eyes to look at her. She was gone; I lay in the tall carpet of grass next to Catherine's crypt alone! Tightly clasped between my hands was the remnant of a lavender blossom.

Chapter 36

Where was Hope? What happened? Had I been taken on another vision quest? Everything that just took place seemed way too real!

My visions were always preceded by an intense headache, but that wasn't the case this time! Or was it? I couldn't remember. Only that I was sitting here with a lavender blossom, alone next to Catherine's crypt. My legs felt cramped. I needed to stretch and get the blood pumping through them. It was still a beautiful sunny day and I decided to take advantage of it by walking around the graveyard. I guess what happened was just a dream! At least that's what made the most sense to me.

I chalked up the experience to over imagination and exhaustion, and decided to explore the nearby woods. It had been such a long time since I visited here and I missed my daily walks. Not much had changed. I still had to fight my way through the tangled mess of nettles and ivy that had overtaken everything since I'd been away. *Survival of the fittest,* I thought.

The sheep grazed in the distance and I found the soft rustling of the rooks in the pines soothing. I pushed my way through the nettle and turned back to gaze at the guardians perched on the corners of the gabled tower. They were silent today. Their clawed feet clung tightly to the stone and their blank dark eyes seemed to stare right through me.

The church and graveyard were peaceful in the light of

day. Waves of emotion cascaded through my heart. I was going to miss this place! Through all the turmoil and darkness I'd awakened here, there had also been joy and love. I discovered a part of me I'd never known existed. I learned to become vulnerable and to listen to my heart--something very difficult for me in the past because I protected myself by not letting in many people. I didn't trust easily. I now saw how the pattern evolved through the years—lifetimes, actually!--to bring me to this place of awareness.

I walked the narrow trails through the woods and welcomed the smell of dampness and decay. The pungent aroma of mushrooms and fern, mingled with bluebells and snowdrops, was intoxicating and I sensed the magic hidden within the shadows of the ancient trees. *I'll miss this-- I'll miss this! I could lose myself here,* I thought, as I continued on.

A storm brewed in the distance--I heard the rumbling of thunder. It sounded tinny, and echoed through the dark grey sky that threatened to release a downpour any moment. As if on cue, small droplets of rain thumped down upon my head. I didn't care today. I had nowhere to go, nowhere to be. It seemed I had an abundance of time...

As the storm raged around me, one brewed within me as well. I was sure I hadn't faced my darkest hour, though I'm not sure how I knew this. Something deep inside warned me: Don't let your guard down, not yet! I ducked in amongst the dense fern and tall trees, their leaves a canopy that protected me from the downpour of rain as heaven opened up its floodgates and sent buckets of water pouring down onto the forest floor. Deep hollow thunder rolled and rumbled through the sky, followed by streaks of wicked lightning that fingered its way through the thick black clouds. I could wait it out, but who knew how long this would last? *I'll take my chances,* I thought, and rushed out from the safety of the trees into the bitter wind and rain. I jogged the few miles back to the shelter of the church.

By the time I made it to Trevor's field the rain had stopped and the sun began to peek out from behind the clouds. The weather changed so rapidly here! Rays of sunshine danced and glistened on the rain-soaked grass. The field was transformed into a thousand sparkling diamonds! There truly was magic here! One last walk about the graveyard and I'd call it a day...

I rounded the tower and couldn't help but notice the stone marker that lay flush to the ground with fresh flowers arranged around it carefully underneath the old pine. Who had placed them there? I approached the pine and, as I stooped to get a better look, I understood. *Not possible!* I thought as I read the words scrawled across the marker: *Hope Langston, Keeper of the Light, May You Rest in Peace...Forever Will Your Memory Linger On...*

I wasn't crazy! It hadn't been my imagination! I did have a conversation with a ghost! I reached down and touched her grave. Cool to the touch, the tingling sensation of her spirit coursed through my fingers. I reached into my pocket, pulled out the crushed lavender, and placed it beside the other flowers.

"For protection," I whispered. "Not that you'll really need it. I sense you're a very powerful healer, but this is the only gift I have to offer. Thank you!"

It was growing dark, and a light mist started to form throughout the graveyard. I hated the mist and didn't relish the thought of being out in it. One last glance at Hope's grave. *Her body may be buried here,* I mused, *but the essence of her power and spirit is everywhere...*

Chapter 37

I hurried inside the safety of the church and out of habit flicked the light switch in the hall. To my surprise it worked! Naturally I assumed the power had been turned off since no one lived here. Maybe the solicitors had forgotten! I breathed a sigh of relief knowing that all the corners were filled with wonderful bright light. Of course, this cast light also on all the residents that did live here! The eight legged variety, that is. Seems they had quite a nice thing going on. Cobwebs of all shapes and sizes greeted me from the high rafters.

"Victory is yours!" I laughed before I realized that during the excitement of the day I'd forgotten about the tower. It was pitch black outside. The church was surrounded in mist by seventy graves--correction seventy-one, with the recent addition of dear Hope, the newest resident.

I couldn't put this off another night--I needed to gather up the necessary courage to climb to the inside of the tower. *What if I never made it back out?* I wondered. *Would anyone really miss me? Would anyone know where to find me? Did it really matter?* I had nothing to prove to anyone anymore. But I did have a score to settle with a very powerful spirit! The problem, though, was that I didn't have a plan. All I knew was that everything had to end here and it needed to end tonight!

I was tired and drained from the constant attacks and, even though I managed to soldier on through them all, I needed to finish this, return home, and move forward with my life. All of the shadows and darkness needed release!

Catherine's story nearly finished, she deserved to rest, finally. Sebastian could no longer hold her back from moving into the light! Never mind that I had absolutely no idea how I was going to do this and it would be only me walking into the line of fire without backup...

I possessed Catherine's journal still, and I thumbed through it now looking for any clues that might help me with my mission. Sebastian was mesmerized by Catherine and her light—I wondered if it was possible to destroy him with it? He relied on the Book of Souls and its power. *How can I use this to my advantage?* I pondered. *Could I somehow call forth the Keepers of the Light and somehow harness enough energy to send the darkness back to hell?* I knew it would take more than the power of the trinity to achieve this goal. Hope was here now, and I believed Monique was still connected to her. *What if I could somehow connect with Aggie and the coven? I need to bring them to me—I'd be foolish to attempt this alone!*

I hated going back into the mist. I placed my boots on the narrow graveled path as shivers of darkness crept in all around me. It took all I had to force myself to run down to the end of the narrow drive, where I struggled with my keys and finally opened the car door. I slammed and locked it, turned on the engine, high beams, and found myself driving back out onto "Hells Highway" once again.

Chapter 38

Something was trying very hard to keep me from getting to my destination--the nearest warm pub I could find this late at night. Sleeted rain whipped against the windshield and the wipers did double time trying to clean it off. I could barely see, the fog was so thick, and the wind whipped my little car back and forth along the winding road. What should have been a thirty minute journey took two hours, as lightening struck a nearby tree and sent a large branch crashing down onto the road that nearly hit my car. I swerved to avoid a collision and ended up in a small ditch.

No damage to the car. I gunned the engine and rocked the car back and forth until the tires dug in and spun me into reverse. I swerved back onto the wet pavement. *Damn, that was close!* I thought, as I focused on the drive and held my breath until The White Swan Inn came into view.

"Thank you," I whispered to no one in particular, except the invisibles, who I was sure must have helped me maneuver through the disruptive energy that seemed to follow me that night.

First order of business, straight to the bar where I downed two shots of peach brandy--Aggie would be so proud! *Damn, that burned!* There was only one other couple sitting in the corner near the fireplace. I had the rest of the place to myself. It seemed much later than it was--only a little past ten-thirty. I rented a room for the night. I was not going back to the church without reinforcements! Now where the hell was my cell phone? I punched in the number and swear it didn't even ring before I heard the soft Scottish brogue.

"What took you so long, lass?"

"Aggie, how'd you know it was me?" How did she know it was me?

"I've been expecting your call. It took you long enough! Saw you in my dreams the other night, told the girls and we made a plan. Naturally we had to wait for you to call, lass! We'll be there in the morning with bells on!

"But you don't know where--"

"You live? Lass, give me more credit than that," she laughed. "You forget who you're talking to! Now have another peach brandy and go to bed!"

"How did you know I was drinking--"

"Peach brandy," she laughed. "Just do it and expect us in the morning."

I didn't have the chance to argue, as the line clicked off and the humming of the dial tone sounded in my ear.

Chapter 39

I sat outside the church on Catherine's crypt watching the sun rise. I love the dawn. This morning it appeared as though an ancient artist had dipped his brush into the sun and, using the sky as his canvas, painted pastel colors of pale liquid pinks and golden yellows in between the white billowy clouds that drifted by.

I could get lost in this moment, I thought, until my daydream was interrupted by the loud cries of the women as they pulled up in their caravan and rushed out to greet me. Aggie followed, carrying a large basket of goodies--I hoped--because I was starving! Too nervous to eat at the inn I left at first light to have some time on my own before they arrived. I wanted to watch the sunrise, sit in silence with Catherine and reassure her everything would be all right.

"Lass, you're looking well, but I see you still haven't managed to put any meat on those bones! Here, take this!" She shoved the large basket into my arms, kissed me on the cheek, then led me toward Catherine's crypt where she immediately whisked the basket from my arms and opened it to display peach cobbler, sausage, and tea. I couldn't get a word in edge-wise as all twelve women fussed over me and bombarded me with a million questions. If I'd gotten a word in, I might have answered one of them.

"Okay, enough!" Aggie laughed. "Let her speak!"

Too busy wiping the tears from my eyes, now I couldn't answer, I couldn't even focus. So many emotions washed over me, and the best I could do was make gushing noises before I started to cry all over again. Finally, after what seemed like forever, I composed myself long enough to say "I missed you guys!" I know it was lame, but that's all I had...

"We missed you too!" they all chimed, staring at me with their worried anxious faces. *Damn, twelve sets of eyes focused on me, no pressure!*

"Okay, first things first," laughed Aggie. "Let's eat before it gets cold!"

She took me aside after we finished; she wanted to catch up. I told her everything, exhausted by the time I was done.

"How'd you know I'd be calling you?" I asked. "How did you know I needed you?"

"Come, lass." She walked toward the old pine and knelt beside Hope's grave. "This is my sis," she said, looking up at me with her golden gray eyes, "buried here now for the past ten years."

"That's not possible, Aggie!" I responded. "This grave wasn't here when I first moved in, and Hope is the woman who helped me at the library. This grave is fresh."

"Sorry, lass, but you're wrong. Hope did love the library though! She volunteered there in her spare time when she wasn't working at the crystal shop with her daughter."

"I'm sorry--run that by me one more time, did you say her *daughter?*"

"Yes," Aggie replied, "my niece Monique, beautiful girl that one."

"But she's French!" I sputtered. As if that had anything to do with anything!

"Yes, yes she is," Aggie said absentmindedly. "Hope was always the wild one. Ran off to France and fell in love with a gorgeous Frenchman, and then came Monique! Hope's the eldest of my sisters and the most powerful, as you already witnessed. But she's been buried here for a decade now, so before you ask if she's the one who told me you needed help, you should know she communicates with me in my dreams."

"What about the crystal shop?" I asked. "I know that's real! I was there and I met Monique!"

"Sorry, lass, when Hope passed away, Monique closed the shop and went back to France to be with her father. He passed shortly after Hope, unfortunately--died of a broken heart. They were separated for many years, due to the nature of Hope's accomplishments, if you will. He never understood the elements she worked with and why, and it drove them apart, but they never stopped loving each other."

"But she told me Monique was her niece."

"Ah, that's Hope for you! She liked to keep one guessing, I'm sure you sensed that. We're all connected, Evie. We're a sisterhood that's been around since the beginning of time, and each new generation has managed to evolve and perfect their gifts in order to bring balance back to the darkness. It's had control far too long, if you haven't already noticed."

"Of course I agree, Aggie--I'm just not sure how to make things right."

"We focus on your lineage," she replied.

Her words took me back to the Tor and my intimate relationship with the druid priest who said the same thing: That we needed to protect our lineage. He also mentioned the Book of Souls, but I had no idea how to get my hands on it.

Confused, I replied: "I don't know what to do!"

"I need you to show us the tower," Aggie said calmly. "It seems that most of the negativity is centered there. His energy seems to be slumbering at the moment. Somehow you've managed to disconnect yourself from him--good girl!"

I didn't want to go up there. The last time I did I'd witnessed a murder, been trapped in a fire, and seen Catherine chained to a wall! Bad things happened in that tower! Something evil lived up there! Aggie saw the look of sheer terror cross my face, and must have read my mind.

"Sorry, lass, you have to go up there--it's the only way to fight him! You don't have to stay long--just enough time to clear it. We'll perform the actual ceremony in the living room downstairs. But first there's something else I must share with you."

"I'm afraid to ask," I said, waiting for her to reveal some dark mysterious secret.

"I'll tell you after we've been to the tower," she said. "Girls, follow me!"

"The space is small, Aggie, we won't all fit up there unless we separate and each of us concentrates on different levels. There are three floors, but the activity always seems centered on the middle one."

"Right then, Margaret, you and the other five--to the top! Mind your step and focus all of your energy down toward the middle! Evie and I will be where the darkness is the thickest, meaning the second floor, and you six girls"--she pointed in the direction of the others--will remain on the first level and send your energy upward!"

"Right, let's do it!" they all agreed.

"One more thing," said Aggie. "We're just clearing the space, nothing more. Our intention is not to awaken the beast just yet."

Dear God, I thought, as I placed my foot cautiously onto the first step and climbed upward into the tower. *Famous last words...*

Chapter 40

For a simple clearing, as Aggie called it, everyone looked as though they'd been through a meat grinder! I felt like my organs had been sucked inside out with a vacuum cleaner, spun and stirred around a bit, then replaced--just not in the right order. That's the only way to describe the intense energy that ran through me and hadn't stopped since the clearing of the tower.

I glanced around the living room, and saw I wasn't the only one who felt that way—except Aggie. She sat cross legged on the floor sipping tea. How did she do it? I dragged myself over to her slowly and gratefully accepted the cup of tea she placed in my hands.

"What now?" I asked, as I sipped the hot tea, scalding my tongue in the process.

"You did well up there," she said. "I'm proud of you--all of you!" She surveyed the group of weary women, all of whom managed to respond with what looked like smiles. I wasn't sure, since my head still spun from the ritual we managed somehow to survive.

"We rest," she said, "and we gather our strength! Whatever happens next, ladies, will be dangerous and I can't promise we'll all come out of it in one piece!"

"Well that's reassuring," I laughed. I couldn't help myself. I still couldn't believe this was happening.

"We can't banish Sebastian here," she added.

"What exactly are you saying?" I asked, dumbfounded.

"Where do we go? I assumed this would be the place since this is where I experienced the most attacks."

"Oh, it *is* the place," Aggie replied, "just not the right dimension. We can't fight him here in the present. We must fight him on his own turf."

"How are we supposed to do that?" Margaret asked, gingerly sifting her fingers through her mass of thick red wavy hair.

"Evie's going to take us there," Aggie responded.

The women turned to stare at me. Uncomfortable, I didn't know how to respond. Shivers of dread, mixed with excitement, coursed through me as I mulled over the idea-- because to me that's all it was...what was Aggie thinking? There was absolutely no way I could take them back! I scanned her face quickly to see if she was joking.

"It's going to take every ounce of courage from you all," Aggie advised, standing up for emphasis. "I've not come empty handed," she continued, "I brought a very powerful weapon for our defense."

That got my attention, along with everyone else. "What weapon could possibly fight something so powerful?" I asked.

"In time, lass," replied Aggie. "The thing still slumbers within these walls, and I plan to use that to our advantage."

"But--"

"No buts, I'm starving. Where's the nearest pub?"

Chapter 41

A heavy mist blanketed the graveyard as we returned from the pub. Midnight, the witching hour, had arrived, and the only light illuminating the church--and hopefully keeping the darkness at bay--came from strategically placed candles. The full moon cast slender beams of pale light through the large window in the living room and the skylight above us in the loft. It felt as if the residents of this place were holding their breath in anticipation of what was to come. The owls were silent tonight, or maybe they'd abandoned their nest in the old pine in search of safer hunting grounds.

We held hands and formed a circle in the center of the living room. Somehow, someway, I was supposed to take us back to Sebastian's time. I wasn't sure how I was supposed to accomplish this--I only knew it didn't work that way. My visions came of their own accord, I didn't will them. I felt silly standing in the quiet, all eyes upon me. I'm not sure what Aggie wanted me to do.

"Hurry Evie!" she whispered. "It's beginning to stir!"

A light breeze danced and swirled through the church. The candle flames flickered and weaved from side to side, slowly at first, until the breeze grew in strength and whipped the candles to the stone floor, leaving us in darkness. Only the full moon's light—sporadic at best, as it danced in and out between the clouds—remained.

The clouds parted, and once again the moonlight streamed through the church's large window. That's when I saw her standing in the middle of the circle, dressed as she was the night we first met.

"Catherine," I whispered. Her deep emerald green eyes glistened as she beckoned me toward her. I wasn't sure if I should break the circle. The last time I'd done that all hell had broken loose.

I searched for Aggie. "What do I do?" I asked

"Go to her, lass!" cried Aggie. "Enter the circle!"

I released my hands from the others, who carefully joined theirs back together to maintain the energy coursing through the circle. Visions of the past--brief flashes of memory of her life before Sebastian--came rushing in as I walked toward Catherine. She had been so happy before he came into her life! Her undying love for David shot straight through my heart. Her innocence, mixed with her phenomenal beauty and special gifts, had been her undoing. She was powerful in her own right, but everyone who might have helped her was taken away. Alone and abandoned, her faith in all that was good had been tarnished through repeated abuse and the betrayal of her father and Sebastian.

Sebastian manipulated and coerced her, and threatened to destroy the only thing she had left--the life of her unborn child! Yet, the most disturbing betrayal of all was that of her father, who'd willingly given up her child--*his grandchild*--to something so monstrously evil. I couldn't begin to fathom her depths of despair and sadness but, as I stood within the circle and connected to her memories, her pain came crashing in and brought me to my knees.

"Catherine, I'm so sorry!" I cried out as the pain of her loss swept through me.

"Stand strong!" yelled Aggie. "Do *not* break the circle! If you do, we'll all be lost forever, do you understand?"

I could barely hear her words as they filtered in and out

of my awareness. The damned jackhammer had returned and, between Catherine's intense energy and the terrific pounding in my head, I found it hard to focus. The familiar embrace of darkness closed in all around me. Once again, this energy dragged me down into the rabbit hole--only this time the tunnel was filled with thorns of anguish and despair at every turn. My heart felt like it might explode on this emotional roller coaster. *Make this end!* I pleaded silently.

I wasn't alone in the tunnel. It seemed others followed not far behind. I could hear their high pitched screams and wails as I was tugged further into the thick dense blackness.

"Am I going insane?" I panicked. *Boom! Boom! Boom!* The jackhammer beat like a drum. "Make it stop!" I wailed. My body felt like a giant pin cushion; sharp pain pierced through me mercilessly. It vanished as quickly as it had come, and suddenly I found myself free-falling through open space.

"Is she okay?" screamed Margaret.

"Quiet, lass!" shushed Aggie.

I could make out only the briefest outline of her face. I could tell it was her by the intense flashing of her wolf like eyes. But she wouldn't hold still and kept disappearing from view.

"Give her some room!" cried Aggie.

"I'm okay!" I said, trying to sit up. The pounding in my head was intense and I felt sick to my stomach.

"Easy, lass, you've a bit of a concussion," soothed Aggie.

"Where are we?" I asked. I could see outlines of shapes all around me but I couldn't quite see straight. I struggled to wipe away the residue that blocked my vision.

"You did it, Evie!" Aggie said. "I'm not sure how, but you got us here!"

My vision returned slowly, and I realized immediately

where we were. *Why would I choose to bring us here?* I wondered. The place oozed with dark malevolent energy, and I smelled the stink of decay everywhere...

Chapter 42

I had managed to land us smack dab in the middle of the tiger's lair--with Catherine's help, of course. I found myself lying in the center of a pentagram and beside me sprawled twelve confused and frightened ladies. After confirming I was alright, Aggie left my side to survey the huge cavernous room. Catherine was here once and paid for it dearly.

"Is this where all his power originates?" I asked no one in particular. "Are you with us Catherine?" I whispered.

"For now, we're safe," Aggie said reassuringly. "I'm not picking up any of Sebastian's energy--just residual darkness from a past ceremony performed here, nothing more."

"This is not a happy place," I informed them. "Catherine wrote about it in her journal." I looked around. The huge dark and damp cavern stank of death and decay. Bloodstained chains hung against the walls, and remnants of discarded bones littered the floor. Flashes of red glowed in the darkness as beady-eyed rodents scavenged for food. The only light came from dim torches that hung against the stone walls. Instead of the catacombs beneath Hawksworth Manor, it felt as though we'd been dragged into the very bowels of hell. To me, they were one in the same.

"This is where we make our stand," said Aggie defiantly. "At the moment we must sit and wait."

"That makes us a perfect target," I argued. "Like sitting ducks!"

"No," she replied, "because we have the element of

surprise, and I've brought a very powerful weapon." She reached into the satchel she'd somehow managed to drag along on our wild roller coaster ride. *How'd she managed that?* I didn't care and I didn't ask.

She pulled out a small black leather book. I moved closer to get a better view. Inscribed on it in gold lettering were the words "Al-Kimiya."

"Oh my God! How did you get your hands on that?" I asked, as I reached forward to run my hands across its smooth surface. Instantly, they began to throb and vibrate, and I pulled away immediately.

"I see you connect with it," said Aggie. "I thought you might!"

"We'll be fighting fire with fire?" I asked.

"The only way!" she nodded. "Girls, come close--all of you have to connect!"

We formed a semi-circle along the outer perimeter of the pentagram. This pentagram, according to Aggie, would set the trap and, instead of infusing Sebastian with power, would do the exact opposite! Aggie's plan was to siphon off Sebastian's power and drain him completely. He'd make sure he was well-protected, of course. The pentagram's power was intense, but Aggie assured us that when the time was right, it would turn against him.

And there was something else--we had the element of surprise! I liked the way Aggie thought. She really was an old witch in more ways than one. Truth be told, she hid her age well. I had to appreciate the fact that I was in the company of some very powerful women, all of whom were risking their lives for me.

"Aggie," I asked hesitantly. "Do you think this will really work?"

"You know, lass, if I could see into the future I would

have called myself a fortune teller."

I couldn't tell if she was joking or serious. She had on her poker face. I had to admit we were attempting something so out there--not to mention extremely dangerous--that I couldn't explain why the two of us were acting so jovial. *Why do people do what they do when they find themselves in extreme danger?* I mused.

"If anything's going to happen, it'll be around midnight," advised Aggie. "Lass, are you listening to me?"

"I'm sorry--what?" I replied.

"Focus!" Aggie snapped, as she clapped her hands to get everyone's attention.

"What happens now?" I asked.

"Why don't you ask her?" replied Aggie, pointing to the dark stairwell that led up to the interior of the magnificent manor.

Chapter 43

"Catherine!"

She placed a slender finger against her lips and shook her head from side to side. "Shhh, he's very close!"

"Can you all hear her?" I asked. "It's not just me right?"

"We see her!" everyone replied as they nodded their heads in unison.

"How is this possible?"

"Because we're in her world now," replied Aggie. "She has just as much at stake as we do--maybe more!"

Catherine walked slowly toward the pentagram. "Stop, you can't go in there!" I whispered loudly.

"Let her go, she knows what she's doing!" Aggie commanded.

Suddenly, deep booming thunder rattled the manor and sent painful chills up and down my spine. He was coming! The air grew thick and frigid, and was accompanied by what seemed to be an intelligent mist. It rolled down the winding staircase, shifting and sliding up against the damp cavernous walls. And then the unexpected happened: Sebastian walked out of the mist, tall and slender and just as handsome as Catherine had described him in her journal, and standing beside him was the Coven of Nine, silver daggers clenched tightly in their fists.

"Evie!" Aggie cried, "get your ass inside the circle *now!*"

Our coven of twelve women stood tall like sentries as they prepared for the attack. I rushed into the circle to join

Catherine, and I swear I saw them all wink.

"Well, what have we here?" Sebastian growled as he circled the group of women. "You don't actually believe you can beat me--*or them*--do you?" he asked, signaling the Coven of Nine to advance. "We've been waiting for this for a very, very long time! And, as fate would have it, you've been served up to me on a silver platter!" He smiled an evil smile.

I couldn't stand there and watch him destroy the sisterhood! I had to do something! I started to move toward them, but Catherine signaled to me to stop me.

"Be still!" she whispered. "They know what they're doing!"

I watched as Aggie thrust her hand into her satchel and pulled out the tiny black book. She held it high in the air and I saw it begin to glow. *Aggie's secret weapon!* I marveled. One by one, the sentries left their posts, and placed their hands delicately onto the book. They began to hum, and I watched with sheer fascination as their bodies merged together into a huge beam of intense white light! *How was this possible?* I wondered, utterly amazed. The women transformed themselves into a giant ray of blinding white light, and all around me their soft chanting grew to an ear-splitting crescendo!

"We are the keepers of the light! Let no harm come to this circle or those who stand within it!" they continued to repeat over and over, calling forth others to join them, as the light grew brighter. Ancestors of the past clasped hands with those present, creating a most formidable energy!

"Catherine!" screamed Aggie, "do you have the book?"

I watched as Catherine lifted her delicate hands into the light and displayed Sebastian's most cherished possession.

"No!" he screamed as he rushed toward the circle, the Coven of Nine close behind. As soon as they entered the circle,

Aggie thrust the book she'd been holding into the pentagram and it burst into flames, feeding on the coven's energy as it drew them further into the circle. One by one, I watched as they each shattered and dissolved into the light.

Sebastian, held prisoner by a powerful vortex opened within the pentagram from out of the flames, stood right in front of us, but the light radiating from the book was so powerful he couldn't see! He placed his large hands across his face to shield his eyes from the intense heat flowing out from the book's pages. The light was so bright, I could barely make out his dark silhouette, and it appeared as though he was blind. When Catherine saw this, she made her move and--rushing toward Sebastian--cast the other book into the flames.

"No!" I screamed, as I reached out toward the blinding light. The intense heat of the fire prevented me from moving any closer. The light from the swirling vortex closed in around Sebastian, highlighting the look of terror on his face. He began to scream obscenities and threats; his deafening cries made me want to cover my ears! I could tell he was suffering and in great pain, and just when I thought I could take no more, one last blast of heat surged forth, struck Sebastian dead center in the chest, and lit up the pentagram like the Fourth of July! It felt like a nuclear explosion!

Catherine wrapped her arms around him and pulled him further into the fire until the towering inferno engulfed them both, and I heard her cry "Thank you, Evie!" above Sebastian's deafening screams. Then they were gone! The flames began to dissipate and, to my surprise, Catherine stood there still! She moved toward me slowly, and my body shook with the intensity of her emotions as they washed over me. I reached out to embrace her as she continued to glide through me, and I heard her whisper "Victoria!" Overwhelmed with emotion and unable to move, I felt her spirit pass through my soul and watched as she walked into the light...

Chapter 44

I awoke face down on the cold smooth surface of the marble floor to a throbbing headache. I looked around and saw that I was back in the church. Aggie and the others were beside me still, in a semi-circle, looking a bit disheveled and tired but--upon closer inspection--unharmed.

I felt different somehow--as if a heavy weight had been lifted from my shoulders--but weak, as though I could have slept for months. *Who knows, maybe I will when this is all said and done!* I thought. The church, too, seemed different. It appeared brighter, and the dark energy I always felt in the tower was completely gone.

"You sure know how to throw one hell of a party!" laughed Aggie. "How are you feeling, lass?"

"I'm okay," I mumbled as I ran my fingers through my long blonde hair. It felt damp to the touch, as if I'd stepped from a shower and been cleansed and released—finally!--from the oppressive energy.

I rose, and all twelve women approached me. We embraced, and I felt enormous amounts of energy pass through me and into my heart. I was a part of the sisterhood again, reunited with my lineage--stolen from me so many lifetimes ago! Their embrace anchored me in the light, sealing me forever from the darkness.

I could tell Aggie sensed my question before I even asked it. "Sebastian's gone!" she assured us all.

"What about Catherine?" I asked. "Is she finally at

peace?"

"When we banished Sebastian it released the hold he had on her, and she was finally able to go into the light," Aggie explained. "Her one and only concern was the safety and welfare of her daughter. It took tremendous amounts of energy for her to get you here, Evie, and when she finally did everything started to fall into place. Painful as that was it had to play out the way it did in order to reestablish balance. She was protecting you from Sebastian all along!

"Wow, I feel kind of lost without her," I said, "like I'm missing something very precious." I turned away from the group. I didn't want them to see me cry.

"No lass," she replied. "You've gained a grand treasure, and your life will never be the same again! Look how far you've come! You never gave up! Do you know how much courage and strength that took on your behalf?"

I inhaled deeply, and as I did experienced a flash of realization so incredible it surely could have blown me away! Aggie looked at me and, recognizing my revelation, did a double take, her eyebrows arching as her golden grey eyes opened wide. Clearly she knew what she was witnessing, as slowly it began to dawn on me that Sebastian had been the culmination of energy in at least a part of every man—father, boyfriends, husbands, including Michael—who manifested in my life until I was able to stand my ground and fight back! Finally I realized I could fight back without losing anything but a lack of their love--which was never love in the first place!

"Aggie!" I cried, "I see the light now! Sebastian's power followed me throughout this entire lifetime through my father and my marriages, almost breaking my spirit until--through the grace of God and Catherine--I was pulled to England, where I finally once and for all stood my ground and reconnected with my healing gifts! He's tripped me up my entire life, and I've *always* felt a darkness hovering over me. Now I see Sebastian had a way of deceiving me and taking what he wanted when he wanted it, and he got away with this because of his *authority!*

"I've always feared standing up to authority figures even when I knew I was right!" I continued, on a roll now. "So instead I became a doormat who never wanted to rock the boat! Sebastian is the shadow cast on all of my past lives where I wasn't allowed to walk my talk, follow my heart, or heal others, because I might be exposed as evil, or not good enough, or for not following the rules!"

I raised my fist in triumph. "Now I *must* venture out into the world to share my gifts with everyone—the gifts passed down to me through Isabella and Catherine!

"Aye lass, now you're talking!" Aggie exclaimed, as she turned toward me abruptly and pulled me into a tight hug.

"Thank you!" I cried, hugging her back. I stepped back again in order to look at her clearly. "In banishing Sebastian, with your help and the help of the coven, I healed an inner child who's been devastated and afraid for years and years! Sebastian was in my father—the father who ridiculed my sensitivity and diminished my psychic talents, *and* in the step-father my mom married who spied on me and degraded me, *and* in my first husband who was jealous of my artistic talents, and *even* in Michael, who always felt the need to diminish my light and control me!"

"Yes, yes, and yes!" Aggie agreed gleefully, as she grabbed my hands and we swung each other around in the middle of church. The other women smiled and gathered round us, sharing in the joy of the moment.

"Sebastian tried to destroy Catherine but, unfortunately, he ended up with me!" I yelled to them all. "Catherine, Victoria, and I are so much more powerful--we *kicked his ass!"*I dissolved into laughter, exhausted, joined by Aggie and the coven.

Just then I realized I'd completely forgotten about something. "I need to get something," I called to them all, and quickly rushed outside to my car. Once there, I reached inside my bag and pulled out Catherine's tiny journal, then walked toward her grave.

"This belongs with you now, I whispered.

The sun was just beginning to set beyond the horizon, and I watched as deep liquid purples and pinks appeared in the evening sky. I loved this time of night. No longer afraid to be caught out in the mist, I watched as it swirled and danced throughout the graveyard, darting in and out amongst the seventy-one tenants that called this place their home. I knelt next to Catherine's grave, moved the fern away from the crumbling bricks, and reached my hand inside to place the journal back from where I'd taken it so many months ago.

"You're free now, Catherine," I whispered, as I withdrew my hand from the crypt. I brushed the loose gravel from my trousers, and sat on the cold damp ground to watch the last remnants of sunshine before it completely disappeared from view. The owls returned--I could hear their soft rustling in the branches as they began to stir. Somehow the sad grimacing faces of the sentinels perched atop the gabled tower now seemed less ominous and more comical.

Once again I found myself overwhelmed with bittersweet emotions as I said goodbye one last time to everything I'd come to know here at the church. In a flash I realized there are no coincidences--I was placed upon a path in order to fulfill my true purpose. Although I'd gotten sidetracked at times by the mundane aspects of day-to-day living, I knew now that my heart would never allow itself to lose sight of who I really *am*.

Through the love and support of a young spirit named Catherine, I was able to heal the wounds of my past, and hers. She was no longer a prisoner and—ironically--neither was I.

"Rest in peace now, Catherine," I whispered softly as I placed my cheek against the smooth cold surface of her grave. "Thank you..."

I remained by the crypt and watched as Aggie and the women filed out of the church. Then Aggie closed and locked the old wooden door behind her, walked over to me, and smiled as she handed me the key.

"Do me a favor, Aggie, and mail it to the solicitors," I requested.

She tucked it into her pocket, wrapped her arms around my shoulders, and said "it's time for you to go home now, lass," as she wiped the tears from her beautiful golden gray eyes.

The End

Afterward

It's time to honor my power, and who and where I came from. I know now I've never been alone on this journey. Always, I had support and help from the other side. I never lost that--only closed myself down and shut myself off based on the choices I made. Through the support of Catherine--my mother--and the guidance and inspiration of sweet and wise Victoria, I trust the intuitive knowing that comes from my heart and *own* my inner strength.

Born a healer and intuitive unable to share my gifts freely in the past, I've sworn to honor these gifts in this lifetime--even if I had to take the long way around to get there! I am here to assist others with similar stories and broken psyches. I know many others have been brought to their knees and broken through past experiences. I know that childhood traumas and old wounds keep them stuck and unable to see the light at the end of the tunnel. Petrified to open their hearts to something new, what they have is all they've ever known.

I am here because I've lived it. The good, the bad, and the ugly, and I've survived. I saw the light at the end of the tunnel and dodged some bullets along the way, but had I not experienced this I would not be who I am today...I know how it feels to walk through darkness, but darkness is a weak energy that can't stand up to an open heart's shining light. Love and hate are the two most powerful emotions in the world. We *are* the sparks of love by nature, and when fear enters the picture we become something we are not. We disconnect ourselves from the divine and forget our true nature.

I am proof that we can shed the layers of betrayal and fear and step into a new, honest, and loving reality. I felt the fear and did it anyway; stood my ground when everything around me was falling apart (or so I thought.) It was the most difficult thing I was ever guided to do, but coming out of the funk and fear of victim mentality was my saving grace. This I learned the hard way, but I am so grateful my blinders were removed and I was allowed to see through and beyond the darkness.

No longer afraid to speak my truth or share my light, I use it to heal myself and others. Confident of my abilities, I attract those who seek clarity within their own lives. Taking back one's power is the ultimate gift of unconditional love--this is what I share and convey to others. Unconditional love has no stipulations, no small print, no hidden clauses! It's something with which we are born and to which we are entitled, but sadly something we often forget. We--every single one of us-- have all the answers we need within, though some may have lost their way and merely need to be reminded.

I no longer hide my light, but shine it out toward those who may have lost their way. The parts of me that carried darkness and insecurity have slowly slipped away, replaced by powerful beings supportive of my actions and assisting me in my healing practice. The past no longer serves us but keeps us stuck, as does thinking only of the future—which creates fear and anxiety. I am living proof that focusing on and becoming aware of every *now* moment creates unexpected miracles, and heals and empowers the heart. How blessed are we who walk through the valley of the shadow of death and emerge reborn into the light and love of our soul!

Namaste...

Acknowledgments

Special thanks for my amazing and insightful editor: Sheri Horn Hasan.

About the Author

Stefaunia currently lives in Utah with her little Jack Russell, Kiah. She is a Reiki Master/teacher/practitioner and Intuitive Counselor and has just completed her second novel, **Keeler Moon,** a futuristic story of Indigo children. You may contact her at www.fragileangel.com

Books by Stefaunia Dhillon

Fragile Angel

Keeler Moon

Keeler Moon

Chapter 1

"We need to figure out a way to get inside that school," voiced Sade as she wiped a thick mop of curly red hair from her forehead.

"I agree," replied Ruby as she scooted around the carousel just in time to dodge a black stallion as he raced by.

Even though they were twins, identical in every way, it was their eyes that gave them away. Sade's deep green flecked with gold shined with enthusiasm as she hopped from the carousel to join her sister, whose blue eyes flashed with sheer intensity as she withdrew from behind her back a small brown satchel.

"What are you doing with that?" asked Sade. "Under no circumstances were we ever to unearth that." She gazed at her twin, who twitched nervously from side to side. Her dimpled cheeks sagged in dismay.

"Don't scold me. You're not my mother." She said lashing out.

"But mom's the one who told us never to dig that thing up," yelled Sade pointing at the satchel Ruby held in her delicate hand.

"Yeah, but mom's not around anymore," cried Ruby as she stomped her feet, sending a thick clump of dust soaring into the air, she quickly turned and walked away.

"Okay, I'm sorry," shouted Sade, racing to catch up with her twin. "Look, it's just that I haven't heard from him for

1

several hours. I'm a little freaked out right now, aren't you?"

"Why do you think I dug this thing up?" cried Ruby, holding the satchel up in front of her. Her sister watched as it dangled from side to side, almost as if it has a mind of its own.

"You know," said Sade eyeing her sister. "You're incorrigible."

"Do you even know what that word means?" asked Ruby. "We wouldn't be in this mess if it hadn't been for dad. I hate him. I wish he were dead."

"You don't mean that," cried Sade, reaching out to grab Ruby's hand.

"He abandoned us. What kind of father would abandon his kids?" she asked. "It's his fault Keeler's in that horrible school. It's his fault mom is dead." She raced off towards the little trailer they now called home; before Sade had a chance to catch her, she'd ducked inside and locked the door behind her.

"Come on Ruby, I'm sorry. Let me in. Please."

"Go away," cried Ruby. Her soft cries were muffled by the closed door.

Sade knew better then to push the issue. In some ways she felt the same way. She was the oldest by a mere minute or so, and felt she had to try to keep things together. Sade knew her sister couldn't hold a grudge for long. She planted herself down on the wooden steps in front of the thin metal door of the shabby trailer, waiting for Ruby to come to her senses.

"Geez, this place is a dump," she thought, as she slumped up against the door and looked over at the rickety wooden roller coaster. It was near dusk. Bright neon lights flashed along the weathered tracks. She watched the old carts slowly climb to the top. The sound of the rusty wheels, clickity clack, click, click, and clack echoed in the air, as the carts spiraled down into a circle eight before disappearing from

2

view. Squeals and screams from excited passengers echoed softly back. Each time she watched it took her breath away. She hated the roller coaster. Her father had brought them here when they were younger and she just didn't relish the memories it stirred within her.

"Keeler, can you hear me?" she asked inside her head. She closed her eyes beyond tight and willed her heart to send out as much energy as possible. She waited a few minutes but there was no response. Usually when he'd contact her, her heart would begin to flutter slowly at first until she adjusted her breathing to match its rhythm. Once she did, his voice would come in loud and clear almost as if he was sitting beside her. Of course he wasn't. He was locked up in that dreadful school. Supposedly, it was to help him understand his abilities. At least this is how the Headmaster had sold the idea to her parents. According to Keeler, that was not the case. He was in a place that was dark and scary, filled with creatures' right out of someone's worst nightmare.

"Keeler, please. I need to know that you're okay."

A slight fluttering stirred within her heart until the pounding became so fast she thought it might leap from her chest. "Slow down," she cried. You're going to give me a heart attack; I truly want to live to see seventeen."

"I'm okay," said Keeler. "But they have me separated from the others. I think that they are afraid of me. Dr. Saunders shaved off all my hair today. She screwed metal tubes onto my head. It really hurt. I hid inside my safe place until the pain went away. It only hurts when I come out. That's why I haven't been talking much to you today. When I come out, she sends sharp bursts of electricity through my skull. I stay hidden so she can't find that part of me that feels pain."

Sade couldn't respond. Her heart was beating so fast

3

and a slight wave of pain threatened to squeeze down tight. "You had such beautiful hair," she whispered. "All my friends were always so jealous of that thick brown mop of yours. You should have been born a girl, you know?" She hoped this would make him laugh, instead she felt his sadness. Besides being able to speak to her brother telepathically, she also had the misfortunate attributes of an empath. She focused her breathing and tuned in to where he was being kept. All she found was darkness. She searched the dark foyers and hallways of the fortress, sensing things that scuttled past, and hiding in the corners just out of reach of her sensitivity.

"We'll find a way to get you out, I promise. I know this is stating the obvious, but just sit tight. If you have to stay in the safe place I'll understand when I don't hear from you right away."

"Where's Ruby?" he asked.

"Sulking," replied Sade. "But she'll be okay. " She felt the connection between her and Keeler starting to fade. The tightness in her heart was beginning to ease up a bit. His words seemed garbled, distorted and distant.

"Sade, are you there?"

"Yes, I thought I lost you," replied Sade. "Are you okay? What's that clicking noise?"

"It's her, the Pretender. We hide inside our minds when we here the clicking, because we know she's coming for us, he replied. The clicking grew louder and echoed throughout the dark hallways. "She smells like rotten eggs," he whispered.

The Pretender stopped a few feet from Keeler's cell, tapping her stiletto heels against the smooth surface of the marble floor.

"Keeler, are you there?" asked Sade. "Keeler, answer me."

"She's here," whispered Keeler. "Gotta go."

www.ingramcontent.com/pod-product-compliance
Lightning Source LLC
Chambersburg PA
CBHW071309200626
46813CB00015B/655